A Nickel's Worth of Road Measles

S.L. Funk

Published by Stephanie Funk, 2020.

This is a work of fiction. Similarities to real people, places, or events are entirely coincidental.

A NICKEL'S WORTH OF ROAD MEASLES

First edition. April 1, 2020.

ISBN: 978-0-578-64736-4

Written by S.L. Funk.

For Ed, whose belief in me keeps me going.

Acknowledgements

No man, or woman, is an island. Throughout the long journey that writing *A Nickel's Worth of Road Measles* took me on, I was guided and supported by many along the way. As a brand new author, even just figuring out how to edit and publish something is a daunting task at times. To that end, I would like to thank author Steve Ulfelder for his encouragement and direction in recommending that I join the Mystery Writers of America and Sisters in Crime. And to the many members of the Mystery Writers of America and Sister's in Crime, I wish to thank you for your support and guidance, from published authors to other aspiring ones. You all made a huge difference.

Prologue

I can just see the hood and part of the windshield of the little Toyota Corolla through the narrow window. Bland, cookie cutter lines, designed by bland, cookie cutter engineers someplace far away. A constellation of pale speckles is sprayed across the dark blue nose. 'Road measles' they're called, the result of grit and stones thrown up from the roadway.

I can't see the entire car, but it looks like it might be the DX package, the sedan with cloth seats, a CD player and 14" wheels. Unless it's been swapped, there's a 1.8L single overhead cam under the fading hood, likely with upwards of 200k on it now. It's probably a '95 or '96 judging from the headlight shape.

A shudder works its way unbidden between my shoulder blades. "Goose walked acrosst yer grave." Gramma would have said. More like drove across it, I'd say.

I turn away from the grimy window, beads of sweat popping out under my hair.

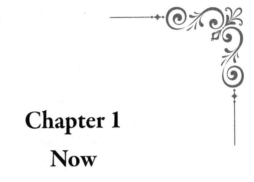

Chapter 1

Now

"Hey Howie!" I bellow across the shop, my voice momentarily drowning out the hard metal crap squalling from the radio. Howie's thin shanks were visible underneath the Honda Civic he was laboring on, the one with the plugged cat, stinking of rotten eggs, stumbling like your grandmother after three sherries. A blue clad leg wiggled, a muffled, "Hang on," from under the grimy undercarriage. Mrs. Howland's car, damn thing was in every few weeks. Half the problem was age, the other half Mr. Howland who ignored little things like making sure it had oil on a regular basis, or that the tires were so low they bulged like a herniated gut.

Howie slid out from under the car. "Whaddya want, Ger?"

Not the brightest bulb in the pack. But not the worst kid ever walked through these doors either. Beggars can't be choosers, especially when you're begging off the side of old Route 9, the Hudson a glint through the empty mill buildings across the road, the new shops up on 200 gleaming with glass and multiple garage bays, neon blaring "BRAKES

– EXHAUST – TUNEUPS- FOREIGN- DOMESTIC! Mechanics on duty 6 days a week!" Acne scarred cheeks, sunken where the teeth were already going.

Shame in this day and age, but fame, fortune and dental plans don't always come to tech school drop-outs.

Wiping my hands on a soiled red shop rag, I jerked my head towards the outside of the shop.

"Go give Luther a hand dropping that car."

Yellow lights bounced off the bodywork of the cars parked in a ragged row; the chug of diesel audible over the din of Lazer 103.9 as the rollback loaded with a breakdown from the Northway maneuvered into place. I could see Luther, greasy, curly gray hair, a perpetual cigarette hanging from one side of his mouth, working the controls.

Dipping his head, Howie wiped his hands on his legs and shuffled morosely towards the shop door. I snapped off the radio, my ears ringing as comparative silence set in.

Over the chugging of the diesel, the shop phone blatted, once, twice, then stopped as Bill picked it up in the cluttered little room that served as his office.

I heaved a sigh, feeling the muscles in my lower back contract as I did. Wincing, I reached around and grabbed it a moment, massaging the knot. On my lift a Ford Ranger sat, suspension drooping, a hole visible where the exhaust system usually resided. I grabbed the pipe I had just finished bending up, a shiny new muffler and tailpipe already in place. Wouldn't look like that for long in this almost-upstate New York town. Job security, I guess, about as certain as anything I had in my life.

I heard the door to the office creak open as Bill stuck his head out. I didn't look at him.

"G.L., how much longer you got on that turd?"

I shrugged. "Coupla hangers at most. Why?" I glanced over my shoulder at him.

He ran a black nailed hand over his equally black hair. "That was Tim Mathers just now. Needs something small and economical for his daughter and wants a new work truck for himself. He says he's interested in the Dodge we got, but...I got nothing for his kid, and that's the deal breaker. Needs them both like yesterday. I was thinking maybe you can shoot over to the auction today and see what you can find. We oughta start looking for some more for inventory anyway."

I flinched as the pain lanced up my lumbar again, slowly lowering the exhaust back to the floor. Bill noticed, didn't comment. "Have Howie finish it up. Take Gertie and see what you can get. Computer's showing a coupla prospects coming through later today."

"What's he looking for?"

"Cheap. This is Tim we're talkin' about, man who has the first nickel he ever earned." He wasn't kidding. Tim Mathers was the poster child for tightwad. He spent nothing until he had to, then it was like he couldn't wait for the pain of the money leaving his hand to be done. If we didn't have anything for his kid, he wouldn't buy the Dodge, the rust speckled work truck that was past time to be off our lot and in someone else's yard.

I glanced at the clock. Leaving now gave me just enough time to drive a few before they ran through the lanes.

Stretching, I heard a pop from low down my back. Bill heard it too. "Jesus." he muttered. "You sound like a bowl of Rice Krispies."

"Yeah, well it's still better'n what you sound like...half the time you sound like a fart in a tin can." Bill was about 15 years older than me, but still in pretty good shape, except for a few pieces that he had busted up over the years. Wrenching on cars most of your life and doing motorsports in your spare time will do that to you.

"What's the budget like today?" I ran water over my hands and arms in the saggy sink along the wall. Bill shrugged. "Coupla k tops."

Black water swirled down the drain, bubbles from the handcleaner spiraling down out of sight. A discomfiting thought came as I watched it go: One day I was a kid like Howie then bam, here I was 25 years later and life was bubbling away down the drain, black stained with broken dreams and dappled with toxic memories.

I blinked, pushing the thoughts away, Bill's eyes on me, unspoken concern in them. Pissed me off, even though it shouldn't. Man ought to be grateful that anyone gave a shit for him, instead of pissed. Just one more shortcoming to add to the ever-growing list, the one that Amy recited to me on a regular basis.

Drying my hands on a black stained rag, I grabbed the keys to Gertie off the pegboard, Bill a shadow as I headed towards the light outside. "You want anything else specific for the lot?" He scratched his eye a moment. "Think we should start looking for winter beaters. Not too early yet. Here..." he disappeared back into his office, emerging with a stack of papers. "I printed out the lines that have some stuff we might want." I took the papers from him wordlessly, folding them into quarters and shoving them in my pocket. There was a clang as the car from the Northway rolled off the rollback, Howie's head jerking as he steered it to a halt.

"Gertie" as she was so named, sat in the corner of the small chain link fenced back lot. A '93 Ford 450, she was a rollback with a 19' bed that Bill got a couple of years ago from a guy retiring to Florida. A diesel, she was balky when the mercury dipped below 32 degrees and had some noises we hadn't bothered to figure out yet. A car dolly was already strapped to the bed, the only way we could take more than one car at a time with her. Probably wouldn't get more than two maybe three today anyway; Howie would gladly go for any stragglers. Bill's head popped out the window of the brown block building as I climbed into the seat. "Hey! There's a Toyota going through that might be perfect for Tim, lot number 2578. Red one, only has 105 on it." Gertie fired up with a belch, partially drowning Bill out. I nodded, already on autopilot. "Alright. I'll check it out."

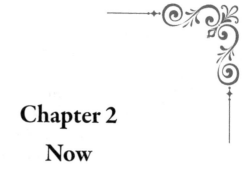

Chapter 2

Now

The auction was a huge enterprise, sprawled all to hell and gone alongside the highway. Acres of cars, trucks, the odd boat or RV gleamed in the harsh sunlight as I steered Gertie through the chain link gates. Transporters were busy unloading off to the east side of the building. To the west, rows of cars sat in lines, numbers marked on the windshields with wax markers.

Gertie rumbled and protested as I threaded her through the ranks of tow vehicles to an open spot, the lot a beehive of activity as dealers, small shop owners and wholesalers bustled around.

I spotted Glenn Harrison over by a triaxle transporter, talking to someone. He spied me and waved. I returned it, glad to see him. Despite my earlier reservations when talking to Bill, I was sort of happy to be here today. The sight of the thousands of cars and trucks always awakened a shadow of that emotion of being a kid on Christmas morning to me, a feeling of anticipation.

And happiness didn't come very easy or often to me anymore.

I registered at the office, then pulled out the printout of the offerings for that day's sale from my pocket, scanning the list for possibilities and the one Bill had mentioned. Engrossed, I almost collided with Dan Gardner as I was leaving the office. My new-found anticipation began to wither.

"Gerry! Surprised to see you here today. Didn't think Bill would let you out without a chauffeur. Or your parole officer's permission." He bellowed a laugh, so amused at himself. Poison coiled in my gut. I had a DUI last year, a fact this dick rubbed my face in every chance he had.

"Hey Dan." Walking on, trying to push by him. Not so easy. He had three men with him, an audience. He shifted to one side, blocking my way down the stairs. I felt the waves coming off him, struggled to block them out.

"You're lucky you didn't take someone out, driving shit-faced like that. Christ, do you know how many people die in drunk driving accidents every year? Of course, you probably drive better drunk than sober, huh?"

"Yeah Dan...Whatever." I tried to move forward. He blocked me again. I looked up into his brown, red rimmed eyes, meanness shining through them, felt the waves rolling off him, brushing my face, a tendril snaking into an unguarded crack, instant bile rising in my throat.

She curled on the floor in front of the couch, hands over her head, blood flowing from her nostrils. Excitement coursing through my body as I kicked her in the stomach again, hate her, hate her, hate this bitch, knowing the stupid cow would never dare tell anyone...

Grayness around the edge of my vision, desire to turn and flee. I stood straight and still, tremors coursing up my spine. Slowly I looked into his mean, piggy eyes, nastiness glowing through like brilliant embers of plutonium. I felt my face tighten, coils of rage awakening in me as I looked him in the eye.

Smiling, I ever so softly asked, "So Dan. You still beating your wife? You really messed her up last time. You know, you almost ruptured her spleen. You really ought to just come out of the closet and make peace with yourself." His face flushed red, mouth working silently.

"I know Dan. She didn't tell anyone, but I know. And if it happens again, you're a dead man." Fear, a tiny spark in his eyes. He hated me because he feared me, because he thought I was weird. And he was right. I am weird. But I'm not a prick, not like him.

Taking advantage of his sudden muteness, I pushed past him and continued down the short flight of stairs, tremors running through my gut.

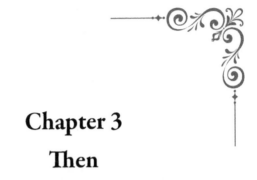

Chapter 3
Then

"Mommy!" I shook her arm. She mumbled weakly, rolling over on the couch away from me. Purple marks dotted her neck and upper arms. My stomach rumbled again, bile burning the hollow feeling into my brain. "Mom-MEE!" I gave her a hard shove, rousing her from her comatose state. "Wha? Leave me alone..." She rolled further away.

The kitchen door rattled. My dick shriveled up as I heard the key in the lock. HIS key. My room, where I was supposed to be, all the way across the little apartment, the kitchen between me and it. The door opened. Trapped, nowhere to run, no place to hide, HE was in the doorway already, swaying, mean ferret face with red rimmed eyes staring at me, hatred evident.

"What are you doin' out here you little shit? I tole you to stay in your room! Now you're gunna pay, you little fuck!" The belt slithering out of his jeans, the one with the metal studs.

Whimpering, I grabbed my mother's arm again and tugged. She muttered and pulled it away from me. He advanced, excitement and rage in his eyes, the belt snaking free and brushing the ground...

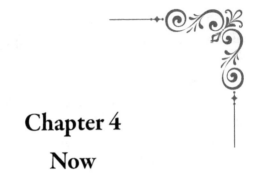

Chapter 4

Now

I practically leapt off the last step, heading blindly into the colorful sea of automobiles. My stomach heaved, threatening to disgorge itself into my mouth. A couple of guys sent sharp glances my way and moved aside. People don't like weird dudes.

That was me. Strange Gerry Lee Donahue, the weird dude wrenching over on Route 9 in the falling down block building run by Bill Alberti. The charity case. The messed-up guy that Bill kept on. Black clouds streamed across my brain. I moved faster, deeper into the mess of cars and trucks.

Finally, I halted half doubled over, my breath rasping in my chest like I had run the entire distance. I leaned against the fender of a navy blue Astrovan and waited for my heart to slow down. The clouds receded, the glints of colors coming back slowly, oh so slowly. Slowly I straightened up and looked around, taking in my surroundings.

Rows of compact cars, vans, sport ute's and small trucks spread along the lot in front of me, gently sloping downhill, blues, greens, reds, whites, silver, the windshields reflecting bright stars at my eyes in the late September sun. A few people moved among them, this area of beater cars my feet had taken me to automatically. I stayed leaning against the van, letting my racing heart slow.

My head hurt, a dull throb in the dent that I carried on the right side of my skull, the one just visible under the edge of the hairline. The one that started everything, this entire freaking mess, the mess that wouldn't go away even now, 39 years later. I would never be 'normal' again, the cyst I carried that festered in my soul, poisoned blackness threatening to eat its way through the protective membrane that surrounded it, a membrane that weakened as each passing year went by instead of strengthening.

I stared blankly at a pair of guys two rows away who were inspecting a Kia, a red and black windbreaker on one, denim jacket on the other.

For a moment, a fierce envy reared up, envy of those guys, so utterly clueless of the entire other world that surrounded them, blissfully unaware of the shadows and ghosts that brushed across their faces as they opened each car door and inspected the interior. Envy of the singular insulation they carried, insulation provided by an undamaged brain, a 'traumatic insult to the frontal lobe' that bashed open doors best left closed, doors that only let insanity into your sane brain. The door I struggled to keep closed as much as possible.

A struggle that got worse every day.

Chapter 5
Then

Pain. Red hot lancets on my back when I rolled over, wetness where the blood was seeping through my pajama shirt, the Winnie the Pooh set Gramma had given me last Christmas. Pain, pain from the hot tears that burned my cheeks yet again, tears of pain, tears of fear.

Tears of rage. Through the thin door of my bedroom, I could hear HIM, that hateful beast my mother married, the devil with the quick temper who always stunk of alcohol, I could hear him grunting as he did that weird thing with mommy again, that thing that scared me so much I had wet the bed the first time I heard it. The first beating had happened the next morning.

They happened regularly now.

I hated him. Hated, hated, hated him, wanted to spear his eyes out like the superheroes would, wanted to hurt him, make him go away, save my mommy from him, make her love me again.

He beat her too. I heard it. I heard it.

I hated him.

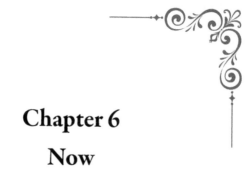

Chapter 6

Now

I didn't ask for this. I didn't want this. I paid the price for it every time it happened. Heard some bimbos on TV one night talking about the 'supernatural', and 'telepathic powers' they claimed to have.

I knew they didn't have it. If they did, they wouldn't look so smooth and unlined. They wouldn't be in front of television cameras under white hot lights talking about it. They'd be home, cowering in the darkest corner of the bedroom, hidden in the shadows, hiding from the insanity.

I didn't always have this either. That was the hell of it. Maybe if I had been born with it I'd 'a gotten used to it or somethin'. I thought I could use it when I was a kid, I thought I could control it, master it, use it for my own good.

What does a stupid kid know?

Even now, I struggled to only allow it in small inklings, for benign reasons, like here at the auction. If you didn't let it through at all, it would swell and swell until it burst like an abscess, spewing purulent tissue everywhere. Problem is, it's that much harder to push out the unwanted stuff when you are trying to only open the door a crack.

The hungry wolves are always waiting to tear at the wood of that door, rending it from the hinges.

Pushing myself upright, I considered leaving. Going and getting back into Gertie and driving back to the shop. Tell Bill I was sick or sumpin', book off the rest of the day. I didn't know if I could face him, face his sympathetic eyes, feel the gaze on me as I left. I just wanted to be anonymous sometimes, work in a place where I was a cog, a number, someone no one noticed or cared about.

That thought made me feel crappy again, another notch on the list of failures. Not everyone had someone who cared about them.

I stiffened my spine, ignoring the pain. Railed at myself in my head, "Get to work, Ger. Go choose a couple cars and get them loaded and out. Suck it up buttercup."

I can do this. Yes I can.

How I wish now I had chosen to leave.

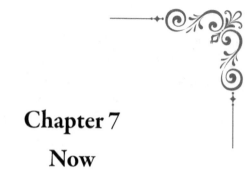

Chapter 7
Now

The Auction was a bizarre place, sprawling beyond comprehension for the uninitiated. Cars, vans, trucks, all makes, models, colors and conditions stacked hundreds deep with apparently no rhyme or reason. But if you came to them enough, you would soon see how the system worked.

This one had 25 lanes running. A car ran through each lane every 45 seconds and was sold in that short time frame. They say upwards of three thousand cars sell here every auction day, held fifty weeks of the year. Incomprehensible numbers until you've seen it, then it feels like it should be higher.

You had to know which ones you wanted before they hit the lanes. Cars were parked with numbers greased onto the windshields, numbers that corresponded with the line they would run through, then what number they would be in that line. The dealer that consigned them had their name scrawled in wax pen up the A post of the windshield. You had everyone from high end dealers and off lease vehicles to junkers that came in on trade that were too weary for resale through the dealership.

This auction had the higher end stuff running through the first lanes, with the best stuff coming early. A car marked '512' would be the twelfth car through line number five. An early seller generally got more money, sent through when all the players were here. Late stuff ran through with empty seats on the bleachers, wallets already thinned from earlier purchases.

The cars out here in the higher number lanes was a mixed bag, a real crapshoot. Wrecked cars, or cars with bum transmissions that would come through on a hook. High mileage Japanese cars with tarted up headlights. Older models with high mileage. The odd gem, your late gramma's low mileage, always garaged twelve year old sedan. Stuff that could be had cheap, get a few bucks thrown at it and resell still on the cheap. Bread and butter stuff if you did it right.

Wallet emptiers if you did it wrong. Like I said, a crapshoot.

The area of the lot my feet had taken me to automatically was where these cars always wound up. Beater alley, Crapcan Avenue. The higher number lanes, the later cars to run through them. My eyes scanned the pocked windshields and rust spotted fenders, noting the paint chips on the fronts of a number of cars. "Road Measles" they called them, chips from the stones and grit constantly flung up on these almost-up-state New York roads.

My heart still pounded heavily, the adrenaline dump playing hell with the nerves in my back and hands. Steadying myself, I fished a battered pack of Camels from my shirt pocket, trembling fingers fumbling with the match, once, twice, yellow and white flame flaring. Acrid smoke bit my lungs and eyes as the first hit took.

Taking a deep pull, I felt my stomach finally settling back down where it belonged. Sunlight hurt my eyes, bouncing off the metal and glass. I pulled my sunglasses down off my head and covered my eyes, knowing how they looked right now.

Normalcy, such as it was, began to return.

Rows of cars sloped down the gentle grade towards the perimeter fence that lined the road beyond. People moved between the sparkling rooftops motors fired up as vehicles were test driven around the lot. I pulled the printout that Bill had given me from my back pocket and scanned it.

We had a few set policies in place for our resale cars. It couldn't have too much rust, we weren't set up to be a body shop. We specialized, if you could call it that, in foreign cars and light trucks, dabbling in heavy domestic trucks from time to time.

Our bread and butter cars were Hondas, Toyotas, Subarus, Mitsubishi's, Acuras, stuff like that. All-wheel drive always a plus. 4 cylinders even better, what with gas going close to $3 a gallon now.

Turning away from the sun's glare, I scanned the sheet. Three Hondas, a Ford Escape that looked intriguing, a Subaru and two Toyotas, including the one Bill had mentioned, caught my eye. I circled them on the page.

I blew out my breath, feeling my pulse rate steadying out finally. I focused on the cars circled. A '96 Honda Civic LX with 101k on the odo caught my eye. Four-door, automatic, located in row 23, number 49 to run through. I looked at the windshields in front of me. The numbers started with 21. Pushing off the fender, I made my way through the rows, looking for the bland lines of the Honda.

You were usually better with an automatic, especially in a Honda. Less chance of it being some kid's street rod. And a four door, that was a bonus. No self-respecting homey wanted his bro's seein' him in a baby daddy car. This one may have been a one owner car, maybe even spending its life garaged. The mileage hinted at that. A ride around the lot would tell me if that was the case.

Number 2349 was a white sedan, sitting between a '00 Hyundai Sonata and a '96 Dodge Stratus with a laser like crack across the windshield. I walked around it, eyeing the panels for tell-tale ripples that would mean the car had suffered serious trauma. Most people pull up Carfax reports on their purchases. I rarely needed it. I cocked my head to see the consigner's name, 'Midvale'. Midvale Ford was a medium sized dealer down south of here, located on the 'Auto Mile' outside of Poughkeepsie. They had stuff in every week.

I opened the driver's door and stuck my head in cautiously, breathed deeply. Faint mustiness, a ghost of scent like talcum powder. Driver's seat worn through the covering on the left side, okay on the rest of the seats. A broken knob on the radio. Dirt, probably recent, dragged in by the guys who drove it here, on the driver's mat, clean on the passenger side. Keys dangled from the ignition. Taking a deep breath, I slid into the driver's seat, focusing fiercely on keeping that door closed.

The key turned smoothly. Lights came on in the dash, the little four-cylinder motor cranked over once, twice, then fired. I heard a wheezing up high in the exhaust, probably had a header leak. Shifting it into drive I pulled forward out of its row and headed down the lot, joining the line of cars trundling around the perimeter of the grounds. Cautiously, I allowed the tendrils of sensation to sneak into my brain.

Late for the doctor's again. Had to learn to pay better attention to the time. Estelle sure knows how to talk though. And that daughter of hers! My land that girl gets herself into a million scrapes. This dang car is making that noise again, that hissing sound. Don't really want to trade it in, but Johnny won't let up on me about it. Says he wants his mom in something better for the winter, something with all-wheel drive. Shame really, still think of this car as new. Maybe it was time. Better remember to stop at Jim's Market on the way home, need some coffee, also should check out their sale this week. Janice wants me to bring something Sunday...

I felt the corded muscles in my back relaxing as the waves of mundane ordinariness washed over me, allowed myself to roll in the rhythm of it as I turned left through the big parking lot to the rear, then right, following the shape of the building around.

This was my Carfax. This was the only thing from the dent on my head, the 'traumatized frontal lobe' that was of any value, far as I could see.

Used to be I let everything in all the time. That about near killed me. Then I tried nothing ever. That too about near killed me. Finally, I reached a balancing point where I would crack the door once in a while, use it to find out what kind of previous life these cars had, weed out the ones that had been ridden hard and put up wet.

No one around me knew I had this...this...weird skill. Sure wasn't no gift. Bill suspected something. But he never asked. Amy, well Amy didn't know what to think. She just thought I was holding out on her; what she thought I was holding out, I didn't know.

It wasn't perfect. For one thing, the sensations faded every time you got in the car. Your first was your strongest. And if enough people test drove one before I got into it, it could be a confusing babble of psychic voices. You also couldn't pick up much on owners before the last one either. A car that passed through four hands had as big a chance of being a dud as it would be if you couldn't 'feel' the old owner. Sometimes too, the old owners were assholes, their asshole feelings washing over you, making you feel like you needed a hot shower when you got out of the car.

I never bought cars that assholes had owned, no matter how clean or perfectly suited the car seemed to be.

Same token, I once bought a Ford Focus that was every bit as wrong as right, rusted through along the fenders, seat covers all torn, transmission slipping from time to time. Bill had looked at me really strange when that rolled in, and even stranger when I fixed everything over that winter, right down to the pocked fenders, then turned around and just plain gave it to a daughter of a customer of ours, a smart girl with no money who was working her way through college.

How could I tell Bill it had belonged to an eighteen-year old girl who died of cancer? That the rust came from sitting in her family's yard for three years after, sitting because they couldn't bear to see it gone, this trace of their daughter? How the mother used to sit in it and cry, thinking of it in the crusher. I had taken a couple of photos of it fixed up and mailed them anonymously to them, a simple note saying the car would live a long and useful life. I couldn't tell him that, either.

I may be weird, but I'm not an asshole.

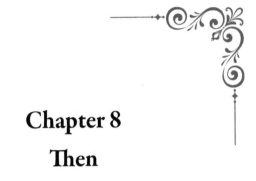

Chapter 8
Then

G ramma keeps asking me how my arms got all bruised up. I can't say, I'll get in trouble if I say. I wish Gramma wouldn't ask me anymore. I wish she would let me and mommy live with her. I love my Gramma. I wish I could talk to her, but mommy says that if I say anything, HE will hurt her. And I don't want her to get hurt. Because it's already MY FAULT that she gets hurt. I feel bad that it's MY FAULT.

Gramma looks at me all funny sometimes, her face all red like. I wish she would take me to get ice cream and stop asking me stuff. I wish we would never come back. It would be fun, like those movies I seen, the ones with all the big dogs that talk, and Mickey Mouse. I seen kids there too, kids littler than me. I wish I was one of them kids. I hug my knees and stare at the television, Gramma stops asking me questions finally. She looks so sad sometimes. I know about sad. I stare at the television and try to forget being sad.

Chapter 9

Now

The Ford Escape is a bust. Interior trashed, broken ball joint in the left front, kid who traded it in used to take it down this rutted up road to some quarry to party. They could fit a coupla kegs in the back...and about fifteen of his friends hanging onto every part of the car. I back it into its slot and strike it off on my list.

Up at the auction building, a dull roar of noise floats down to me; all 25 lines are starting to move. All of my prospects have higher numbers on them; I've been working my way from the lower numbers to the higher ones. I have one Subaru, and two Hondas checked off as good prospects. Bill's suggestion, the Toyota Corolla, number 2578 is next on my list. I peer over the roof tops of the cars in row 24 looking at row 25. I spied a dull red roof about twenty cars over, almost hidden behind a Jeep Grand Cherokee.

A chill snaked its way up my spine, unexpected and unbidden. Gooseflesh pimples my back between my shoulder blades, my head gave a thump. "Goose walked acrosst my grave, Gramma." I muttered. Gramma was always saying that. Came at the oddest times sometimes, like now; bright sun shining, people having all drifted towards the faint ringing of the auctioneer's voices. I was alone, a feeling I usually relished. Except...right now, it was kinda creepy. Shivering, I twisted my head and shoulders, loosening up the knots, a rat terrier shaking it off, and headed towards 2578. "Last one." I muttered, "Gotta get up to the auction."

The left front tire was soft. The car had a decided sideways lean to it. The antenna was kinked, the end drooping down towards the ground. I walked around it, eying the body panels. Sun faded, missing body trim piece on the door, but no visible rust. I glanced at the printout again. A '99, it was seven years old now. I scrutinized the lines of it critically, looking for dents and dings.

The panels lay flat and smooth. A faint constellation of road measles were visible across the front of the hood, about a 'nickels worth', as they say. Opening the driver's side door, I scanned the interior. It was clean, almost remarkably so. Like they had used seat covers the whole time they had it.

That uneasiness again, gooseflesh on my shoulders in the bright sunlight. Pushing the door to, I cocked my head to read the dealer's name on the A pillar; Beckwith. Not a name I was familiar with.

Faint chanting floated on the wind behind me, rising and falling, the auctioneer's voice too far away to make out. I saw cars twinkling in the harsh sunlight moving forward, the ones in front disappearing in the huge bay doors, the next ones creeping forward to take their places and wait. I looked at the dash of the Toyota, spotted the silver glint of keys hanging from the ignition. Felt a strange reluctance to get in the car and take them.

Weird.

I glanced at my watch. Enough time to do a quick spin in this one. Pulling the door open again, I looked into the driver's seat, the fabric looking new, too new, rough and jagged like teeth, dark gray, the color of my soul, the seat sinking down in front of me like a hole you would fall through, right through into the maw of the devil, spittle caked lips and hideous breath, teeth waiting to tear into your flesh and rend your soul...

My butt hit the door of the Jeep next to me, startling me out of my trance, or whatever the heck it was. Startled, I realized I had backed away from the car, *pushed* away from it, cringing backwards until I was pinned by the gold Jeep. My breath rattled in my throat again, heart pumping wildly.

What the hell was this?

I stared at the car, the car that was just...a car. The seats well-kept and bland, typical Toyota seats. Fidgeting, I pushed the door to, ready to close it and walk away, Bill's voice in my head, his face, eyes watching me, worrying about me. "Just tell him it wasn't right." I muttered. My brain wouldn't let me off so easily. "Why isn't it right? You haven't even sat in it. What the hell is wrong with you?"

This kind of reaction, this....*feeling*.... never happened to me. Ever. I could pick up what people left, but I had never had this...this bizarre vision, this...curdling feeling. A feeling that was.... gone.

The car sat there, a little forlornly, sagging on its left front. It was just...a car. A seven-year-old car with about a nickel's worth of road measles across the hood, and a too clean interior, a car that we could probably sell to Tim Mathers and make a few hundred bucks, plus get the old Dodge off the lot and free up the cash again.

Taking a deep breath, I yanked the driver's side door back open and slid into the seat in one motion.

Chapter 10

Then

"Ricky Guy is a Pig Pie, stick a needle in your eye!" Jimmy was jerk. He was dancing around, yelling his stupid jerky song. I ignored him, looking down at the ground, wishing he wasn't walking to school with us. Ricky, walking next to me, looked up at Jimmy and yelled back. "Shut up, you dipshit!"

Ricky was bold. He made me nervous when he yelled back like that, nervous that the yelling was going to get worse than that. I hated yelling.

Darlene laughed. She was weird. She liked Jimmy the jerk. I didn't know if I liked her or not. Sometimes I did. She was a lot older than us, like a year or two at least. But she walked with us a lot, and every time she did, Jimmy was a huge jerk. Maybe I didn't like her then.

"Don't be such a PUSS Ricky!" she stuck her tongue out at him. Ricky's cheeks got real red, like he was mad. I shifted my backpack and shuffled alongside, trying to be small.

"I am NOT a puss!" he hollered back at her. I risked looking up. No one yelled at Darlene. She was gonna be mad!

But she wasn't. She laughed again and tossed her head. She had long, skinny legs, her skirt riding way high up. Jimmy was always dancing around poking at her legs, making fun of them. "You are TOO a puss! Here puss puss!" making kissing sounds, skipping as she walked.

Ricky's face was really, really red now. I wondered if he was going to hit her. "I'm not a puss! You want to see a puss? Here!" a hard shove on my shoulder sent me sprawling forward, almost falling down, "HERE'S a puss! Gerry here is a big, fat PUSSY!"

I stumbled a bit as I stopped, suddenly scared. They were all staring at me. Jimmy had a mean look on his face, Ricky was all red and mad, and Darlene was running her tongue over her upper lip, shifting her weight from side to side, staring at me. I felt tears prickling the back of my eyes, Jimmy saw it too. "Ha ha! Gerry, Gerry, was a big fat fairy! Look at him! He's *cwwwying*!"

"Am not." I whispered.

"What? I can't hear you, fairy boy!" Jimmy held his hand to his ear. I hated him. "I am NOT CRYING!" my voice squeaked. Darlene laughed out loud. "You are TOO! God, you are such a faggot." "Hey! Come on Darlene. Leave him alone." Ricky, red faced, glaring at Darlene and Jimmy. She sniffed and glanced at him over her shoulder. "*YOU* started it, puss boy!" "Did not. HE started it!" Ricky balled his fists, glaring at Jimmy the jerk. Jimmy just laughed.

"You two are such faggots, you and the skank's kid."

I stopped dead, jagged icicles in my belly. "What?" a whisper. Darlene had stopped too, her eyes bright and shiny as she watched us. Jimmy laughed, that stupid, stupid nasally laugh he had, the one that sounded like he was blowing his nose. I stared at him. "Whut? What you want, you skank bait?" he puffed his chest out. "What did you call my mom?" He walked closer to me, blonde hair gleaming in the gray light. "I called her a skank. Because she IS one. My dad says she's one of them 'two-bit horses.'" He smirked. Beside me, Ricky shifted nervously. "A two-bit horse? What's a two-bit horse?" "Oh my God!" Darlene clapped her hand over her eyes. "You guys are SOOOOOO stupid!" "What?" Jimmy's face was turning red now. She lowered her hand. "It's not two-bit HORSE, you stupido, it's two-bit WHORE!" It was Jimmy's turn to look puzzled. "What's a two-bit whore?" "Oh my God! You are too stupid to talk to!" She turned and stomped away from us.

Chapter 11
Now

I hadn't realized I was holding my breath until I let it out, slowly, slowly, slowly. The seat creaked under my weight; the fabric rough on my back where my shirt had ridden up. I sat still for a long moment. Nothing. I looked around the interior, noting the trim, the scuff marks on the passenger side door, looking for flaws. I grasped the keys and turned. The four cylinders coughed to life, evenly, smoothly. I listened to the hum of the engine, noting the smoothness. Reaching up, I grasped the wheel and reached for the shift lever, allowing my 'damaged frontal lobe' to open up a crack to feel....

No!No!NOOOOOOOOOO! Ohmygodohmygod! Blood gushing from the cunt's upper lip, excitement coursing through my body, right hand twisting savagely on the wire that wrapped around her wrists, hands in a praying position, legs apart, gaping gash showing, gross, fucking gross, fucking pig, excitement gone now, anger blooming, the knife in my hand, jamming it in, again and again, twisting it hard and up, her squealing a gurgle now, my excitement back, plastic crackling under her butt as I jammed her down into the backseat, my knee between her legs, JAM HER that fucking stinky bitch, stinky stinky stinky...

Flashes of light, trees whirling over me, rough pavement hitting my cheek, vomit bubbling up, spewing out, retching again and again, rolling, rolling, get away, get away, crab crawling up against the Jeep, mewling sounds coming from some primal place deep inside, bile burning my throat, panting roughly, ears ringing.......holy Mother of God! Oh my God no!

My panting gasps tore at me as I crouched on the pavement, the red car that was just a red car again sitting there, engine running smoothly. My head ached fiercely, a pounding in my brain. Footsteps crunched on the pavement. I grabbed my face, hiding, hiding, hiding.

"Jesus Christ, man! What happened to you?" A shaggy haired kid, no more than 21 or 22, cap turned backwards, one of the drivers moving cars into the bay. I couldn't answer him. He backed away a little. "Um, you want me to, like, call an ambulance or something?"

I shook my head roughly, no, no, no, no. The car purred softly.

Shaking, I lowered my hand from my face, tried for words, amazed that sound was coming out of me. "Bad night.....food poison...caught up to me..."

The kid eyed me suspiciously. "Yeah. Sure, man." A glance at the car. "You ain't gonna drive that are you?"

Shook my head roughly again. No no no no no...

"Good." He leaned in and shut off the motor. I heard my heart pounding in my ears in the sudden silence. "You probably shouldn't be driving anything anyway." He eyed the puddle of vomit in disgust.

On shaking legs, I pulled myself upright, pushed off the Jeep and moved away from him wordlessly.

Chapter 12
Then

I pushed my hot dog around on my plate, drawing lines in the grease. Mommy was sitting at the other end of the table, a glass of red stuff in front of her, a cigarette burning in the ashtray. HE wasn't here. I wished he would never be here again.

I was mad. Mad, mad mad. I hated him. I hated her. I hated me. The smell of the hot dog made my stomach hurt. I hated hot dogs. I wanted Spaghetti-O's. I liked Spaghetti-O's. I didn't want a stupid hot dog. Why couldn't I have Spaghetti-O's? I shoved the plate away suddenly.

"Hey." Her voice was all slurry sounding again. It made me mad, mad, mad. "Eat your shupper." I folded my arms across my chest, kicking the underside of the table. She hated that. I kicked harder. "I don't want hotdogs. I hate hotdogs." "It's what you got, so eat it. Shtop kicking the freaking table." Her glass shimmied. I kicked again, harder. "I want some Spaghetti-O's. Why can't I have those?" "Because we don't have any. Shush your mouth and eat." "I don't WANT this!" My voice was high, crackling through unshed tears. I hated her, hated this. I gave the table a tremendous kick. Her glass

36

hopped, fell, red liquid spilling like blood across the scarred wood surface. "Dammitall!" Her face red, she leapt up, mad, mad, mad, "I told you to STOP IT RIGHT NOW, you little shit! Lookit what you did!" A bubble of pain welled in my throat, swollen, hot, bursting in the middle, made me yell, "I HATE YOU! You're just a stupid...stupid..TWO-BIT WHORE!" Her face whitened, "WHAT did you just call me?" Mad, mad, mad, shouldn't say it, but I did, bold like Ricky, but scared, "You're a two-bit whore." Must be bad, if Darlene knew it was bad, something big kids called each other. Her hand was a blur, the crack of her palm against my cheek loud in the space, the shock blossoming in my chest. Mommy never hit me. HE did, but she never did.

In the sudden stillness, I stared at her, flames on my left cheek, her face frozen as she swayed on her feet, eyes wide and shocked. "Oh my God..." dark eyes welling with tears. "OH my God....oh my God...baby....I'm so sorry..." Don't cry, don't cry, don't cry, you're tough, you're a big kid now, don't cry... I burst into tears. She swayed and dropped to her knees next to me, tears flowing freely, arms wrapping around me, "Oh baby, I'm so sorry, I'm so sorry..." I felt something break in my chest, hot pain and fear running down my face, mingling with the snot. We cried together in the mean light cast by incandescent bulbs.

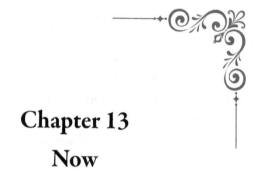

Chapter 13
Now

The white Honda Civic and a blue Subaru Outback are ours, waiting for me in the lot outside. The auctioneer's voices mingle in the bays, a din of noise I'm on autopilot, that numb place I retreat too when my mind can't handle the blows thrown at me. It's my safe place. My default setting when I just can't handle it.

I look around the bay at the faces of the people here buying cars, wondering if any of them had a clue what went on around them, all the time, every day, unseen and unheard by most, but not all of us. I wondered if any of them would go crazy if they could hear and see the things I did. I wished fiercely that I could be clueless, and content like them.

I glanced up at the cars moving through. The red Toyota would be coming through in a few minutes. I wanted, no, *needed*, to be out of here before it did. I needed to get to the office, pay for our cars, load and leave. Now.

My feet refused to move. 2576 rolled into the bay in front of me, a tan Ford Taurus SE. Seconds ticked by, the bidding ending at $1,100.00. The driver, red plaid shirt, black shaggy hair, dropping it into gear and rolling out the other door. 2577 rolled in, the gold Jeep Grand Cherokee. My heart gave a double thud. Auctioneers voice chanting, the light over the bay red, telling us there was a mechanical problem, commotion in the bay across from us, a wrecked Saturn rolling in on the hook of a wrecker, bidding ending at $950.00 on the Jeep. Gold panels reflected dull light back at me as its driver, this one female, piloted it towards the back door.

Leave Ger. Leave now.

The red Toyota came in, still sagging to one side, older man driving it, hood winking dully under the fluorescents. The light above the auctioneer stayed green. No problems as far as the auction house knew. Too late to leave even if my feet would let me.

I sat still as the bidding began, watching the subtle signs of the buyers. $1,700, $1,750, $1,800...I knew the guy across from me who was bidding on it, Sean Hackaman, ran a small shop down towards the city...$1,900, bidding slowing, almost done...my head nodded, seemingly of its own volition, the spotter yelping as he saw it, auctioneer looking back at Sean, Sean made eye contact with me, bid again, I countered, $2,200, Sean stopped bidding, lip curling slightly, auctioneer all done, car in gear again, the red car that was just a car, rolling out the bay door, mine, well, Bills. No...not Bill's. Mine.

Chapter 14
Now

The bottle was cold and wet, condensation rolling down the sides, comforting in my palm. I pressed it to my forehead, leaning forward on my elbows, eyes closed against the dim light from over the stove. An owl hooted somewhere down across the river, once, twice. Moisture pressed to my hot head heated and dried. I slumped into my elbows more.

The mates to this bottle were lined up in front of me on the rickety Formica table, fallen soldiers. I took another pull on the one I held in my hand. Deep into a twelve-pack and...nothing. It was like drinking beer flavored soda. No peace for me tonight.

The red car was sitting in the corner of Bill's lot, still leaning to one side, Bill confused as hell when I told him I bought it. I had winched it onto Gertie, hooking it on to avoid sitting in the thing, sending Howie to come along home with the Subaru. I needed some time to think, to figure out what the hell I was going to do. I pressed the bottle harder against my aching head.

Over by the sink my phone buzzed against the counter-top, vibrating like a pissed off rattlesnake. I ignored it, third time tonight I had done so. I kept my eyes closed as the owl hooted again, closer this time. Over the sighing of the wind, I could hear faint noises from my neighbors here in the park, a TV mumbling someplace, a woman's voice out in the roadway, a dog barking somewhere across the county road. Usually I liked having people near me, made me feel less alone, like I belonged somewhere. Tonight, it just made me feel even more isolated, a strange explorer wrapped in a hermetically sealed suit walking on a foreign landscape, unable to breathe the same air, feel the same sun.

I thought about what would happen if I just left. Quit my job, packed my shit in my F150 and headed west. Maybe go towards Colorado, or Utah. Check out Wyoming maybe. There might be a little cabin someplace that a man could find peace in, someplace with a bright little meadow in front of it, aspens rattling in the wind, high peaks that wore snowcaps in the fall all around it. Someplace where I could fish and hunt, spend my days watching the hawks circle overhead. For a moment, the image was so real, it pierced the knotted fibers around my heart with an aching longing, a feeling of homesickness for a place I hadn't even gone to yet.

But wherever you go, there you are. I could travel for years and never get away from myself. My own soul would poison the very waters of that eternal spring, turning them dark and bitter with the metallic taste of fear and loathing. I could never hope for peace anyplace as long as this 'damaged frontal lobe' kept opening doors best left shut. Even if there were no people around for miles, they would have passed through, leaving imprints on the very rock of the land, imprints that would start atomizing into the atmosphere and into my exposed psyche, piercing my heart, my own humanity with their memories, their fears, and hopes. They would slowly kill me with their needy remembrances.

I had to do something. The images, the *memories* I had experienced so vividly, so wrenchingly, roared back through me again. Shuddering, I leaned forward, clenching my fists around the bottle and pressing it hard to my head as they tore through me again, trying to hang on and glean what little hints I could, see details I had missed in the initial wave of madness.

Brown hair, overweight, she was wearing a red sparkly tube top thing, with a white button down shirt over it, short black skirt, high heeled boots...she made me mad, FURIOUS...jam that stinky bitch...blood running down her wrists....coppery taste in my mouth...plastic crackling loud like gunshots, red painted lips wailing...tiny gold earring...ribcage under my quivering palm...bitchbitchbitch...always laughing at me bitch...

I dropped the bottle to the white speckled top, slapping my hands on my face and groaning loudly. Tremors started at the base of my spine and ran up my back unchecked, stomach clenching, rebelling against the beer and the memory that wasn't mine...I dry heaved a moment, concentrating fiercely on not letting it erupt.

The clock on the far wall swam in and out of my sight, second hand ticking around. I stared at it glassy eyed, watching the quivering needle as it ticked along.

Time was ticking away. He would do this again. He had done this again. There had been many of them.

In that car.

Chapter 15

Then

Mommy told me we had a secret. She said I couldn't tell Ricky about it. I 'speshully couldn't tell HIM about it. I don't talk to HIM anyway. I hate him.

Mommy said we are going to Gramma's house tomorrow for a vacation. She said that we were all going to go to floor-a-duh, me, Mommy and Gramma. I never heard of floor-a-duh, but Mommy said it's where the big mouse and all the castles and talking animals are! I want to see the castle. I want to go to floor-a-duh!

She said HE wasn't coming with us. I couldn't talk about it because HE would get mad. She said this very seriously. I know about serious stuff. I'm not a little kid anymore.

Mommy looks different. Her eyes are all bright. She is like the Mommy I remembered. She even smiled at me. She got down on her knees and looked me right in the eyes and told me we had a SECRET. She knows I can keep a SECRET because I am a big, brave boy now.

I feel funny, like all floaty and light, weird. I think I am happy.

Chapter 16
Now

The deck on my trailer feels unsteady under my feet, like standing on a dock in the lake. Overhead, a fingernail moon winks at me through the swaying leaves on the big maple tree, winking like some signal light from far away, danger, danger, it says, go back. I tilt my head back to look at it, reward myself with a spinning head rush. Damn...the beers did more than I thought.

Stumbling, I half fall down the stairs to the ground, my truck gleaming in the light spilling from the kitchen window. The owl hoots again, booming voice rolling through the little valley. Route 20 is illuminated briefly as a car whooshes by, heading west, tires humming as they head on through to someplace else, anyplace else but here.

I fumble with the door handle on the truck, half staggering as another head rush hit me. I dragged myself up into the seat, focusing on finding the ignition before the light went out. Briefly, it crosses my mind that this isn't a good idea.

I have to go to the shop. I have to go now. I need to get back in that car, to 'see' what happened in it. The title is in the office, still in the envelope. I hadn't opened it before, couldn't open it. I needed to now. He was out there someplace, out there hunting, crawling through the streets in some bland sedan, trawling for the next high, the next gut filling package of flesh and lipstick, teased hair and cheap perfume. He was invisible to police. But I knew he was there.

My headlights stabbed the darkness as I kicked gravel up, slewing the back end around, turning east, towards town. Towards the shop where a little red car that was not just a car sat.

I was always surprised that I could still drive as well as I did when I was this buzzed. My hands firm on the wheel, the truck arrow straight, the road kinking and winding under me. I was on a mission finally, like I had spent years waiting for someone to need me, someone to be calling me to help them, to please find them and lay them to rest. My head and heart felt swollen with it. My purpose.

The center of town was dead still at this hour, the lone traffic light changing colors with a click to empty lanes. I sailed through on a green, further proof that this was right and just. Brown blocks glowed in the headlights as I swung into the lot, windows glinting like stars were winking inside of them, a flash of the sign BILL'S REPAIR. I turned off the ignition, killing the lights.

The motor ticked in the stagnant silence, its dying song. My sense of purpose, my feeling of euphoria, purpose and destiny oozed away, leaving me naked, vulnerable. Sobriety rushed back in, carried on the wings of a fluttering sensation that I knew too well.

Fear.

A chill snaked up my back, lifting the hair on my neck. My stomach clenched, assaulted by the liquid that sloshed in my otherwise empty system. The darkness held deeper shadows everywhere, shadows that held secrets, secrets with glowing eyes and razor-sharp mouths. Secrets that could kill you. Leaves rustled in the freshening breeze off the river, cool air brushing my arms, the fingers of long dead men and women, trailing jagged nails up my arm to my shoulder. I've heard that fingernails grow after you die, long and curled, sharp and demanding. Better tools to tear your way out from the rosewood prison you inhabit under tons of worm laden dirt, moisture from the rains seeping down and puddling on the once shiny surface. Even the most elaborate, glorious casket is nothing but a prison cell for the undead.

"Jesus." My voice is raspy in the sodden silence. "Go home." Home. The sensible solution. The easy solution. The solution I now desperately wished I had chosen instead of driving all the way over here, three sheets to the wind, but not so drunk I couldn't feel the menace all around me. Rolling the window up to keep the dead fingers off me, I sat behind the wheel for long minutes. Stay or go....shame at my cowardice. Fear at the night.

A chain link fence separated the back lot from the front, where we kept our cars. A key to the lock dangled from my keychain, as did one to the office door. Bill in his infinite patience had been trying to partner me in with him for a few years now, convinced that I could be an asset to his operation. Grudgingly, I had accepted a few responsibilities with it, the keys being one of them. I wondered how he would feel about having me as a partner if he knew what lay below the surface of my bland exterior, the deep black currents that ran through my soul.

I suspected I wouldn't be welcome here anymore.

The truck door creaked loudly, rending the thick silence that enveloped me. My heart rate jagged, pounding in my ears. I looked over at the lot, unable to see through the blackness that slithered against the dim light the truck interior threw. Sliding out, I pushed the door to carefully, loathe to make noise, fear of drawing attention to myself. My head swirled again, images fighting to crowd in, coppery blood, glint of jewelry, smell of perfume and hairspray, body odor underneath the surface. I squeezed my eyes closed for a long moment, fighting to keep them at bay.

It took several tries before I fit the key into the padlock in the gate, then several more tries to undo the latch and push the gate open enough to slip through it. Alcohol roared through me in waves, my steps turning unsteady as I made my way across the little lot towards the dark shape that crouched over in the back corner, where I had deposited it that afternoon. I wanted desperately to turn around, walk away, go home and finish up the bottle of vodka that sat in the cabinet over the sink, find some oblivion again. I knew I would never know oblivion again as long as that creature walked free.

Sometimes we are held hostage by our own ideals, facing emotional death if we back down and surrender.

Leaden feet took me to the driver's side door of the red car.

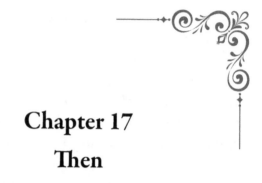

Chapter 17
Then

G ramma and Mommy are sitting in the kitchen talking. I'm so excited, I can hardly sit still! Tomorrow, we are leaving really, really early in Gramma's car to go to floor-a-duh. I didn't say anything to anyone at all, not even Ricky. I'm really, really proud. I can keep secrets. I'm a big kid now.

Gramma's face was all funny when we arrived. I thought she would be happy, happy, happy like I am, but she looked mean. I started feeling a little scared again. Mommy said I could go watch Lassie while she and Gramma had coffee in the kitchen.

Mommy made me turn the sound down though, so I scooch up close so I can hear it. I notice that I can also hear Mommy and Gramma in the kitchen, they're talking louder and louder, almost like they are arguing. I hope they aren't. I hate fights

I pull my legs up tight to my body, wrapping my arms around them while concentrating fiercely on watching Lassie bark at Timmy. Their voices get louder; I wonder about turning the TV up. I can hear them over the sound. I try not to listen, but I can't help it.

"I don't think coming here was safe....first place he'll look....don't underestimate him."

"Mom, he's not coming over here. He's up at the camp with his buddies, he won't even know we're gone until Wednesday. Besides, he wouldn't really do anything to us."

"How can you say that? The number of times you and Gerry have shown up with bruises all over you! You don't think I didn't see that?"

She mumbles, too low for me to hear, then, "Look, you want us to go then? You're just a scared old woman!"

My stomach clenches. Go? I don't want to go without Gramma! I want all of us to go to floor-a-duh.

"I'm scared is right! Scared that he's going to kill you and Gerry! Jesus Christ! You need to leave NOW! Take my car, here..." some rustling, "Here's some money. Car's full. Get going and get on the road. NOW!"

"What about you? I want you to come with us!"

"Who is going to head him in the wrong direction then? Girl, you aren't using your head. Mark my words; He will find you if you stay here and it won't be pretty. Don't wait until morning, go now."

"But what about you?"

"He won't mess with me. I've got a double-aught with that bastard's name on it."

"Mom, we need to get some sleep before we go. It's late. I can't drive very far now; I'll drive right off the road. And where would we stay tomorrow night? If we leave early in the morning, I can make it to Aunt Kelly's place by early night tomorrow, then Orlando by nightfall the next. No, we'll wait a few hours then leave."

Their voices dropped again, too low for me to hear. I stared at the screen without seeing it. I wished Gramma wasn't mad at us. My eyes prickled with tears; my happy, happy, happy feeling gone.

I heard footsteps behind me. I held my legs tighter to my body, refusing to look to see who it was. Mommy knelt down on the floor next to me, her face all smiley and fake. "How's the show, Ger?" She wrapped an arm around my shoulders and hugged me.I don't want to cry. I don't want to cry. I'm a big kid now, able to keep secrets and stuff. But tears start sliding down my face, unbidden and unwanted, a sob hiccups through my ribs.

"Honey, what's the matter?"

"I...don't....wanna leave Gramma...I'm scared!"

She wraps her arms around me tighter, her chin on my head. I feel her chin move as she speaks, not to me, but to Gramma, who is standing just behind me.

"Honey, it's alright. Nothing is going to happen to us. I promise."

Chapter 18

Now

"It's just a car." I sway slightly in the strengthening wind, startled at my own voice. I laugh, a bone-dry giggle. "What the hell, man? What'sh the deal? You're being a pussy."

Pussy, pussy, pussy, my whole life spent in a circle around that word. Trying not to be one. Trying to find one. Trying to leave one. Back to trying to not be one. Funny stuff, right?

So why wasn't I laughing?

The skin on my back was crawling, like a thousand ants on pinfire feet were marching up my spine, up my neck, burrowing into my hair. A chill spread across my scalp and ears, prickling my forehead.

The car was a black shape in the gloom, a spark of reflected streetlight glinting off the windshield. I had a flash of a vision, of gleaming eyes lit from within, red tinged, a black hole where the face should be.

I fought the urge to back away again. What the hell was I doing here? My vision blurred, wavered into two images, then back to one. The damn beer; didn't have all that much, just a twelve pack, 'cept on a stomach that held nothing,

51

maybe that was enough. What a pussy you are, can't even drink beer properly.

The door handle was smooth as a polished bone under my hand, cold and dead. Half-heartedly, I tugged on it, unable to remember if I locked it, hoping I did, hoping the keys were back at home. It opened with a snick, of course it did; it was waiting for me. The interior glowed with a cosmic blackness, a palpable *wrongness*, a whoosh of air from a long-sealed grave, dead breath washing over me....

The interior light glowed, illuminating bland gray upholstery, am/fm radio with a tape deck, automatic transmission, Japanese efficiency, totally....nothing. Just a car. Disoriented, I shook my head, staggering a bit. Around me, the night receded, katydid's raspy songs suddenly filling the dense darkness, light from the streetlight painting thin gray stripes across the hood and seat. Swaying slightly, I held onto the edge of the roof a moment, then took a deep breath, held it like a diver, and slide back into the front seat.

The upholstered surface sighed and settled under me, releasing a faintly dusty smell, old fabric and dirt. Something else, deeper, more subtle. I sat bone still for a moment, aware of the other eyes and hearts that had seen and pounded in this car, raced and....stilled forever. A trickle of sweat beaded up and rolled down my face. I took another deep breath, "Just do it..git 'er done." Closed my eyes and opened my mind up wide.

The air was cold, cold like that bitches' heart, stinging my face and lips. A low growling hunger inside of me, growling, insistent, not satisfied with food, not satisfied with booze, not satisfied with smoke, or blow or anything else blown into your veins or nose. Hungry tonight, hungry...there. Under the light by the convenience store, iron gates pulled tight, there...honey skin, high raggy ponytail, same bitch was here two days ago.

She comes to the window willingly, boldly, she knows you, she doesn't fear you. Her fragrance fills the car as she settles onto the plastic covered seat, her voice grating on your ears like metal skidding across a concrete floor, you smile, smile, smile, crap flowing from your mouth, the blocks flickering by, to the special place you've selected just for her and you.

Your skin quivers with the anticipation, the need. Catching a glimpse of your eyes in the rearview mirror you marvel that she can't see what deep blackened pools they are, can't see the dangerdangerdanger in them.

She's strong, that surprises you. You're stronger. That demoralizes her, flailing, wailing into the night that has no ears for her, no pity, as you twist the wire tighter around her neck, her hands zip tied together in mock prayer.

A blow, another to your ear, fucking bitch hurt you, hurting you with those hands, tighter, tighter, blood exploding like a fountain from her lips as you twist the life out of her, jamming her, jamming yourself hard against her, rubbing on her, exploding into your own jeans as the life flickers and dims in her eyes, that magical moment of ending flashing right in front of you like a firework. La Petit Morte the fucking French call an orgasm; the little death. You heave in the throes of yours as she heaves in the throes of her big Morte, her big death, the empty hollow in your gut filled, filled to overflowing, sated and relieved, the sex ten thousand times better than if you had it with her when she was alive.

Release....for you. For her.

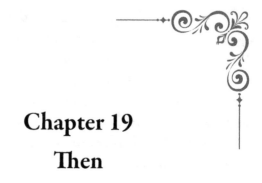

Chapter 19

Then

I can't sleep. Gramma's house is noisy, different than mine, smells different, is hotter too. Sweat trickles down my face as I kick the covers all the way off. I think about taking my PJ's off, thinking that Mommy doesn't like it when I do that.

I toss and turn, darkness in the room strange and unfamiliar. A rattling, whirring noise from the kitchen rings through the little room I am lying in, a spare room with a saggy cot. Mommy is sleeping on the couch in the living room next to me, Gramma in her own bed upstairs.

The little house seems huge in the darkness, noisy, hot and huge. I try not to think about it, thinking instead about floor-a-duh, wondering what floor-a-duh will be like. I can't believe we are going! I hug myself in the noisy darkness, unable to believe we are actually going to the magic castle. I need some magic. Maybe things will be good now, better, more fun. Maybe HE won't care that we are gone, and Mommy won't go back to him. I think of just Mommy, Gramma and me in floor-a-duh, and my belly gets all happy happy happy.

I have to pee. The sensation of fullness, of wetness, comes from nowhere suddenly. I don't want to have to get up. Gramma's bathroom is all the way down the long, long hallway, clear the other side of the house, past the stairs going upstairs, the kitchen and everything. The house is really, really dark too.

I toss and turn, trying to hold it. Images come unbidden into my head; Darlene, Jimmy and Ricky calling me a pussy. I don't want to be a pussy. But it scares me, walking through Gramma's house, in the noisy dark. Pussy, pussy, pussy, little Gerry never going to be a big man, little Gerry always going to be a pussy.

Covers slither down to the floor as I sit up, swinging my legs over the edge. Fear and determination mingle in my throat. I can do this. I'm a big kid now. My feet slide off the edge of the cot and hit the floor.

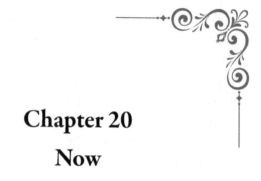

Chapter 20

Now

"Jesus Christ! What the hell Gerry?" Bill's voice slices the numbing fog that cushioned my brain, layers of sleep and alcohol that shielded me from the world shattered, leaving behind piercing pain.

Gray light was shining through the square windows. I struggled to assimilate what was going on. Bill's office, the sagging couch along the side wall under me, the bottom drawer of the file cabinet open, the spare bottle of whiskey he kept there out and empty on the floor next to me, Bill an angry presence, back lit against the mean, soupy grayness that soaked the room.

"What the hell did you do?" he asks again, pain and anger in his voice. I'm mute, unable to formulate an answer even if I had one. I cover my face instead, trying to block him out, block out what happened, block out every crappy thing that has happened to me in my life.

It doesn't work.

Bill snaps on the overhead light and stalks across the room. I cringe against the flare of the fluorescent, pain spiking through my eyes, my mouth dry and furry. I can smell a stench coming off of me, not just alcohol, but worse, deeper.

I pissed myself.

I look down at the floor, a floor that still moved and heaved in my vision, clasping my hands together on my knees, mute, waiting for the ax to fall. Bill's feet in the corner of my vision, savagely he kicks the whiskey bottle across the room where it hits the file cabinet with a deafening clang. He snarls through clenched teeth, "I can't BELIEVE after all the SHIT we went through LAST YEAR that you would do this AGAIN! God DAMN you!" Swiveling, he kicks the wastebasket into the air, paper and empty coffee cups flying out in a shower. "Dammit Gerry! Why the HELL didn't you CALL me?"

Why indeed? To be honest calling Bill, or anyone, wasn't on my mind. Ever. I continued to stare at the floor, his anger raining down on my head.

"I spent thousands on you, spent hours and hours on you, went to the mat for you, and this? This is how you respond? You come in here, drink my booze, trash my office and...and...Jesus! You pissed all over my couch? You don't even call me, don't give me a single chance, you just come in here and crap all over me!"

Shame burned bright and hot in my gut, my damp pants sticking to my crotch, stench to my own nostrils. I could smell the underpinnings to the stink of urine, a stink I recognized, even if Bill didn't. Fear.

I had no memory of after I got in the car, none. I had no idea what I would find when I looked outside in the lot. Would I have torn the car apart? Ripped the interior out, kicked in the glass, pounded on the faded red skin? Or did I spend hours in it, wallowing in the memories and sensations that swamped my psyche when I sat in the seat? I remembered one thing all too clearly, despite wishing desperately that I could forget it, or better yet, never have experienced it at all: I had enjoyed some of the sensations.

And what did that say about me then?

My gut curled. I hunched lower over my knees, grasping my hands together tightly as Bill yelled. I remembered my irritation over his caring about me yesterday. I wished I hadn't completely blown it last night. Because things would never be the same.

I was probably unemployed now, likely to be thrown out of here in short order, my meager savings wasted on the red car that sat like a malignant tumor in the corner of the lot. My mind, sluggish and alcohol laden, struggled to move through the maze of confusion the daylight had brought, problems buried under the 90-proof magnified now. Bill's voice had receded to background noise, like the noise of a washer running, white noise.

The silence pierced the fog. Slowly I realized he had fallen silent. I cautiously raised my eyes from the floor, saw brown Timberlands in front of me, duct tape patching a hole on the side. Painfully, I raised my eyes to him, the light sending lancets of silvery pain through my head. The dent ached fiercely, like a snare drum. Bill's face was a thundercloud, hands on his hips.

"Well? Did you even hear me?"

What answer could I give to that? I shook my head no. He pursed his lips and exhaled in exasperation, sadness suddenly replacing the anger. "God damn you. Get your ass up off my couch."

Unsteadily I rose as he fished a pair of keys out of his pocket. Eying me warily, he grabbed several sections of newspapers off the stack on his chair, pointing towards the door silently.

I took one wobbling step, then two, then a third, surer step as I acclimated to being upright. I patted my pockets for my keys, finding a lump in the front right pocket. I pulled them out as we stepped out into a drizzly gray morning. Bill reached out, yanking my keys from my hand.

"Like hell. Get in the Dodge."

The Dodge. The used truck we had that Tim Mathers wanted to buy. Bill bent and slapped the repair plate in place, held on by two powerful magnets, twisting a strand of safety wire in place as a surety.

Dazed, I looked around. My truck sat at an awkward angle to the fence, half blocking the back lot. I craned to see the car, the edges of my vision swimming. Behind me I heard newspapers rustling in the truck, then Bill telling me. "Get in."

Ignoring him, I shuffle stepped the half dozen steps to where I could see into the lot, my damp pants chafing my crotch and inner thighs. Bill yelled for me to get my ass over to the truck. I don't respond.

Wetness sparkled on the hoods and roofs of the cars lining the lot, dull clouds reflecting back in the glass, sodden leaves blown down by last night's wind plastered all over everything. The little red car sat where it had been dropped yesterday, doors closed, hood and windshield undamaged, looking untouched.

I swear it had a malevolent air to it.

Chapter 21
Then

Gramma's hallway is long, long, long in the dark house. Mommy softly snores on the living room couch, her blanket on the floor like mine. The rattling whirring noise continues, from the 'frigerator I think. It's loud, drowning out everything. I peer down the hall, wishing Gramma had a night light on for me.

Taking a deep breath, I start, one step, two, three, down the long black hallway towards the bathroom. Fear tingles in my belly, making me want to pee even worse.

About halfway, I hesitate. I can hear Ricky, Jimmy and Darlene in my brain, pussypussypussy Gerry the pussy...and I shuffle forward, past the black hole leading to the upstairs where Gramma snores, louder than Mommy, finally reaching the wood paneled door to the bathroom. All by myself.

The door is open a little bit, the wood smooth under my hand. For a sickening moment I have a vision of a monster in the shower, sniffing the air, smelling me... The thought hits me as I step all the way into the bathroom, too late to stop, too late, open and defenseless...

Gramma has a big old bathtub there, the kind with the funny feet, no shower curtain or nothing. I'd forgotten that. There's no one in it, no drooling demons with razor sharp teeth. Faint light comes in the little window over the toilet, letting me see enough to at least not pee on my feet. I leave the door to the hallway open though...if there's something in the sink or toilet, I want to get away quick.

I shove the heavy toilet seat up. Gramma has this old one, it's all gray looking and heavy, not like ours, ours looks like it's wood and doesn't weigh nearly as much. Fumbling with my pajama bottoms, I slide them down and pull my weewee out. I briefly think about sitting down to pee, cuz sometimes my aim isn't so good. But I'm a big kid now. I can keep secrets and I can stand up to pee. Leaning into the bowl, I release my bladder and let my stream out. Instant relief.

The water tinkling down into the bowl is almost silent, with all the noise from the 'frigerator going on. I start to relax a little, the tight knot of tension in my back easing. I'm no pussy.

The 'frigerator shut off with a rattling bang. I gasped a little in the sudden stillness, startled by the silence, the silence I had been hoping for. A nervous little laugh worked its way up my throat. "Pussy." I whispered.

Finishing, I shook myself then pulled my bottoms back up, feeling a burst of pride at doing this all by myself, a BIG KID now. I reached for the toilet handle to flush just as I hear a noise from the living room.

Chapter 22

Now

B ill is silent as he maneuvers the noisy diesel through the empty streets, gray rainwater shining dully in the gutters along the curbs.

I sit in miserable silence, pain flaring with every bump, the newspapers Bill spread across my seat rattling loudly in the cab. Tire rumble changes to a whine as we reach Route 20, water spraying on the underside of the truck. I wonder when he will tell me to take my tools and get out, wonder if I can somehow apologize.

It's too late for that.

The sad little cluster of buildings I call home appears on the right, a few lights gleaming in the wet dawn. My head spins slowly, I long to lay my head down on my pillow and sleep for another 8, 10, maybe a hundred hours. Maybe for so long that when I wake up, this will all be long done. The tire whine dies as Bill slows to make the turn into the park.

My trailer looks sad and defeated in this dank light, the lamp still glowing in the kitchen. Wordlessly, I open the door and slid out to the ground, swaying slightly as gravity plays hell with me.

A door thuds behind me; Bill has gotten out and is walking around the front of the truck, a grim expression on his face. Staggering slightly, I follow him up the three steps to the deck outside my kitchen. He holds the door open for me. Confused, I enter the trailer.

The beer bottles stand in a mini forest on the kitchen table, my dead soldiers. I feel Bill taking it all in; the bottles, the overflowing ashtray, the stench in the room. I say nothing, my numbness starting to be pierced with another emotion; anger. Clenching my jaw, I finally speak to him.

"Thanks for the ride home. I'll be by to collect my stuff."

"Like hell you will."

I turn to look at him. He stands, arms folded, an expression on his face I know all too well. Stubborn.

Great.

"Look, take what I owe you out of my check then, for the couch, the whiskey..." I trail off, waving vaguely, "I'm...I'm sorry, okay? Just do what you gotta do and leave me alone." I sink down into the kitchen chair, reaching for the pack of Camels still lying there. The acrid tang sears my lungs. I drag deeply.

Bill doesn't move. "I'm not taking anything out of anything. What's going to happen is YOU'RE going to take a God damned shower, get dressed, and we are going back to work."

"What the hell? Work?" I laugh, a bitter, mean sound. "Work? You don't have enough insurance for me to go back to work like this..." A buzz hums through my veins as the nicotine mingles with the alcohol.

"I mean it. Get moving."

"Look. I screwed up last night, okay? I get it. But all I want to do right now is sleep. We can talk about this later."

Bill crosses the room in one step, shoving his face in mine. "If I leave now, there isn't going to BE any kind of later, you get it? Your laters are all gone Gerry. You owe me, big time! We have work stacked up today, work I can't do all by myself, work that I sure as hell can't trust Howie with. You owe me...big time. Now get your ass up and into that shower if you want to hang onto any sort of future at all. We have to be back to the shop..." a quick glance at my wall clock, "in twenty minutes."

A real man wouldn't let anyone talk to him like this. A real man stands up for himself, for what he is, for the man he has become. A real man doesn't just hang his head and mumble, "yessir." I silently stood up and headed for the shower.

What can I say?

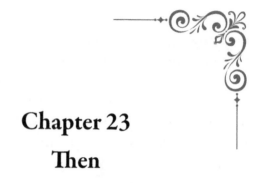

Chapter 23
Then

I'm not sure it I really heard that noise or not. I freeze, my hand on the handle of the toilet. Then, from the living room, a sudden crash!

Noise explodes in a wall, freezing me in my place. My Mommy's voice, screaming, screaming, screaming, thudding sounds, terrible, horrible wet whacking sounds, from above me another crash from Gramma's room, thundering, thundering, then sound, sound, more sounds from the living room, my Mommy! My Mommy! She's yelling my name! Mommy!

I run, I run and run, fear so big and large that I have to run, run, run, run, down the hallway, into the living room where there is a swirl of black shapes in front of me, a whirl of demons locked in a death dance.

I can smell HIM. It's HIM! He found us! He's making wet noises, my Mommy is screaming, and I suddenly am Gerry the Pussy no more, suddenly I'm Superman, scared, scared, scared but launching myself at him, I'm screaming now too, my voice high and razor thin as I land on HIS back, causing him to grunt as Mommy screams, screams, screams, and Gramma screams, screams, screams, and I'm kicking, and biting HIM, his blood foul in my mouth, my strength borne of terror, amazing strength, and he bellows, swiping at me, and Gramma is screaming, screaming my name, screaming for me to get out of the way, get out of the way, but I don't know what the way is, or how to get out of it, and I'm kicking and clawing...

He stumbles and falls to the floor, taking me with him, the floor wet and foul smelling under us, and Mommy isn't screaming anymore, the stench of booze sharp in my nose, and he's grunting, grunting words I can't understand, and he's clawing at my back, trying to dislodge me, and I'm scared, scared, scared because now I'm going to GET IT! And IT is going to be really, really bad, and I'm trying to get away, get away, get away and his hand closes around my neck, a claw, hurts, hurts, hurts and Gramma screams and there's a huge BOOM.....

And then there's nothing at all.

Chapter 24
Now

BRACK BRACK BRACK BRACK BRACK...the air hammer reverberates through my damaged head, piercing pain bringing tears to my eyes. Stopping, I readjust my grip and lean into it again. BRACK BRACK BRACK BRACK. The left side ball joint on the '01 Ford F150, 4wd, finally comes loose.

Sweat beads my forehead, stinking like old booze, I'm panting slightly. Too many cigarettes, too much booze. Too much everything.

In the next bay, Howie is dismounting a set of worn tires and installing a new set, clean black donuts with stickers bright white against the blackness. He is operating a tire balancing machine and an air powered impact wrench, more noise that shatters like glass across my forehead. The shop compressor kicks on with a clattering roar, drowning both of us out for a moment. The onslaught of noise is almost more than I can bear.

Bill is outside, in the back lot. He disappeared out there shortly after depositing me in the bay, where the forest green F150 already waited, both front ball joints in need of replacing, one of the worst possible jobs when you're feeling this low. I take a long slug off my bottle of water, the left side joint almost done now.

Too bad I still have the right side to do yet.

I see a flash of light off the metallic surface of a car turning in out in front of the shop, an E36 BMW. It disappears behind the brown Volvo station wagon, one of those all-wheel drive ones that got deposited here by Clark's Towing an hour ago.

The car parks just out of sight as I glance up at the shop clock hanging over by the coffee pot. Just after 9:00 a.m. now. Two hours since we returned in dead silence to the shop, me washed and sullen, Bill hard mouthed and grim. I glance out towards the lot, wondering about the Volvo. I didn't know we had one coming in.

Taking a deep breath, I lean into the right-side ball joint with the air hammer. BRACK BRACK BRACK BRACK.

Bill comes around the corner from the back, the driver of the BMW a step behind him, a skinny white-haired guy. They step into the office as I brace myself against the noise blowing back at me, wondering if I can get everything done early today, get home and get into bed. The last vestiges of the buzz are gone, leaving me nothing but ill; ill feeling and ill tempered. I wonder, not for the first time, about just quitting there, quitting mechanic work, just...quitting. A vision comes into my mind unbidden, the mountain meadow, bright in the late summer sun, yellow leaves flashing like stars on the flanks of the slopes above me.

I push it away hurriedly. Learned a long time ago there just isn't any use in thinking about stuff you can't ever do.

Gritting my teeth, I lean harder into the air hammer again, surprised as the second ball joint pops loose easily, probably already been replaced once. Maybe I will get out of here before lunch.

The office door swings again; Bill and the BMW guy walking back out, stopping in the doorway of the shop, backs to us, talking about something. Bill's hands move, gesturing up, down, to the side, white haired guy nodding, laughing once, then looking over his shoulder into the shop for a moment.

At me.

Shaking Bill's hand, he walks out into the light, heading back to his white BMW E36. Bill turns to look at me as taillights flare and the BMW is gone.

I don't have a good feeling about where this is going.

My hands are shaking slightly, from exertion and the hangover, as I install the second ball joint. My mind keeps trying to go back to the red car, to the memories that are seared on my 'damaged frontal lobe'. I push it aside, pull up the meadow someplace in the Rockies instead. Safer to think of things I can never have then to give in to the malevolent pull the little car is exerting on me.

A rattling rap-rap-rap comes through the open doorway of the shop. Looking over, I see Bill drive past in his race car, a yellow and green Honda CRX he races with a club called Sports Car Club of America. I realize then why he has been conspicuously absent in the shop this morning; he's loading the trailer to race at Watkins Glen this weekend. Something I normally help him do. A leaden feeling settles in the pit of my stomach again.

In the bay beside me, Howie has finished mounting and installing the new tires on the little white Honda Civic I brought back from the auction. Tim Mathers is supposed to come in to see it and hopefully seal the deal on both cars.

Howie doesn't look at me as he wipes off his hands before getting in the Honda to back it out of the shop. He pulls it off to the side of the door and parks, looking for Bill. Bill walks over from behind the building, listens to Howie as he talks and points at the Volvo, then shakes his head; no no. He points towards the lot, towards the blue Hyundai along the outer fence. Howie walks towards it in his usual shuffle step, head perpetually hanging.

Bill walks over to me as I lower the Ford back down to the ground. I don't look at him.

"Tim's coming by at noon for those two vehicles. Don't need to do nothing except be here for it. Howie's gonna finish up on that Hyundai, and then he's got two oil changes scheduled, both of them are waiting. Make sure he puts the God damned drain plugs back in this time, okay?"

I finally look over at him. He doesn't look at me. "You taking off?" Dry mouth slurs words. He nods.

The Ford reaches the ground with a soft hissing noise as suspension takes up the slack again. He tilts his head towards the lot, towards the brown Volvo. "Got one job out there for you to do today. New customer, got that Volvo. I told him we would have it back to him by tonight."

I kick the arms of the lift back out of the way, preparing to drive the Ford out as Howie pulls in with the Hyundai. "What's it in for?"

"Fuel pump's gone. Auto House should have parts over for it in the next half hour or so." I stare at him, speechless. He returns my stare, defiant, daring me. "What? You afraid of a little work now?"

I can't speak; my tongue is stuck to the roof of my mouth. A fuel pump replacement on that car is an 8-hour job according to the computer program. On a good day, a day I'm not sick to my stomach, I can do one in 6. Everything has to come off; wheels, suspension, fuel lines, brake lines, sub-frame and then you finally reach the gas tank so you can take that off too. Then it's put everything back in again, piece by piece. It's a tedious, noisy job.

The feeling I had before crystallizes into certainty; Bill told this guy we would get it done today, instead of whatever day he was originally going to do it. This was his revenge on my screw-up, his punishment.I know about being punished.

I say nothing, nothing at all, afraid of what I would say even if I could. Bill stares at me a long moment, anger and sadness in his eyes, then he turns and walks away. With trembling hands, I climb in the Ford and back it out into the lot.

Chapter 25
Then

Noise, noise, so much noise, white light stabbing my eyes, searing, burning, pain, incredible pain, a drumbeat in my head. I cry and wail through stilled lips, begging for mercy, begging, begging, begging. Numbness washes over me and blackness crashes down.

Visions, dreams, they dance through my shuttered eyes, weird, wild dreams that scare me, scare me, scare me. Old lady, gray faced, gray haired, yelling, no, *howling* in pain as she leans over a still form in a bed. Throngs of people wearing blue and white clothing clustered around something I can't see, their faces all funny looking, some kind of masks on them, one woman with black framed glasses and no mouth, she scares me, pain, pain, pain, no, no, no!

Darlene, Jimmy and Ricky are walking with me again, only this time they're talking like I am not even there, talking *about* me! Puffs of dust kick up under my feet and I hang my head in silent shame, listening as Darlene tells Ricky and Jimmy that I am just a pussy, pussy, pussy and that my old man killed me and my mom because I was a *faggot*, and that my old man was NO GOOD and had done this before. You watch, she says all adult like, Gerry ain't gonna be much if he makes it. My daddy said his brains are mush now. I wonder how I can be dead and alive. I try to ask her this, my voice quavering, but she doesn't hear me.

She tosses her hair, for Jimmy I suddenly realize, she and Jimmy have been going under the bleachers down at the end of the field and she's been letting him stick his hand under her clothing, feeling her up with sticky, nasty fingers, and my cheeks bloom with shame like I've done something wrong, because Jimmy is looking at her and thinking about doing that today, and Ricky is looking away because he knows what they have been doing, and it's gross, gross, gross.

And I'm aware suddenly of only a dim, gray light punctuated with noise; beeping, hissing, humming, and there's no Darlene, no Ricky, no Jimmy, just me. I can't get the light to go away or come all the way in, it's just gray light, sometimes darker, sometimes lighter, just gray. The only color comes from the dreams that steal in on cat feet, bringing terror and color, so the terror is welcomed because anything is better than just gray, gray, gray. At least I think they are dreams, because how can I be two places at once? I wonder where mommy is. I try to call for her, but my mouth is frozen solid. I long to sink all the way through the gray and fall into the blackness.

Chapter 26

Now

I didn't think a man could feel this bad and still be alive. My head was banging huge, dull throbs in time to my heartbeat, my stomach coiled and empty, but full with shame, bile and need.

The Volvo was parked back outside, a shiny new fuel pump in place of the dead one, the streetlight reflecting off the windows as I locked the gate behind it. I looked at the corner of the lot the red Toyota lurked in. It was a dark, humped shape among the other dark, humped shapes. Just...a car.

Yeah. Right.

The title burned in my pocket, the envelope still unopened, a reluctance I couldn't name nagging at me. Wearily, I backed the truck out and pulled out of the lot, heading for the Hudson House of Pizza. I tried to remember the last time I ate, couldn't. The puddles of light thrown from the streetlights swam in my vision.

Inside the pizza shop, light and noise assailed me, turning my stomach over in place. The acne pocked kid at the register looked at me funny as I handed him a twenty but chose to say nothing as he slid the pizza across the counter at me.

I knew what I looked like; wild hair, thousand-mile stare, black bags under my eyes. He was afraid of me; I caught a whiff of that sneaking under my defenses. Wondered how he would feel if he knew the things I had seen and experienced. My own cheeks bloomed with shame as I backed through the door, clutching my large pepperoni pizza protectively.

Inside the cab of the truck, the smell hit me full force, instant saliva overdrive. Putting it in reverse, I tore a piece off hurriedly, almost moaning as I stuffed it in my mouth, my body craving the calories, craving the grease and the pleasure of something as simple as food. I felt some strength coming back as the food burned into energy in my belly. I tore a second piece off as I turned onto Route 20.

The lights were burning in the windows of the trailers haphazardly parked behind the closed restaurant, the partial moon hanging over the treetops again, some twenty hours after I left the first time. My headlights swept across the back end of a Volkswagen TDI parked outside my trailer, a "Co-exist" bumper sticker partially visible under the diesel grime. My heart sank.

Amy.

The engine ticked over in the silence as I sat for a moment, trying to gather myself up to face her. I had a memory of my phone buzzing, buzzing, buzzing like an angry snake on the countertop, the same phone I had left there this morning, the same phone she probably had already scrolled through, searching for more transgressions to hang on me.

She wouldn't find any; my transgressions aren't the kind to take place in such a mundane fashion as through a telephone.

Inside the house, a light glowed, and I saw a shadowy form looking through the kitchen window at me. No escape now. The very thought made me feel shamed and....angry. I loved Amy, loved her as much as I could love anyone. But it wasn't enough, it was never enough, she always wanted something more than I could give her. I wondered, not for the first time, why she stayed with me. Why she didn't dump me like Carol did and take off with someone else. The only answer I could formulate, as dim as I am, was that Amy was maybe, just maybe, even more screwed up than I was. And that thought made me uneasy too.

She was at the kitchen table, the newly cleaned kitchen table, all dark eyes and wild hair, anger pouring out of every pore, saturating the very air I breathed as I carefully deposited the pizza on the table, my appetite gone now, longing for sleep, deep and oblivion, wishing she hadn't chosen tonight of all nights to come here and blast me with her anger, her rage, her need. Feeling empty, like I had nothing to give her back except my own anger.

Silently, I went to the refrigerator to grab a beer. Empty shelves greeted me. Anger crystallized into rage. I knew there were at least two or three bottles I hadn't gotten to last night. Turning around, I met her lioness stare.

"You want some pizza?" deliberate, knowing that kind of mundane question would infuriate her, incense her.

She stayed silent a moment, her stare brittle ice points. "No thanks. If you're looking for something to drink, there's ice tea in the door."

Her way of telling me what I already knew; the last beers, the survivors, resided someplace in the septic system, the empty bottles nestled with the ones from last night. I clamped down on an almost overwhelming anger, aware of how much like HIM it felt like, a thought that brought fresh shame to me.

"Thanks." The word clipped from my mouth. I pulled a plate down from the shelf. I didn't want more pizza, but I had no choice now. "Sure you don't want some?" spoken to the cabinet I looked into.

I heard her shift in the chair. "No...thanks."

Such a strange, stilted conversation between two lovers, two people who supposedly loved each other, volumes of words unspoken flowing underneath the spoken ones, words that held far deeper, far more complex a conversation than the one our ears heard.

The plate clattered as I dropped it on the table in front of my chair. "Suit yourself then."

She eyed me, a wild, smoky air about her, this translucent young Gypsy woman with her colorful, billowy scarf around her neck, her soft, crinkly flowing skirt tucked around her knees, feet clad in brown, knee high boots pulled tight under the chair. My Gypsy, flown here in her coughing Volkswagen, the same one she had flown into my life in some nine months ago, her colorful, flowing presence striking me dumb with wonder the first time I met her, a blaze of burning light in the dark shop. A dumb wonder that flowered into full out, bewildered love/lust when she pursued me, actively seeking me out until we fell into her bed that first time, a tangle of flesh and need, her ferocity scaring me a bit, me wondering how this creature had come to be here in my life, amazed and thrilled at it, scared by it.

Frustrated by it when I got to know her a little better.

I tore a third piece off the rapidly cooling pie, aware that she was looking at the fat globules on the meat with ill-concealed disgust. Amy was a sometimes vegan, she was an earthy crunchy activist who hated anything that resembled change, hated windmills, hated fossil fuels, hated nuclear power. Why she was with a man that made his living on vehicles powered by dead dinosaurs was beyond me.

I wondered what would happen if I just asked her to please go home tonight and not harass me. I decided it probably wouldn't end well.

And truth be told, part of me really didn't want her to leave.

"So..." one word, laden with meaning, as treacherous and unpredictable as an IED in the roadbed, "Where were you last night?" The buzzing phone. My leash.

"At the shop." Muffled through dough, grease and pepperoni.

"Really?" eyes narrowed at me. "Looked to me like you were home at least long enough to drink ten beers."

I shrugged, didn't answer, chewed slowly.

She sat back in the chair, pinning me under her stare like a science project being dissected.

"The shop, huh? You mind enlightening me as to why you were at the shop all night?"

The title burned my chest through the inside pocket of the navy-blue uniform coat I still wore, 'Donahue' written in a white box over my left chest.

"I needed to go back for something." Took another bite, chewed slowly as my stomach rebelled against it.

"You 'needed to go back for something'. What would be *so* important that you would leave here, probably, no, *definitely*, shitfaced, and drive across town? Look at you...you look like total shit! You mind filling me in here? What the hell is going on with you, Gerry?"

What indeed? What could I say to her, to Bill, to anyone, that wouldn't make me sound like I was completely and totally crazy? How did you explain being able to see, hear, feel and taste the memories of other people, in all their crazed glory?

How could I possibly tell her that I had experienced at least three, maybe more murders last night? The answer was, there was no answer. I chewed my rubbery pizza and said nothing. I felt her anger sparking into a full-blown rage.

"God damn you!" hissed through clenched teeth." I am so sick and tired of you fucking with me it's not funny!"

Inside, I cringed at the words, the anger. Outside, I kept my face impassive, my only defense. She pushed away from the table suddenly, violence in her every movement. I worked on keeping my breathing still and even, keeping the coiled rage in my gut at rest.

"Where were you?" snarled at me from eight inches away from my face. "Who is she?" Who is she? I didn't know who she was, who *they* were. But I planned on finding out. I said nothing.

Amy's rage flowed over me, hardening my exterior again, glassing me over, allowing me to recede into my numb place, my safe zone. I could handle her, could handle anything when I was like this. I slowly chewed the last bite of pizza, secure now that she was safely locked outside of me. She stared at me, dark anger from her eyes, something more, anguish maybe. Amy was like that, all the time. Needy, angry, sucking you dry into her vast empty spaces. Part of me needed to be needed like that.

Part of me was terrified of it.

I wiped my mouth, trying to figure out how to ask her to leave without escalating things even more when she suddenly crossed the space between us, grabbing my face roughly, hands on each ear, yanking my mouth around to hers, attacking it with her mouth, lips full and wet on mine, tongue intruding roughly, not ladylike at all, not subtle, a full blown rape on my mouth, my body, conditioned like Pavlov's dog, rearing up in response, begging for a treat, begging, begging, her way around my safety zone, the chair under me crashing backwards to the floor as she landed on top of me, legs straddling me, hungry tongue probing me, and then all thought and logic was gone.

Amy. She was more screwed up than me. And that scared me.

Chapter 27

Then

I don't like it here. I know there's something other than this, but I can't picture it, can't feel it, it's like my life began here, in this flat lackluster place and I can't move on. Every day, people poking me, moving their mouths at me, making me do things, things that hurt.

I hate them all. I want them all to die.

Everything is hazy, flat, green walls, white ceiling, people in their white or blue clothes, bugging me, bugging me. I'm mad, mad, mad. I hate them all.

The dreams, everywhere the dreams, they won't leave me alone. In the dreams the colors are bright, vibrant, oh so bright. They scare me, none of them are good, they all are pain, fear, violence and death.

Sometimes the dreams feature people I know. How I know them I couldn't tell you, but I *know* them. Darlene, Jimmy, Ricky, Mommy, Gramma. Hollow names with images attached, names that mean something, but are holes that can't be filled. I toss and turn against the onslaught of dreams from them, until people poke and prod me, making me hurt, making me long for the dreams again.

The old woman with the gray hair and skin is here again, her mouth moving, sadness in her eyes. I stare at her, flat like a lizard, until she leaves. Her words to the blue clothed woman with her black glasses cuts through the noise around my brain.

"He's never going to be normal again, is he?" Words like a cry, words like unshed tears. My anger towers, anger at her for something, the blue clothed woman's reply lost in the buzzing of my brain. They are afraid of me; I can feel it. That makes me feel strong, full, huge...powerful.

I like being powerful.

Chapter 28
Now

Another gray dawn. This one seeps in around my eyes slowly, gently prodding my brain with fog-like fingers. I lie still, waiting, feeling for it. Nothing, no pounding, no drumming, no vibrating from my dented head. My stomach lies still, hollow, but still. I listen for another long moment before deciding that I am probably alone. Slowly, my eyes open against the shell colored light. Tangled sheets, rumpled pillows, a single strand of long hair across the one next to mine, a light scent I can smell even over my own, sour one. Pushing up on my elbows, I scan the small room, as if she somehow has hidden herself in a small space.

The trailer is empty. I smell coffee.

Swinging my legs over to the floor, I yawn widely, aware that my body is dumb with the events of the past couple of days, the emotions and experiences wrapped around me like a thick quilt; anger, fear, lust, coppery blood smell, rage. It's too much.

The first throbbing starts, low on my forehead, under the deepest part of the dent. Pushing myself upright, I shuffle into the bathroom to pee, aware suddenly of how full my bladder is; and how sore my penis is, the fresh crop of tiny bruises that are spattered over my upper arms, my back.

Amy's revenge. Swear to God, after a night like that, I find myself thinking that if I never had sex with her again, it would be okay.

Finishing, I pull on a pair of shorts and make my way into the kitchen, where a partial pot of coffee steams gently on the counter. My hand is steady as I pour a cup, my eyes on my blue work jacket, strewn across the kitchen floor where it was roughly thrown last night, aware that the title to the red Toyota was still in the inside pocket.

That is, if Amy hasn't taken it with her.

She hadn't. She had opened it, the torn flap evidence of that, but deciding it was harmless, left it in my pocket. I felt a frisson of anger starting.

The first streaks of light are painting the sky beyond the maple tree. I sit at my kitchen table sipping my coffee slowly, the white rectangle with the title inside set in front of me. I hold my cup with two hands, reluctant to see the name in black and white that will give a face to the nightmare that is roaming the streets, the nightmare I have been privy to already.

The cup leaves a wet streak on the table as I push it to one side, sliding the envelope carefully towards me, my scarred fingers probing the torn open edges of the seal. Holding it open, I peer in enough that I can see the green and white title paper, different than our New York titles, this is a different state, looks like Connecticut.

I grasp the title and slide it out. My eyes scan it for the name. There; Robert F. Blake of 67 Stanton Way in New Fairfield Connecticut.

I stare at the black words typed across the face of the title, so innocuous, so deadly, wondering how something so *evil* can look so mundane. I try to open up, to allow something, anything from this scrap of paper and I get....nothing.

I turn the title over, looking for the chain of ownership, finding that the Toyota was purchased new by him in October of 1998, traded last month to Beckwith's down in Danbury, Connecticut. Beckwith...not a dealer I am familiar with. I wonder briefly why they sent this car all the way up here instead of using the auction in Windsor Connecticut instead.

Traded. Beckwith would know what he was driving now.

Rising, I fumble through my kitchen drawer, searching for a pen and a piece of scrap paper. Finding both, I scrawl a note about that. Taking another sip of my cooling coffee, I spy my battered road atlas on the shelf in the living room. Pulling it down, I run through the pages until I have Connecticut spread out in front of me. Beckwith's address is easy to find, just off the junction of 7 and 84 in Connecticut. Blake's is not.

I scan closely, but the roads on the New Fairfield map don't include a Stanton Way. I think about the computer at the shop and decide I will take a few minutes today to pull Google Maps up. I glance at the clock, realizing that it's time, no past time, to be showering and heading into the shop. I wonder briefly if Bill really left for Watkins Glen yesterday or if he would show up to check on me today.

I realize with a start that I'm feeling oddly energized, full of purpose and meaning today, a strange feeling for me, a departure from my usual ennui .

I'm on the hunt now. And it feels damn good.

Chapter 29
Then

I've been here, like, forever now, this institutional mess of a place. They come in every day, pull me up from my hard, stinky bed, make me move, make me walk, make me hold a pencil, put my clothing on. They tell me it's 'rehabilitashun' making me whole so I can go HOME, and aren't I happy to GO HOME?

I don't answer them. How can I be happy to go someplace that has no meaning to me? Words are empty holes to me. People gray phantoms around the edges of my mind.

Only the dreams are real.

They come every night, or is it every day? Vivid, bright, colorful, terrifying. Faces, names, emotions, needs, fears, all these thoughts and memories, memories far more intense and meaningful than my own hollow core. It wears me out, this constant pouring of a cascade of images into my empty soul, leaves me blank eyed and exhausted.

Try as I might, I have not pulled up one single thing that I can call my own 'memory'.

And so, I go through the motions. Let them herd me around, feed me, dress me, move my arms and legs. I feel nothing except anger from time to time, flatness the rest of the time, pain, physical pain, all of the time. My head throbs in time to my heart, sometimes harder, sometimes slower, but all the time.

There's other kids here too. Sometimes they confuse me, because my dreams, I swear my dreams are their dreams, and I can't figure out why that would be, why I would feel like I know them so well. I don't want to know them.

But I do.

Emily, the little girl with almost no hair over in the first room, she got sent through the window of her dad's car as he roared home one night. She got splattered across a big pine tree, and now she lies there in a perpetual twilight, except I can *see* what she saw, *feel* what she felt, and know that she prefers where she is now to where she was then. She didn't have no good home. Her grampa was touching her sometimes and telling her not to tell or he'd hurt her dog...or maybe her little sister. And now she lays there, not wanting to come back when actually she probably could.

Kristian is across the hallway from her. He had something growing in his brain, something bad. They opened him up and took it out, and said he'd be fine, just fine. Except he isn't, because it's growing again, filling the hole they left, and Kristian isn't fine at all. Kristian is dying.

Juan is scary. I try not to go near him, but sometimes I have to. He's getting out soon, because he's ALL BETTER. Except he isn't. He's all messed up now. He's mad, scary mad, and he loves it. He has a dent on his head too, like me, except his was caused when his mother pushed him down for making a mess, and he fell, hitting his head on the coffee table.

She blamed his daddy for it to the social worker and the cops, and they believed her. But Juan knows better. And he's going home to her...soon.

I put my hands over my ears, trying to block out all the noise, all of the input these kids are giving me, aware that I can't. And aware that try as I might, I have no idea of who I am or what I am.

It's a blank space.

Chapter 30
Now

My energy carries over to work, a rare thing for me. No Bill when I arrive at 6:30. I open the shop, turning on lights, start the coffee, check the answering machine.

Howie shuffles in at ten past seven, late. He ducks his head as he punches in. I say nothing, just offer him a cup of coffee. He takes it, looking at me out of the corner of his eyes. He's uneasy around me, unsure. I tell him what his work orders are for the day; three sets of tires to do, a couple of oil changes, and one front brake job.

I meet with the owner of the Volvo I changed out the fuel pump on, Howard Lansing, and manage to keep a bland smile on my face as he tells me how amazed and grateful he was when Bill called him last minute yesterday, telling him his car was already fixed. That's something I push aside, aware that it evens us back up a bit.

He needs me. I need him. Simple reason we have stayed in business together this long.

At ten, the shop phone rings. I'm in the office, poring over Google Maps as Howie struggles with a set of light truck tires out in the shop.

It's Bill. I was expecting him.

He sounds surprised when I snag the phone first ring, wary when he hears my voice, strong and upbeat even to my ear. I can hear motors roaring behind him; cars are out on course at Watkins Glen, he tells me, a test day before the races that will start tomorrow. I can hear the adrenaline in his voice, the worry. I ask a few mundane questions about the car, mentally urging him to hang up so I can concentrate on what is more important to me right now.

Finding Mr. Robert Blake, of 67 Stanton Way in New Fairfield, Connecticut.

Finally, Bill signs off reluctantly. He isn't comfortable with me, but he can't pin down why. I flick my eyes to the clock, and remind him his group is due on track in less than an hour, and has he gotten the setup on the car changed yet? The reminder that it hasn't been changed over since the last time he raced, in the rain at Lime Rock Park sends him running. I sigh in silent relief as the connection is ended.

A thought crosses my mind again, one that has been bothering me since I first sat in the red Toyota; who are these women, these women whose dying thoughts and feelings I was subject to? Their scents, feelings, emotions, all wide open and revealed to me, but their names remain a secret. I stand up and peek out the shop door at Howie; he is still deep into the truck tire job. Closing the door, I sit down at the computer and call up Google.

But I sit and stare blankly at the white page with its colorful lettering, a white box ready to take my every request and search millions of bytes of data for me. How the hell do you find something like this? Finally, I type in "unsolved murders in Connecticut". To my dismay, I get almost 90,000 results. I try to narrow it down, "unsolved murders, women, CT". Depressingly, this time I get almost 200,000 results.

An hour of fruitless surfing passes, my mood slowly sagging as search after search yields too much information. Howie finishes a second set of tires and comes in the shop, looking for his next job. I quickly diminish the search box as I get the keys and work order for him.

Three hours later, I'm no closer to restarting my search. A flurry of calls, pickups, and a drop off from the thruway have kept me busy, busier than I want. Frustration builds in me as the phone rings again. I'm not very polite when I grab it off the base this time, almost snarling, "Bill's Repair" at the caller.

It's Bill again.

"What's the matter, Gerry?"

"Nothing...just kinda busy."

"Like what kind of busy?" I can still hear engine noises behind him.

I close my eyes briefly, hoping for patience. "Just keeping Howie on track, got a bunch of calls today, and a drop off from the thruway. What's going on there?"

He exhales, a disgusted sound. "A God damned cv joint failed on me. About threw me into the Armco going out of one." The first turn at Watkins Glen, a downhill, high speed right hander. Not a place you want something to break on the car. "I just went through my spares and I don't have any axles for the right side. No one else here today has any either. I need you to go into the back shed and get that black box of spares out for me. It's on the shelf on the right, almost to the ceiling."

I'm listening to him in growing dismay. Watkins Glen is a full five hours from the shop. I don't realize I'm holding my breath until he finishes his instructions with, "John Gasper is coming out tonight. He said he would stop by to get it for me, thinks he'll be there around 2." He swears, then says, "I can't believe I didn't pack the spares for this trip. I just threw a bunch of random shit onto the trailer last night and left."

Because of me.

I don't comment. I don't have the space or energy to. I simply tell him I'll have the spares ready for John, and was there anything else he might need?

He's silent for a moment, then, "No. No, there's nothing else you have that I need."

I don't attempt to think about that statement as I hang up. I can't.

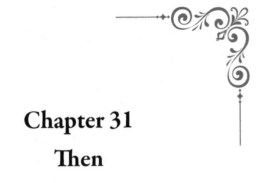

Chapter 31
Then

I'm going "home" today. Big deal. I stare at the floor as the nurse's fuss over me, all happy and cheery. I wish they'd shut up. Home. Whatever that is.

The gray-haired woman appears in the doorway at ten. She looks at me, her purse clutched to her belly. I can feel her unease as she eyes me. I stare at her, flat, lizard like. Dr. Orbison is there, telling her what GREAT PROGRESS I have made, and that he expects I will make A FULL RECOVERY in no time. She nods slowly, never taking her eyes off of me. I sit, a lump. My head hurts.

My stuff is gone from the windowsill, from the little closet, all packed neatly in a red bag that sits on the floor. My roommate, Harold, lies on his right side, staring at us, a white bandage glowing on his skull. His eyes track movement, machines monitor his body. He just got here a few days ago and I don't mind him. He doesn't clutter up my mind like the last kid did. He's a smooth, glass like presence in the room, a blank wall.

The old woman, who they tell me is my GRAMMA, takes the handle of my red bag, her mouth moving as she speaks to me. I hear the words, but they are white noise. I don't listen to her very much. I'm really, really angry at her. For something. I don't know what. But I am angry.

We clatter down the brightly painted hallway, past the rooms with kids lying in beds, me trying to block them out, to concentrate on one step at a time, the blue clad nurse jabbering, jabbering, jabbering. The gray-haired woman hugs her at the door, hugs Dr. Orbison too, doesn't hug me. They speak to me, their words getting through my barrier briefly, words of how good I will be, and how much better I am doing, and how the therapy will continue and that I can go back to school, back to my friends.

I don't reply. The white noise in my head is humming and receding, making it difficult to talk.

"Are you sure he's ready for this?" the gray woman mumbles next to me, her voice cutting through the white noise around my ears. Dr. Orbison smiles at her, barely glancing at me. "He's more than ready. Give it some time. That was quite a traumatic event he went through. You have him lined up for his counseling sessions, right?" She nodded, dabbing at her eyes with a tissue. He smiles again, finally looking down at me. "He'll be fine. He's a survivor." His eyes look flat to me, dark pools. I stare up at him, my own face as blank and still as a corpse. He breaks eye contact first.

Outside, cold wet air, mud stained concrete sidewalk, rows of cars with moisture dotting the roofs and windshields. I tilt my head back and breathe the cold, oddly fresh air, the first time I have been outside of this building in a long, long time. It was hot when I arrived here, I do remember that. Now everything has that flat, wet look things get after being buried under mounds of snow for a long time. Snow. I saw snow, watched it from my window. I remember that I liked playing in it. Watching from my hot, hard bed had made me sad, made scalding tears trickle down my cheeks. I had hoped that I would get to be in it, but now it's gone. Tears prickled my eyes briefly. Voices rang in my head; "Gerry's cwwying! Lookit the pussy!" Voices I couldn't unravel, ghost voices. I swallow hard against the tears, fighting to be a big kid now. I'm not a little kid anymore, never again.

The gray woman, GRAMMA, stops in front of a station wagon, fumbling keys out of her bag. She's turned away from me, slightly hunched, saying things I can't hear. I'm staring at the car. Dread curls in my belly. I'm afraid to get in it. I want to tell her this, but I can't, and she's talking, talking, talking, and the door is open, and I am meekly climbing in the front seat, Gramma fastens the strap across my body, and I am tense, waiting for a blow as she talks and talks and talks...

Sensations like water, warm moving water across my head, across my DAMAGED FRONTAL LOBE, the thing they keep talking about, the aching dent on my forehead, warm, flowing water, soft, gentle. I sit stock still as she turns the key, the motor sparking and starting, still as a stone, water flowing around me.

I've got to go see Gerry today, I need to find something for him, maybe that teddy bear I saw in the window at Albers last week. I wish there was something I could do to reach him, he's so far away and lost now.

We're going to Florida; we will take this old car and ride down long long roads and you'll get to see Mickey and Minnie and go in the giant castle. It will be just us and it will be fun!

And Mommy loves you, loves you, loves you so much. How could I let it get like this? How could I not see what that bastard has done to us? We are leaving, yes we are, and I will be the best mommy you have ever seen.

I hope Gerry gets out soon. It breaks my heart because I just love him so much and he scares me so. I'll never forgive myself for what happened. I just love him so...

My breathing is ragged, my chest hiccuping. I can feel the love, feel my mommy and this woman next to me, who I suddenly remember is Gramma, the same Gramma I loved, the same Gramma who loves me, loves me still. How could I forget about Gramma and Mommy? Memories, *my memories*, flicker through me like strobe lights; this car with its wooden sides, in the back seat, a child seat, Mommy and Gramma in front, going someplace, Christmas time, lights everywhere, me feeling happy, happy, happy because we are going someplace fun, when was the last time I felt like that? The last time I felt anything other than a stone like anger, deep in my gut. I close my eyes, aware that Gramma is speaking to me, the motion of the car stopped, reaching across to touch my cheek, tentatively, then firmer as my hiccuping breaks into full blown sobs. The first ones I have had, maybe ever.

Chapter 32

Now

Howie has gone home, the clank and clatter of compressors and tools quieted, and still I sit here, lost in thought. The monitor has an annoying flicker; it hurts my eyes. Leaning back in the chair, I press my hands to my face, frustrated.

Too much information. A depressing number of people, of women, who never came home again. Dead bodies dotting the country, decomposing in landfills, basements and forests all across the country. How the hell was I going to find out about the three, maybe four women whose deaths I had "witnessed"? I *knew* they hadn't been found, knew it with a stone certainty. He had as much told me so himself, Mr. Robert Blake.

I wished he could have told me where they were now.

I felt a cold draft on the back of my neck. I stayed in the chair, my eyes covered, willing it to leave me alone, to go away.

I feared it wouldn't.

Dropping my hand finally, I swivel around towards the back window of the office, the one looking over the lot where the mounded shapes of the vehicles fade into the background with the dying light. The window, like the other two, is open slightly, the cold draft oozing through it, the only window that has such a dank, rancid air coming through like this. I know exactly where it comes from. I stare into the shifting murk that gathers in the parking lot and shake my head, no, no, no. I can't. A desire for alcohol rears up, sharp, demanding. With shaking hands, I pull my cigarettes out of my shirt pocket and light one, the flame trembling.

To get into that car tonight would kill me.

To find those women meant that I would have to get back into it. I would have to look around while in the car, look for landmarks, signs, clues to where they died.

The shaking extends into my arms, my body. I can't do it. Maybe another day, a day when I am stronger, but not tonight.

I have to do it.

I can't do it.

Grabbing my keys, I shove myself upright and head for the door.

Chapter 33
Then

The little house looks dingy and sad as Gramma pulls up in front of it. I sit and stare for a long, long moment. I don't want to get out of the car.

Gramma is talking, talking, talking, she won't stop talking, her voice like white fire in my ears. I stare at the doors, the windows. The little house is wrong somehow, evil. Windows are blank holes that swallow all light, not shining or nothing. I say nothing as Gramma comes around the car, still talking, talking, talking. I can hear my heart pounding in my ears. She doesn't seem to notice anything, just grabs my red suitcase and says over and over, you're HOME now, you're HOME! Everything will be ALL BETTER now that you are home. She doesn't seem to notice that I am shaking, quivering, feeling like a million thousand ants are marching all over me, biting me.

Without a word, I slide from the seat and reluctantly follow her up the sidewalk. She sets my red suitcase down on the flaking gray painted floor of the porch, her hand trembling as she struggles to slot the key in the door. Don't do it! I scream in my mind. Don't! My lips are blocks of ice, frozen, struck mute. She doesn't hear me, her mouth moving, moving, moving. She turns the key and swings the white door open, gesturing into the blackness to me.

I stop, unable, unwilling to move forward. Gramma is talking at me, taking my hand, pulling me forward into the house, my white sneakered feet skidding slightly as I hit the mousy blue rug on the inside. Smells assail me immediately, familiar smells, then sounds, noise from the inside, from someplace deeper inside a rattling bang followed by a whir of something mechanical, something maniacal. I freeze, my bowels turning to water.

Gramma turns to me then, her mouth still moving, fear in her eyes, her gray lined face suddenly at the end of a long tunnel as I begin to scream long wordless shrieks, high pitched keening noises. HE killed my mommy. Right here. Right underneath me as I flailed on his back. She died in a gurgle of black blood, blood that soaked into my skin as I fought for my own life. I was there, and I remember everything, it assaults me like a movie unspinning at superhigh yet superlow speed as I stand there and shriek. My Gramma shot me, shot me in the head trying to kill him, almost killing me. And HE is still alive.

Chapter 34

Now

Murky red light spills across my face as I pull open the door to Mickey's, the sharp tang of years of spilled booze and old nicotine slapping me in the face. I inhale deeply, gratefully, guiltily.

I'm just going to have one beer and go home.

Pool balls click and bang in the back corner as Willie Nelson belts one out on the jukebox, a television on mute showing a baseball game under lights. The long bar is scarred and uneven, the rows of bottles under the long mirror dingy looking. About half the seats are taken on this Friday night.

Danny is wiping glasses behind the bar, his sleeves rolled up to show impressive biceps, biceps he isn't shy about using when things get out of hand. He casts an eye at me, a hint of a raised eyebrow when he sees me.

I haven't been in since last year.

He drops a coaster in front of me, rolling a toothpick in his mouth from side to side as he does. "Hey Ger. What'll it be?" his only remark.

"Just a beer. A Bud draft."

He draws the glass and places it in front of me, takes my money and leaves change without another word. I dip my head, glad to be alone as I inhale the smell rising from the glass. Budweiser isn't my favorite, the reason I ordered it tonight. My eyes rise slowly to the bottles reflecting dull light back at me, their amber, rouge and golden contents seeming to glow with an inner fire. I feel an answering burn in my belly, a burn I try to quiet with a slow swig on the glass.

Movement in the mirror, a red and white baseball cap, lean face with a handlebar mustache, glasses. Dean Hamilton appears in my vision as well as the mirror as he slides onto the seat next to me.

"G.L!" he elbows me as he says it, "Hey Hammerhead, long time no see!"

I like Dean I guess; I mean he is about as close a friend as I have in this town. He and Tommy Mercer have a little shop over the other side of town, specializing in heavy equipment repair. I'm always surprised at how a man as scrawny as Dean can muscle around parts as large as he is, but he manages.

I elbow him back, "Hey Ferret Face." Brotherly love. "What's shaking in the poor side of town?"

"Well." He takes a slug off his beer, a Corona in a bottle, "Not too much, just moving and grooving, keeping my head above water, ya know?"

We talk then, talk for a half hour or so, just mundane stuff, blissfully mundane stuff. Who is going out of business. Who bought a house. Who is moving out, changing jobs, blissful, everyday things that are like a balm to my soul.

I look down at my glass, surprised to realize it's full, not sure if it is my first or third one now. I decide it doesn't really matter. I need this mundane moment in the midst of the insanity. I take a long pull, aware of how smooth it goes down.

Joey from over Route 200 comes over, kid I don't know well but Dean does. He works up at one of the big shops, BRAKES! ALIGNMENT! MECHANICS ON DUTY 6 DAYS A WEEK! in neon blazing out front. Kid's okay, maybe a little dopey but okay. We talk, yelling back and forth over the rising noise from the jukebox, Led Zepplin replacing Doobie Brothers replacing Creedence Clearwater Revival.

I order a Sam Adams, just one, a treat. The ale has a zip and tang as I swallow it. There are four more guys at our end of the bar now, a regular little mechanics corner happening. I feel the camaraderie, the fellowship as we trade war stories, hooting with laughter. It's as close to feeling normal that I ever get. I have another Sam Adams, or maybe two, to celebrate.

The ground sways under my feet as I stand up to go take a leak. Dean notices, yells over the din at me, beer foam on the ends of his mustache, "Hey Ger! Sure you can hit the hole? Don't be pissing on your feet now!"

It's hysterical, and I belly laugh, grabbing the stool back to slow my sway. "Least I can REACH the hole, unlike you, you sawed off excuse of a midget!" There's a chorus of laughs from the guys at that, while Danny reaches over, taking my glass from the bar top, several inches still in it. "Hey! I wasn't done with that!"

"Oh yes you are. You've had enough tonight, Ger. Time to head home."

What? I only had a couple beers! I stare at him, a rage blooming in my belly. "I paid for that beer! Give it back!"

The guys have fallen silent, Joey staring with his mouth hanging slightly open, looking a lot like Howie. Danny stares back at me, his eyes....sad? I blink at him, confused.

"Ger." He speaks softly, so softly I almost can't hear him. "You've had enough. You should go now." He looks over at Dean, "Dean? Think maybe you should give him a hand and make sure he gets home safe tonight."

Dean nods slowly, setting his empty glass down and dropping a five down. "Come on G.L. Let's hit the road. We'll toss down some beers some other day."

I am bewildered at the turn of events as we suddenly are shuffle stepping through the bar, aware of the glances thrown our way, mute with anger and confusion.

The night air is crisp and damp, slicing across my senses as we hit the parking lot in an awkward two step. I realize Dean has my upper arm, has it to steady me, has it to guide me towards his truck, a saggy Dodge Ram.

Ben, one of the other guys is with us, and he has a set of keys in his hand. My keys. I open and close my mouth silently as Dean hands me into his cab and Ben climbs into mine.

A wave of weariness passes over me as I hit the seat. Screw it. Time to hit the sack for a few hours, try to clean my head out. I stare out the window as Dean turns the motor over, then look at him as we roll out of Mickey's, a thought coming back to the forefront of my mind. "Hey Dean. How do you find a dead woman?" lips numb over a thickened tongue.

Dean looks over at me, eyes big and dark in the dash lights. "Say what?"

"How do I find someone who'sh dead, who'sh been killed? I been looking all day and I can't figure out how to find her. I can see where she died, but I don't know where she is."

"Jesus Gerry. What the hell you going on about?"

"I told you, I can't find her. There's this woman, see...and well...." A wave of sobriety pushed up through the layers, a voice in my head screaming SHUT UP SHUT UP SHUT UP!

I stop talking abruptly. "Jesus I have to pee."

"What woman? Where did you see a dead woman?"

"Ah never mind....I'm popped, don' lissen to me."

He glances at me again, uneasy. I lean against the glass and bounce along in silence.

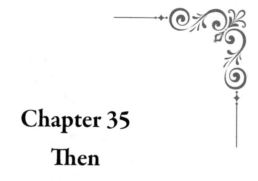

Chapter 35
Then

I started sleeping in the car two days after coming "home". The house is noisy, loud, constant images, memories, terror ripping into me. Every time I close my eyes HE is there again, laughing, laughing, holding a knife, a big, wet red knife, the one he stabbed mommy with twenty-two times. Twenty-two is a lot. I know that. I can't close my eyes when I am in the house.

The car is different. The car is safe. The car is where I can close my eyes, play with the knobs, and dream of the road winding away underneath the wheels on the way down south to someplace like Florida.

Gramma doesn't like the fact I sleep out here, but she lets me. She lets me because she doesn't like hearing me scream in the middle of the night, doesn't like seeing me drift like a cloud in the daytime, insubstantial with exhaustion. My counselor told her to let me do it, that it would help with my PTSD, whatever that is. All I know is that to sleep in that house is to die in that house.

I'm supposed to go back to school. Leaves are turning dusty green and yellow now, the hot, smoky summer days turning to a memory. I think about Ricky, Jimmy, and Darlene, wonder if they are still there. I'm not sure I want to see them. Gramma says I'll be in some 'special class' for kids like me, says that it will do me good to have a 'normal routine' again. I stare at her, too exhausted from the constant battering of my psyche to argue with her. It never ends unless I am in the car.

I don't argue when she brings me down to Lowsen's to buy clothing, nor when she stops at Gilmore's Shoes for a pair of shoes and sneakers. I say nothing as she coos over lunch boxes, makes a big deal out of choosing a thermos. My head just aches slowly, rhythmically, in time to my heart.

School fills me with a nameless dread.

She chatters, chatters, chatters non-stop as she pulls into the little service station with me. I stare out the window, her noise a wave over my stony exterior, my senses focused on the inside of the shop, where a man in stained work clothing stands beneath a sedan up on a lift, wheels drooping. I stare fascinated with the underside of that car as the man does something up over his head, his arms moving. Gramma is talking, talking, talking to the gas station man who has her hood up as I open the door and slip out, Gramma as forgotten as my life was to me all those months.

I can *see* under the car. It's really cool. The man grunts a little, mumbles a swear word as he struggles with something, then sees me out of the corner of his eye. "Oh hey, kid. Where'd you come from?"

. Tongue tied, I fidget, then point towards Gramma.

"Out with your Gram, huh?" I blink, wondering how he knows that, then I hear myself ask,

"Whatcha doing?"

"I'm trying to get this suspension piece off. Car is making a lot of noise when it hits bumps, think he needs some new bushings." I blink, suddenly an image coming to me as clear as the man's face, the bemused look he has fading behind my mind's eye. I look up, up, up under the car and point. "It's up higher. It's the top of that long thing, the thing with the spring on it." I know this. I just *saw* it hitting the pothole and the loosened bolt finally popping off completely, leaving the long tube to rattle and clunk up and down, making a dull thudding noise.

The bemused look is gone, replaced with a skeptical one raised brow look. I look him square in the eye, and something he sees there makes him lower his arms and step out from under the car. "Up higher, huh? Well okay, Mister Certified Mechanic. How about you and I just take a look? Watch out. I'm going to lower this down."

The lift hissed as the car settled earthwards again, me watching raptly him, him skeptically. He leaned in the open hood with a big flashlight, shining the light down to the top of that big, long thing I 'saw'.

"I'll be damned..." he reached down inside, fiddling with something. I crowded closer. "What is it?" He looks up at me, skepticism replaced with bewilderment. "The top of the shock came loose. That never happens with these cars."

He peered down inside the motor, me pushing closer eying the strange metal pulleys and silver metal things that stuck up everywhere, wondering how they all worked. He looked at me again, smiling, showing one missing tooth. "Hey Boss!" he yelled to the man that Gramma was still talking, talking, talking to. Grateful for the interruption, the man turned towards us, "Got ourselves a natural born mechanic here!"

Gramma calling out to me to get back over there, she had no idea I was out of the car, she was so sorry I bothered him, the man waving her off, "Lady, he just saved me a bunch of wasted energy. You can bring him by anytime."

Me, a blossom of pride, red hot in my chest, a feeling I was not used to, cheeks burning.

"You can come by anytime, buddy." he repeated.

Chapter 36
Now

I sit with maps spread out across my table on this Sunday morning, the air already hinting at unseasonal late warmth. Leaves blow across the park, the rustling sound filling me with a restlessness, a sense of time getting away from me.

I have a detailed map of Connecticut in front of me, 67 Stanton Way in New Fairfield circled on one vector, Beckwith's location in another. Taking a last swig of stale coffee, I gather everything up and collect keys, oddly energized to finally be *doing* something.

Amy is at her sister's in upstate, a respite for me from her determined poking at my brain, something she has been doing with alacrity all week, suspicion oozing through every crack in her soul. She's wearing me out.

A week has passed since the night Dean drove me home, a week spent determinedly sober, and just as determinedly away from the red car. Computers shed no light. Sitting in Bill's office sheds no light. Working under a never ending succession of broken cars sheds no light.

Going to visit the dealer that Mr. Robert Blake of 67 Stanton Way in New Fairfield, Connecticut traded the car in to, might shed some light on it.

Outside, I inhale the tangy fall air, realizing it has been awhile since I was aware of the smell, still surprised that I had a sense of smell. Many people with a 'traumatized frontal lobe" like I had never smell anything again.

I'd trade having that sense of smell a thousand times over to lose the window to hell that opened in my brain.

Pavement hummed as 20 turned into 9W, then 9, then 84 and route 7, traffic building as the day aged. Beckwith's was easy to find, a small dealership off exit one, carrying Toyota's and Subaru's.

Unease hit me as I parked, still not sure of what to ask or how. I craned over the hoods of the car at a salesman who was gesturing at a Subaru Outback as two people viewed skeptically, him a fedora pulled low over trendy glasses, her a scarf wrapped around upturned hair. They paid no attention to me as I exited my truck and wandered along the row of cars, angling towards the service area.

The glass window outside the service area was dark, white lettering proclaiming hours Monday through Saturday. I turned to go as a shadow loomed to my right, a stocky black haired man with a too tight shirt and what looked like crumbs on his collar, a gaudy gold watch visible on his right wrist, a wrist he thrust towards me with a hearty, "Good afternoon! Anyone helped you yet? I'm Bob!"

I took the outstretched hand briefly, wincing at the feeling of soft, dead flesh. Bob didn't notice; he was talking, talking, his mouth moving as he looked across the lot, at the building behind me, at anyplace except at me. Bob didn't like his job. Bob didn't like people. I felt a pang of sympathy for Bob. I felt the same way a lot of the times.

I finally interrupt him, gesturing towards showroom, asking him, "Actually, I'm not here to look at a car. I'm here to find out about one you guys took in on trade recently."

Bob's mouth slapped shut, already disinterested in me. "Come back Monday. Shop's open then."

"I can't. I don't live around here."

He waved towards the shiny glass walled showroom. "You should talk to Dan then. He's inside, at the desk. He might be able to help you."

He turned away, fishing a cigarette out of his pocket, me and my need already forgotten.

Chapter 37
Then

I been back in school three days now and it isn't anything like what I thought it was. I don't know any of the other kids and can't stand some of their thoughts. There's seven besides me, a couple of dyslexic kids, one kid who has some sort of sickness that leaves him all twisted up in a chair, and a couple who are faking stuff to get easy classes. Then there's one girl who is completely frozen, wide eyes with nothing showing behind them, her mind a smooth, walled in glass lobe. Something really bad happened to her, something I don't want to know about. Then there's Billy Meeker.

He's this pipsqueak of a kid, dark hair and beady bright eyes like a bird. Billy's too smart, too smart for this, too smart for regular classes, so smart they think he is dumb. But he isn't. He's anything but dumb.

Billy buzzed up to me the first day I was there, plaid shirt, uneven legs on his pants, and cocked his head, looking at me, IN me. I felt invaded almost, ready to punch him. He only said, "How come you're here? You ain't like the others."

I glared at him, "Well neither are you!" his thoughts buzzing, buzzing, buzzing in my head, like a wasp in the window.

He smiled at that, a gap toothed grin that was disarming somehow, his eyes disappearing in the folds of his lids. "What happened to your head? You got a big dent there."

He surprised me, surprised me with his directness, his boldness, surprised me with the anger that I always carried melting away at his question. I just shrugged. What could I say about it? What was there to say about it? He tilted his head forward slightly, speaking in a voice I could almost not hear.

"You can hear me, can'tcha? I can hear you hearing me." My eyes rounded at him. No one understood what I had in my head anymore; no one.

He cocked his head at me again, a dark eyed bird with greasy hair and a funny shaped face. "We're having pizza for lunch. I LOVE pizza!" And he was gone again.

It wasn't until he was all the way across the room that I realized that I wasn't able to hear him anymore, that he had somehow shut down his thoughts from me.

It should have been a relief, so why did it make me uncomfortable?

At recess, we went out in the yard with the other kids, one of the few times we could leave our own two room wing, down a short hall behind the library. The other kids, the ones play acting at this, said it was because we was all retards, losers. They made me mad, scary mad, when they said that. I wasn't no retard.

On the third day back, I saw Darlene and Jimmy. They were all the way across the grounds, standing over by the basketball courts, the bleachers past those, their heads together talking. I couldn't feel them, what with all the kids around me, their heads making so much noise, so much need and commotion, my head hammering with all the psychic sound.

Darlene saw me, saw me just as the bell rang, her eyes wandering over the kids and jerking back to my face. She said something to Jimmy, Jimmy with the mean little eyes, eyes he pinned on me from across the grounds. I stared at him for a long minute, seeing the look in his eyes changing from boldness to something else, something different. Uneasy, maybe even a little bit scared.

He looked away and said something to Darlene as kids streamed past like a rolling river between us. Darlene stared at me, then oddly, smiled and licked her lips.

Chapter 38
Now

B eckwith's showroom was state of the art....for the late seventies. Battered metal desks shoved together in haphazard clumps, fly speckled windows letting in light reflected off the tightly clumped cars in the congested lot. An off ramp and a drugstore hemmed them in from having enough room to grow any more. A bulletin board on one wall of the showroom showed an artist's rendering of the new dealership that was slated to be built next year, two miles down the road; the drawing was dated three years ago. A couple of customers sat across battered desks from the salesmen, otherwise the place was quiet.

I looked around for the desk Bob had mentioned, spotted a central counter, a man on the telephone sitting at it, colorful posters of Toyota's and Subaru's dotting the wall over his head. He transferred the call and hung up as I approached, eying me as I eyed him. I noticed the rough hands, the battered fingers, knew he was from the shop, pulling the short straw to work the phones on a dead Sunday on this warm, fall afternoon.

I fingered the envelope with the title in my pocket as I said, "Hey, how are you? Can I ask you something about a car that you guys took in trade?" He tilted his head, quizzically, intrigued, my question a break from the mind numbing Sunday routine.

"Sure. What can I help you with?" A hint of a New York accent in his rough timbre. I pulled the envelope out of my pocket. "I just picked this up at the auction in New York last week, and I wondered if you had any history on it."

His face closed down again. I hastened to add, "I have a shop up outside Newburgh. We're a licensed dealer."

He relaxed a fraction, although not completely, asking, "You ran a Carfax on it, right?" I shook my head. "That's not what I'm looking for really. Just wondered if you guys saw it for servicing, or why the guy traded it."

He gave me a sideways look, and I didn't blame him for it. Even to my ears, I sounded awkward, a bit strange. Definitely not the kind of question people got on a regular basis. His brain was turning over all the angles, wondering how I was going to bite him in the ass for this.

Taking a breath to steady my increasingly jangling nerves, I said in a casual tone, "I got it for my daughter. It looks really clean...I was just wondering if I could find out the history on it."

His shoulders relaxed. "Uh, okay, sure. I can try anyway. What's the VIN?"

I took the title out of my pocket and handed it to him. His eyes tracked across the paper, then battered fingers moved with surprising grace across the keyboard.

That explained why he got stuck with the short straw for Sunday desk coverage.

He paused and stared, the screen casting a blue glow to his cheeks. He scrolled down. "Looks like we sold this one here. Nothing major happened to it over the years...just services...uh....says here we did a 100k tune-up on..." lips pursed as he eyed the screen, "December 10, 2005. Pretty clean, far as I can see. He ran synthetic oil in it." That raised an eyebrow on me. Most people used "dino", or "dinosaur" oil in a daily driver. Synthetic wasn't seen much, mostly because of cost, and because the only people who used it tended to be serious car people or competition people. Seeing it on a street car as mundane as a Toyota was unusual.

I pressed the slim advantage. "Synthetic, huh? This guy a collector or something? What's he like?" Dan shook his head slowly, flicking a suspicious look at me. "Where you from again?"

"Me? Outside of Newburgh." I felt his unease. "Why?"

Dan raised one shoulder. "'Cuz everyone around here knows Bob Blake, that's why. He's no car collector or nothing. He just likes them to last so he doesn't spend money."

"So, why does everyone know him then?"

Dan finally looked me square in the eye. "Because he is probably one of the biggest businessmen in the area, owns Danbury Acres for one, the new high end condo development. Also he has two other businesses, Geotechnik and Labrynth Industries. Besides that, in his spare time..." here he shot me a wry look, "he's really active in local politics. Was the first selectman in New Fairfield for a number of years and now they say he is looking at a congressional seat. The man is a bona fide entrepreneur."

I felt the floor tilt under my feet for a moment. Of all the news I thought, or hoped, I would get, this certainly didn't compute. A strange expression crossed Dan's face. "Why? What is it?" I looked down at the title on the counter and said the first thing I could think of.

"I...uh...I guess it is just weird that he would own a little shitbox Toyota for a car and keep it as long as he did."

Dan slid the title back across the counter, relaxing again fractionally. "Well, you aren't from around here, or you would know about him. The man is frugal, part of the reason he made his money. He's kinda famous for it actually. At least you can rest assured you picked up a decent car for your daughter."

I slid the title back in the envelope. "So, um, what did he trade it for?"

He pecked at the keyboard a moment. "Says here, another Toyota, looks like a Camry this time, one of them new hybrid ones."

"Huh. So what do you think of that motor?"

He shook his head. "It's a great idea, but there's been a couple complaints. I think they have some bugs to work out yet."

I nodded, one mechanic to another, sensing he was finally letting his guard down. "Yeah, we had a couple in recently, one would randomly lose power when he accelerated, the other one lost the auxiliary battery twice." I shrugged one shoulder.

Dan looked at the screen as he listened. "Yeah? What codes did you get?"

"That's the funny thing, we didn't get any."

"That's not that unusual actually. Half the time, the hybrids that come in aren't throwing codes either."

"Well, I hope Mr. Blake has a backup car then, just in case his Camry decides to start acting up."

"His wife has an '05 Matrix, so I would say that would be his backup car." He pushed the keyboard away.

Sliding the title in my pocket, I turned towards the showroom floor. "Thanks for the help, Dan. I think this car will do just fine for my son."

As soon as the words were out, I realized my mistake. Dan's eyes turned flinty. "I thought you said it was for your daughter."

"Uh..it is, the kids are twins, they're 17 and are going to share it." Lame. I knew it. He knew it.

I felt his eyes between my shoulder blades all the way out the door

Chapter 39

Then

It was almost two weeks later that Billy Meeker sidled up to me during our 'remedial reading skills' class and mumbled, "Hey, G-man, meet me at the stairwell at recess. I got somethin' to show ya." I looked around at him, but he was already skitter stepping away, all wire and energy.

Becka Carlson, the girl with the messed up head was sitting next to me, the closest one to me in the alphabet. I didn't care about her much; she was messed up but she didn't bother me. Not like some of the kids did. Billy was the only one I think I maybe liked, maybe. He was kinda strange though, strange and closed off. It made me mad sometimes.

This was the first time he had asked me to come do anything with him though.

The bell rattled through the hallway, finally signaling recess. I shoved myself upright from my cruddy little desk, my head pounding slowly. From beside me, a little voice; "Be careful."

Startled, I looked around, seeing no one near me except Becka. Becka who was looking straight at me, her face all serious like, her eyes...*there* for the first time since I had met her. Surprised, I simply stared at her. She stared back, then, "He's not...he's not...." Her voice trailed off. As I opened my mouth to ask her what she meant, her eyes grew distant and the glass wall slid back down in place. I stood still watching as she slowly got up and made her way out the now empty door, her steps slow and hobbling.

The hall was empty already, voices ringing from the outside recess court, all of us kids a mix from real little kids in kindergarten to the biggest kids in eighth grade. I headed down towards the doors, the stairwell open to the left of it to go upstairs. I felt him before I reached the stairs, an impatience, an eagerness. Pausing, I looked up the metal staircase, feeling uncertain. Not afraid though. I don't think I could ever be afraid again, not after what HE did to me.

A hiss from above, "Hey, Gerry, c'mon!" My feet found the stairs, the railing snot slick under my hand. He was waiting on the next staircase above the landing, almost dancing with anticipation. "Come *on*!"

I followed him up, into the empty hallway above, the smell of apples, wet shoes and chalkboards heavy in the air. He almost buzzed with energy, head bobbing both ways as he checked for anyone around. "Where are we going?" my voice echoed in the emptiness. "Shh!" He flinched, a finger to his lips. "Come on!" hand waving me on.I followed him.

The teacher's lounge was up here, located along the far side of the building, away from the side that had the recess yard. At this hour, it too was empty, all of the teachers outside with their charges. I froze when he pushed the door open, my mouth suddenly dry, shaking my head, no, no, no.

He grinned, a wild toothy grin, and grabbed me, pulling me into the room. "Come ON!"

The row of old windows threw light across the space, blinding me. A long table with chairs around it was the first thing I saw, piles of books and papers on it. Hanging on the back of some of the chairs were coats, worn this morning as frost nipped, abandoned as the sun strengthened and warmed the earth. A coffee pot steamed on the long counter on one side of the room, the smell of bitter, burnt coffee searing my nose. From outside, the distant shrieks of the kids could be heard.

I glanced up at the wall clock, the same black handed one we had in our classrooms, wondering how long it would be before someone missed us.

Billy was already darting around the table, plucking a blue and white windbreaker from the back of a chair, gesturing impatiently at me. "Come 'mere! We don't have much time!" He held the jacket up at me. "Put it on!"

"What?" I stepped back from him. I knew about stealing; stealing was bad. Stealing wasn't anything I was going to do. I shook my head, no, no, no. Billy crossed the space to me in a shambling run.

"You dummy! We aren't going to TAKE it! Just put it on for a second!" He thrust the jacket at me, tugging at my arm.

"What...why? Whose jacket is it?"

"It's Mr. Hawley's. Hurry up or we're gonna get caught!"

Bewildered, I slipped my right arm, then my left one through the sleeves, sleeves that fell several inches below my hands. The nylon whispered against my arms and neck, a soft sighing sound in my ears, a soft hissing sound...

The little boys were the best, the fresh little morsels, oh how he had to control himself when they wrestled and ran! How he wished he was wrestling with them, feeling their little warm peanut butter scented bodies against his. The photos stashed under the floorboard in his attic helped, helped some, but weren't good enough, photos of children he had mentored over the years, boys from his scout troop, boys he had on his SPECIAL campouts, his glory times. He yearned fiercely for a new boy, a soft, unbroken one, like that little red headed Jimmy Carlson, oh how he would be a SPECIAL one for him. He already had him signed up for next summer's camp, too long to wait, too long....

Black spots danced in front of my eyes as Billy stripped the coat off my numb body, flinging it back onto the chair, tugging me frantically. "Someone's coming! Run!" Then the doorway, banging off my head as we tumbled into the hall and headed towards the stairs, him jogging, tugging me on numb legs, hissing, "Come on, come ON!"   .

A flash of light off the pane of glass in the stairwell door, then Mrs. Donnelly was in front of us, all wide hips and frowns, scowling at us, trapped in the shiny linoleum hallway, my face burning with the shame that belonged to Mr. Hawley. There was sudden, leaden silence in the hall. "What are you two doing up here! We've been looking all over for you!"

Billy chimed in, his voice high pitched, earnest, his face smooth. "Mrs. Donnelly, I been looking for someone to help us, 'cuz Gerry here is getting sick!"

She turned her laser beamed gray eyes on me, doubt evident in her face. "Sick? Why he doesn't look sick to ME! He looks GUILTY of something, but not SICK!"

Which was when I doubled over and emptied the contents of my stomach all over the shiny linoleum floor.

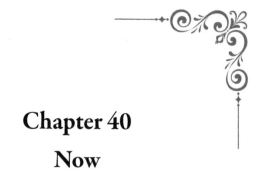

Chapter 40

Now

I felt like a total dumbass. Of all the things I had looked up, I hadn't taken two minutes to research Robert Blake. Something I should have thought of, should have done immediately.

My head ached, a slow pounding as I recalled the hard look Dan had leveled at me in Beckwith's. I had to be more careful than that. That kind of mistake would screw me over. And I had a strong suspicion that screwing up around Robert Blake could be the end of me.

The daylight was sending long shadows across the lot as I pulled into Bill's yard. I could feel the red car, sitting just out of sight behind the building, the tire even saggier than it had been when I dumped it there less than two weeks ago. A lifetime already.

Ignoring it, I concentrated on fitting the key into the lock, carefully unbolting the sequence of deadbolts we had on the door. I briefly wondered if Bill was going to take the keys away from me. He hadn't exactly been overly friendly to me the past week.

I guess until he asked for them back, I still had permission to use them, which is what I did now, closing and relocking the office door behind me.

I fired up his computer and felt my right pocket carefully, feeling the pint flask I had purchased on the way here. I wouldn't open it now, no, not now. It could wait until I reached home. The smooth hardness of it was reassuring to me.

An hour later, I shut it back down, the despair and disbelief I had first felt at Beckwith's having grown a hundredfold. Bob Blake was a local celebrity. Not only was there information about him, there was TOO much information about him. Business articles, political articles, charity articles, ribbon cuttings, tree plantings, donations to the local shelters, there wasn't anything he wasn't involved in. I had photos too, dozens of them, photos from work, with his wife, a puffy faced blonde, professional head shots, him with his receding hairline and solemn face, pictures of him on a float during a parade, people smiling and waving at him, Bob, entrepreneur, philanthropist, business owner. Bob; killer of those nameless women.

My headache was worse, my stomach burned as I closed the shop door behind me and relocked everything. I knew I would have to get in the red car again, to see where those women were. I wavered outside the shop, the gate to the lot to my left, the padlock hanging there, mutely accusing me, pussy, pussy, pussy, you're too much of a pussy to do this.

Before I could question it too much, I was inserting the key and popping the lock off the gate.

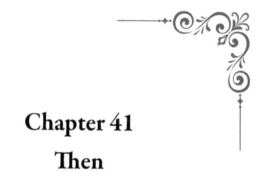

Chapter 41
Then

"We have to tell someone!" My head ached, ached with a steady throb, a deeper, harder pounding than it had done for a while. I felt sick to my stomach.

Billy grabbed the monkey bars and swung gangly legs up and over them, dangling upside down, his goofy face turning red, a grin looking like a frown. "Who are we going to tell, dummy? We're just kids, and RETARDS at that. Ain't no one gonna listen to us." He swung back and forth, then reached up with knobby hands and grabbed the bars again, gracefully swinging his legs free to the ground.

I sat on a pair of bars above him, mad, mad, mad, wishing he would listen to me. Wishing he hadn't taken me into the teacher's lounge three days ago, three days that passed in slow motion, weighted down with the horror and shame of Mr. Hawley. Even now, I couldn't look at some of the kids, the ones he had taken on his SPECIAL campouts, suddenly aware that through the babble and din of the others, I could hear their voices crying in pain, in shame, in confusion. One little black haired kid, an eighth grader, had a gun stashed under his bed at home, a gun he was taking out and caressing, working up the courage to use it.

On himself.

I tried again. "Come on Billy! We can't let him DO this!" Pain, pain in my head, in my soul, in my voice.

Billy swung down from the bars, landing on frost blackened grass. "So who is gonna listen to us? Huh? No one believes me about anything. I tried before, they said I was lying. Uh uh, screw that. I'm not saying anything!"

I realized his face was turning red from anger, shame, the first time I had seen anything other than a goofy slyness in him. I stared at him; tongue tied.

"You think anyone's gonna listen to you?" he pelted the words at me, anger giving him force, "You're just a dummy! A big, dumb ox with a broken head. No one thinks you have any brains anyway. You think I'm wrong, go ahead and tell someone! You're just a dummy! A dummy who couldn't save his mom or have enough balls to get even with his step daddy! You're a loser! A big, fat PUSSY!"

I was swinging through the air, the ground thudding up under my feet, watching Billy's face change to fear as my arms swung out at him, seemingly of their own accord, arms with big fists at the end of them, fists that hit, and hit, and suddenly Billy wasn't closed off anymore, and suddenly the voices in my head were his, voices that cried out as his dad beat him, beat him, beat him, and slammed him into the wall because he was a WEIRDO, and he WASN'T RIGHT, and he was A LITTLE SHIT, and then the other kids were yelling, and Mrs. Donnelly was yelling, and I wasn't hitting Billy anymore because Billy was lying in the dirt with tears and snot slicking his face, blood red snot, and I was crying too, and the voices in my head were saying, "What a PUSSY!"

Only the voices weren't in my head at all, they were in my ears, and Jimmy was standing there, Jimmy with his mean eyes, right there, right behind Mrs. Donnelly, and his mouth was moving,

"You are such a pussy, Donahue."

Chapter 42

Now

The late sun glows on the windshield, fiery, smoke like clouds dappling the smooth glass surface. My tongue feels glued to the top of my mouth, the weight of the bottle in my pocket pulling on me, pulling...

I slide it out and crack the seal, the glass smooth and slick under my sweating hand. The whiskey burns like fire down my throat, then runs smooth like liquid silver. Capping it, I slide it back in my pocket, unable to move from where I stand, just inside the gate, the shadows from the building spilling over my head.

Fire slowly blooms in my belly, fire that chases away the tremors that threaten to spill over into my hands. Slowly, I move my feet and make my way towards the red Toyota. Dread prickles up my spine, shooting tremors that spill down my central nervous system, vibrating through my fingertips.

I slow, fumble the bottle out, take another long pull, smooth, smooth now, soothing. I drew abreast of the front fender. Took another long swig, capped the bottle with a hand that was surer, steadier now.

I still couldn't see past the cloud reflections into the interior of the car.

I felt a sudden spike of anger, of rage, at the car, anger I wasn't aware that I had. Without realizing, my foot was suddenly swinging, swinging hard at the Toyota, my size 12 bouncing off the door with a 'thwock', a dent appearing in the formerly smooth surface.

My tongue was stuck to the top of my mouth, dry, withered like a shriveled fig, desiccated. I felt an unintelligible cry tear through numbed lips, unrecognizable even to my own ears as I swung my fist at the windshield, then gave a yelp of pain as it bounced back off, the glass unscathed, my knuckles popping loudly, on fire.

The pain shocked me back down off the cliff of rage. I stood, half doubled over, clutching my burning, no, hurting like hell, hand to my belly, panting slightly, staring at the bland car. My pulse roared in my ears. I swore the car had just stopped me, slapped me down like a bug, protecting itself. What a crazy assed thought.

Or was it?

I slowly backed away from it, backed away until I was in a waning shaft of sunlight, shadows pooling around me everywhere, feeling slowly, awkwardly for my flask. Finding it, I pulled it out, left handed, and took a heavy swallow.

The bottle ran dry. I moaned slightly, licking the rim of the neck, searching for the last drop, a drop I must have missed.

There was none. I whimpered in the pregnant silence that surrounded me, a silence filled with dread, no, make that outright terror. I wavered, desperately wanting to back away and leave....and knowing if I did my slide was complete. I licked my lips with my dust dry tongue. I had no options, no laters left, like Bill had told me.

Now or never.

Never was starting to sound like a very good thing.

I slowly opened deadened fingers and let the whiskey bottle clatter to the macadam. The roaring in my ears grew louder, my face felt hot, red. With my head hanging like Howie, I shuffle stepped to the car, free will a fading memory.

In the glass of the driver's side window, I saw my face, shape shifting like the red scudding clouds above, a face I no longer recognized as my own, heavy jaw, dark hair, deep, black holes for eyes, red fire glittering in their depths.

I blinked, gritty lids on my eyes, the image shifted subtly and my face stared back at me again, a thousand yard stare, brown curly hair barely covering the mark on my head, my face, mine.

I reached for the door handle, pulled and it popped open smoothly, a faint whoosh of something dark, something foul escaping into the crisp river scented air. A coldness began in my neck, working its way down my spine with icicle feet, a chill spreading and spiraling out from my core. I closed my eyes as a shudder worked its way up from my gut, then opened them to see a flash of a face, that face again, from the driver's seat, there and gone.

Never had a simple gray upholstered seat looked so malevolent. My bowels clenched as I took a deep breath...and slid into the driver's seat.

I was ready for it this time...I thought. It gets dimmer as time goes by...usually. Maybe it was a bit dimmer, maybe. God I hoped so.

The sights and memories hit me with the force of a tsunami, a wave of noise and emotion pinning me in the seat, an unwilling participant, drawn into something I desperately didn't want to be in, something I couldn't walk away from. I gritted my teeth, pain roaring through me as I saw...

Gray streets, side streets crisscrossing, the roar of traffic on the...on the....thundering in my ears, right there behind those buildings. I'm back for the little skinny bitch, the one that's been out here the past couple of weeks, all high heels and short shorts, stinking of cigarettes smoked through mean, painted lips. I can't find her tonight, can't see her, that pisses me off, fucking bitch, I drove all the way here for her.

I see another one, under the street sign saying Linden Court, soft, bread soft, dark rolling hair, smooth faced with fearful blue eyes, a newbie, a young'un, maybe 16, 17, probably a runaway, her fishnets wildly out of place on pudgy thighs, her pimp likely close by, close, can't take her, leave the newbie, too risky, mark her, mark her, come back for her in a couple weeks, when her eyes have gone dead and her pimp has broken her so she won't run off any longer. Damn it, damn it, damn it, all this way, all this driving and nothing. Don't like the dark meat on the next corner; don't want the old shriveled hag stinking of booze and body odor in the doorway.

I want young and smooth.

Circling the block again, store fronts in the gloom and neon, "Girls, Girls, Girls", "The Penthouse Collection", "Latin Market" "Easy Eddie's Fast Cash", and then I am back at Lin-

den Court again, back for the pudgy one, back for the soft downy feeling of her, ready to take a chance, invincible, powerful, only she's climbing into a black Nissan, a white plate with a blue band across the top, a flash of leg disappearing into the car, in the alley across from them, the light reflecting off the profile of her pimp, her man, heavy face, bandana on his head, damn it! I pull away, aware of how close that was, how angry I am.

And then I see her. Emerging from the side street, Washington, onto Linden Court, walking briskly, her eyes stoned, cigarette hanging from her lips, I see her and I am suddenly aware of a hunger, a ravishing need roaring through my veins...

"No!" I can't see this, can't. My head shakes, side to side, no, no, no. "No....don't get in the car...no..." Dimly I am aware of sweat sliding down my face, my stomach cramping violently. I want out, out of the past, out of the car...

She stumbles slightly as she reaches the street corner, flicking a glance at the pimp, who is disappearing down into the darkness of the alleyway, melting back into the night. I am already moving, moving, sliding up alongside her, aware that her lipstick is smudged from the last one, her eyes newly stoned out, gone.

She doesn't hesitate as I stop the car, she thinks this one might be a good night, a good high. Little does she know how high I plan to take her.

But of course I can't stop her, can't change it. It already happened. I brace myself and cringe, moaning, as she gets in the seat, trying to tear myself away, away, away. I don't want to see anymore, don't want to experience another one; I want it to not happen.

You can't change the past. You can only change the future. I moan and hang on as the blood and screaming begin.

Chapter 43
Then

I'm sitting on the side of the shallow hill that slopes down from the playground, my arms resting on my knees. Clouds slip and slide across the chilly October sun, throwing purple shadows across my eyes. Cold is seeping through my jacket, my butt. Billy Meeker appears and sits down on the grass beside me.

We don't speak.

Behind me, the voices and squeals of the kids playing on the playground stuff cut through the air, in my head, their screaming cut through my soul. I close my eyes, rub at them, wincing as the pain from my head pierces me. Beside me, Billy shifts slightly, then says, "You know, you can block them out."

It's the first words we have spoken willingly to each other since our fight four days ago. "What are you talking about?"

I know, but I want him to say it. I realize I can feel him, hear his psychic voice faintly, whereas before I couldn't feel anything.

He stretched his gangly legs out, and slowly picked his nose. Billy was gross like that, always sticking his fingers in his nose, his ears. My Gramma had fits when I did that. "Them other kids. You don't hafta hear their shit all the time."

I finally look over at him. "How do you know this?" No one else I had met knew this. No one else understood what I was trying to tell them when I was still in the hospital. Billy shrugged. "I just do, okay?"

"How come you can do it too?"

Another shrug. "Dunno. I just can. And so far, you're the only other kid I've met that can do it too."

I notice the cut still visible where I split his lip. We got in BIG TROUBLE for that. I had to 'pologize to him, or I was gonna get kicked out. Gramma was mad, really mad, when she heard. Billy just shrugged it off....and didn't talk to me. Until today.

"Whadda ya mean, I don't have to listen to them?" I can't figure out what he means. He draws his legs up like mine, resting his chin on his knees as he answers me. "You can block 'em out. It's like...it's like...you imagine a curtain that you pull over your brain, it's a gray one. You see it and you pull. Then you gotta hold it, gotta pay attention or it opens again. I'm pretty good at it now. Used to be I had to think about it all the time."

We sat in silence, looking down the little hill towards the driveway that rose gently to the front of the building, the playing fields beyond it. Kids race and chase after a round red ball, kicking it mightily, all bright colors and distant yelling. I scuffed my heels in the dirt, watching grass clumps break loose.

In my head, I look for a curtain, like Billy said. I don't see one. But there is...something. Like a blanket, maybe. I think about grabbing it, tugging it loose, then feel it slide across, covering my brain.

For a moment, all noise IN my head is gone. The only voices are all outside.

"Hey!" The blanket disappears.

"What?" Billy has his head cradled in his arms; his voice muffled.

"It worked...kinda."

"Told you so."

I try again, carefully grabbing the edge and easing it across my brain, feeling the whisper of the fabric sliding over the ridges of my brain. All noise in my head goes away again. I realize I am holding my breath. Carefully, I exhale, gently loosening my ribcage. The blanket goes away, my brain is back to being noisy, noisy, noisy again.

Still, I'm excited. This is, like, the first time since I got hurt that I realize that I can control it, guide it. Taking a deep breath, I concentrate hard on finding the blanket, and carefully pulling it across my brain. I can almost feel the soft fabric sliding over the folds and wrinkles in my head.

"Hey." Billy says beside me.

My eyes open, the blanket disappears in a poof. I'm momentarily blinded by the sun that streams across my face, black dots dance in my eyes.

"Lookit those guys." Billy says, gesturing with a pointed chin that holds the first signs of acne speckling the skin.

I look over his knees as the bell rings, signaling the end of recess, peer over and see Darlene and Jimmy, coming from the bleachers on the right side of the field. Kids are streaming up from where they were playing kickball in the field, Darlene and Jimmy falling in like they were with them. Behind us, the littler kids are shrieking and running from the jungle gym and the swings, all of them trying to be first in line to go back in.

I watch Darlene, feeling the shame blossoming in my face as I remembered what they were doing down there. Shame and...something else. Jealousy maybe? I scowled, pushing myself up off the ground, feeling mad. Beside me, Billy was staring at them with a strange look on his face, an almost...hungry look. It made me mad.

I kicked his leg. "Come on, you retard. It's time to go in."

Chapter 44
Now

Amy won't shut up as she guides the car with herky jerky movements through downtown, her mouth moving fast and furious.

I'm silent in the seat beside her, silent and in pain, everything that can move on me hurts, from booze, from work, from fear. The left front corner of the Volkswagen hits a pothole with a slam, causing me to gasp involuntarily. "Jesus Christ, Amy, would you slow down?" before I can stop it.

Mistake.

She swivels to look at me, hurt and a bright, brittle anger showing in her eyes, anger that rides right along the surface these days, anger at life, anger at me. I feel a spark of my own, answering rage.

She's been the spark to my tinder lately, constantly there, there, there in my face, in my space. Waiting for me tonight when I got home, the late sunlight streaming across the kitchen as I entered, all noise and talk, wanting, wanting. I agree to go to dinner with her, even though leaving is the last thing I want to do now that I just got home. I just want to quiet her down some, get her to stop this clinginess and let me have some room again.

I desperately want a drink.

I press my lips together as her eyes start to sparkle, with tears, with rage, with I don't know what. She's wearing me out. I say nothing as she spews sarcasm at me, letting it slide over my back and off. Get the next hour out of the way and get home to bed, get to sleep, lose yourself for the next few hours. Just deal with it, Gerry.

Amy falls mercifully silent, frustrated by the non-response from me. I know this. I know it because everyone I have ever cared about gets this treatment. You can't let them too close, can't let them in you. Best to hold them away some, away so they don't get hit with what splashes off of you as you blunder through life.

A tiny part of me way deep inside, a little fragment of the BEFORE Gerry, feels a lance of pain at this, rails against it uselessly.

I ignore him.

BEFORE Gerry is as dead as my Mom is. He died that same night, died in a soft sinking of gray nothingness. AFTER Gerry is all that is left, crafted of mismatched parts, broken pieces, the big ox with the broken head, the retard, the pussy.

She swings into the lot of the Fish Kill, throwing the wheel harder than needed, sending more pain lancing down my neck. The lot's about half full, pickup trucks, sedans, a couple of yuppie type sport Ute's, likely weekend warriors. I don't see any cars I know.

Cooking fish and steak hit my nostrils as we enter, the wooden double doors whooshing shut behind us. Amy is brittle, her discontent visible on her face to the kid who seats us awkwardly, voices of the other diners rattling in my ears, music overlaying it.

Wooden tables with clusters of people, waitresses moving quickly with loaded trays, aprons over black pants, a bar along the back wall calling out to me, bottles glowing like gems in the half light.

I pick up my menu and pretend to ignore it. Amy leans across the table, her voice a hissing spit, "Don't you think for two seconds that I can't see what you're thinking, Gerry. You are NOT drinking anymore tonight!"

"I haven't BEEN drinking, Amy." A lie. We both know it.

She glares at me a moment, then holds the menu up to study it, as do I, words swimming in front of my eyes. I decide on fish and chips without even reading the menu, knowing that they have it.

A black panted waiter appears with an order pad for drinks, setting two soft doughy rolls down on the table. I grudgingly order a Coke, Amy a gin and tonic. Anger flares as she does so. The kid scoops up the menus and departs, leaving Amy and me glowering at each other across the table.

"So it's 'Do as I say, not as I do', eh?"

A red flush starts at her cheekbones. "I can have one anytime I want to. I'm not the one with a PROBLEM!" Angry hiss. "I'm sick of not living my life because of your fuck ups!"

My belly clenches at her words, rage striking me mute. I feel a warm tingling in my palms, the desire to strike her so strong for an instant it scares me. I have never hit a woman, ever. Tonight, I feel like making an exception.

She reads something in my face, falls silent, fiddling with her fork. I reach over and grab a roll, stuffing it in my mouth, tearing into it, spraying bread crumbs all over the table. I know she hates that. That's why I do it. The red on her cheeks solidifies into two red circles, flowers of rage. She stays silent.

I grab the second roll, do the same thing. Noise flows over us, two silent rocks of anger in the middle of the stream. Our drinks come as we sit in silence, Amy gulping a third of hers down in one gulp, then our food. I put my head down and eat mechanically. Amy picks at hers.

I'm almost done with my meal when a skinny shadow falls across me from my right, a shadow with a ball cap, glasses, handlebar mustache. Dean Hamilton, nudging my shoulder, saying hey, nodding at Amy, who eyes him sullenly.

I haven't seen Dean since the night he drove me home from the bar. My stomach clenches, wondering if he will mention that. He leans a skinny hip against the empty chair next to me, saying instead, "Hey, did you hear about what happened to Ben, that kid from over to Forge's Garage?"

I shake my head, finishing my meal as he launches into a long story of a stupid kid in his father's truck, one that ended with police and being towed out of the Hudson River. Amy's eyes have glazed over, and she looks around the room visibly annoyed at the intrusion. Dean doesn't notice.

Mercifully, he winds up his story, a story that isn't half as interesting as it would have been that night, the night we all met at the bar. Dimly, I remember that it was a kid named

Ben who drove my truck back, wondered if it was the same one, decided I didn't care enough to ask.

Feeling our indifference to him, Dean finally winds down, pushing upright off the chair back. He casts a glance at Amy, a glance that turns sly even as I recognize it, then says to me, "Hey, this the 'dead woman' you was looking for the other night? She don't look all that dead to me!" He chuckles, smug in his humor.

Amy's attention is snapped back to us, her eyes going from far away to RIGHT THERE, assessing, narrowing, staring at me like she can slice me open and examine my insides. Dean either doesn't notice or doesn't care. He chuckles, a dim sounding heh heh heh, low in his throat, unaware of the danger he just conjured up.

Amy cuts her eyes to him, her voice all sweet, syrupy, "Why Dean! Has old G.L. here been telling you I'm dead?"

She smiles, not a nice one either, "I can assure you I am anything but DEAD."

Dean is staring at her, frankly, captivated now, his eyes on the rise and fall of her ample breasts, snugly draped with a tee shirt, tight jeans accentuating the lower half, battered Frye boots on her feet.

Even in redneck regalia she looks exotic. I realize with a start that she is the sole reason Dean came over here just now, his intent to eyeball her from up close. My anger spikes again.

"Amy's far from dead, Dean." I reach for my wallet, pulling out two twenties to toss on the table. "I can vouch for that a million times over."

Amy isn't placated though. She cuts me a razor sharp look, and shifts to push her breasts further out at him, asking Dean, "Why in the world would Gerry say I'm dead?"

Dean is captivated, staring openly at her chest, at the soft half circle of the collar where multiple silver chains disappear into the sweetly scented darkness. He is half a beat slow in his answer. Amy smiles, catlike.

Caught out, Dean stammers a moment. "I, uh, the uh, the other night, when I was taking him home, he was asking me how he was supposed to find a dead woman."

A chuckle at that, an uncomfortable one. "He said he seen her die but didn't know where it happened. You, um, you definitely don't look dead."

"So why were you bringing him home, Dean?"

Too late, Dean realizes the can of worms he just opened, fully realizes it. He's an asshole, but he still is my friend.

Kind of.

He straightens up, turning away from her, a panicked look in his eyes. I meet his eyes stonily, resigned. "Because I had a few drinks and wasn't going to drive home like that. Dean here was nice enough to take me, weren't you Dean?"

Relieved from the direct fire, Dean laughs uneasily, then mimes raising his left arm to check his watch, a watch that I can see from here isn't on his arm.

"Oh, hey, I better get going. Miranda's waiting for me. See you later, Amy, G.L." He tilts his head, his mustache backlit on the left side of his face by the light that streams from the bar behind us and takes his leave, almost scurrying out the door.

I'm already rising, grabbing my jacket off the back of the chair as Amy throws back the last of her gin and tonic, her second one, and kicks her chair back. If she was angry before, she's seriously pissed now.

We head for the exit in silence.

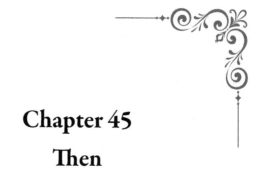

Chapter 45
Then

I can see a sliver of the moon when I lie on my back just right. It peeks over the edge of the station wagon's windshield, just a fingernail moon tonight.

Wind rattles the bare branches of the trees that arch overhead. It's cold tonight, the first really cold night since I came HOME. Gramma didn't want me sleeping in the car anymore, really didn't want it. We almost got in a huge fight about it.

I can feel my anger, sitting right there, there on the surface of me, so real I can see it. Gramma sees it too, sees it and backs off from it. She's afraid of me. I like that. But...but... it makes me feel bad too. My head hurts when I think of it, so I don't think of it. I just...am.

I feel...stuck. The whole entire time I was in the hospital, all they talked about was when I was ready to GO HOME. And now that I am here...now what?

I see a counselor a lot, like every couple days at least. I don't know what to say, to her, to anyone really, so I don't say anything. The only person I ever really talk to is weird Billy Meeker. Talking to him, I can just be me. I don't have to explain anything. He doesn't ask questions; doesn't really care I guess. And that's good.

The seatbelt is poking me in the back again, and I shift, making the moon wobble a bit. I lie still, staring through the windshield at it, seeing the light from a really long way away right there. I'm cocooned in a down sleeping bag, my breath frosty in the cold car interior, isolated from everyone here in my hiding place.

No one knows where HE is, or if they do, they aren't telling me. I've caught hushed conversations, conversations between Gramma and the police, between my counselor and Gramma. Sometimes between the kids at school. He killed my momma, and almost killed me and he's gone, scot free. It's not fair.

I stare at the moon until it wavers in my vision, bracketed between the rear view mirror and the sun visor. I think about crying, but the tears aren't there, haven't been there since that day I came home. It's like I froze up inside.

People say mean things to me, stare at me, try to hurt me and I stare at them through a pane of thick glass, so thick they look wavy. They always back down first, look away, mumble something and leave. My weirdness has given me a power, a strength.

It came with a price though; isolation. I can't decide if I like it or not, and in the end simply give up trying to figure it out. It just is.

I think about something Billy said the day we were fighting, something that has bugged me ever since. He was yelling, yelling, telling me I was stupid, a big dumb ox with a broken head, who was a pussy because I hadn't saved my mom.

Because I hadn't gone after HIM.

I roll that thought around in my head awhile as the moon slowly rises higher, disappearing above the roof line of the car, the dim light spilling over the dash.

I'm a kid, maybe not so little anymore now that a long time has gone by since he attacked us, but still a kid. I spent a long, long time in the hospital and in rehab. I'm stuck going to school, stuck with my Gramma in the noisy little house my mom grew up in. I'm all she has left. And she's all I have left.

And every day, HE is there in the room with us, a big smelly presence. I smell it in the fear that rolls off Gramma. I feel it in my broken sleep, always with one eye open. I hear it in the noisy, damaged house. I've been trying to pull that blanket across like Billy said, but it's hard here.

My only hope is that it seems....to be getting dimmer each time I walk in the house. My first time back, it was like waking up in the middle of it, seeing his fist whacking down, again, again, the screams, the fear, the pain, living it all over, not just seeing it.

Now it's like a television playing loudly as you are going about your everyday things. WHAM, he hits her with a knife, a wet thwacking sound as I am pouring my cereal out, her screams rake my ears as I am drawing my bath, brushing my teeth. BAM! Gramma thunders across the upstairs hall screaming as I get dressed for school. THWOCK, one of the twenty-two stab wounds happens as I load my backpack for school.

I spend a lot of time out on the front porch, where their screams are muted by the walls of the house.

By the time I go to bed in the old wooden paneled station wagon, I'm worn out, hollow eyed, like one of them kids I seen on the magazine, the ones caught in a civil war. The noise finally mutes completely when I close the door of the car, the sudden silence a blessed relief, so much so that I sag into the seat, exhausted.

Here too, the sensations have muted, something that makes me sad because it's all I have left of mommy. I never knew my daddy. Mommy told me he died when I wasn't even born yet, so it was always me and mommy, at least until HE came along. I try and try to remember details about mommy, but it's hard, they aren't there anymore, she's just a blurry shape and feeling to me now.

I think about HIM and details prickle my eyes like needles. Narrow mean face. The white hairs he had in his left eyebrow, from a scar. Missing teeth. Skinny waisted, pants belted up tight, sunken in cheeks. His stink, like bad breath and something else, a rotting smell. Hatred bubbles up in me, hatred so strong I feel like I want to rip the steering wheel right off and throw it at something.

The seatbelt is digging into me again. I roll around some more, trying to get comfortable again. Billy's words ring in my ears, over and over. I wonder if I can do it. I wonder if this broken head of mine can actually help me.

I wonder if I can track him down and kill him. My fingers clench into fists in the darkness. What if I can do it? How would I do it? Could I?

I know even before the thought is complete that while I don't know how I would do it; I have no doubt that I could indeed kill him.

And enjoy it.

Chapter 46
Now

I stare at the moon, nearly full now, just barely visible in the upper right corner of my bedroom window and give up all pretense of trying to sleep.

Amy is long gone, probably rolling around on her own bed in her apartment over by the medical center across town.

She dumped me in my driveway in icy silence and blasted away, her taillights getting smaller as she accelerated down Route 20, me standing in the mottled moon shadows watching her go.

I felt like a part of me went with her.

I finally climbed the three steps and opened the frayed back door to my home. That was five hours ago now. And despite my exhaustion, sleep is a long ways away yet.

I close my eyes, trying to ignore the pain in my head, the waning alcohol and fear buzz banging like a heavy drum, images flickering across my mind, images I haven't had time to process since staggering away from the red car earlier today.

Linden Court. Easy Eddie's Fast Cash. Girls, Girls, Girls. A figure appearing on Washington Street, where it joined Lin-

den Court. A flash of leg as the young runaway climbed into a car with a white plate, blue band across the top.

I open my eyes again.

"He didn't do it in Connecticut. He did it in New York." I rub my eyes, hard enough to cause pain, pressing the images to the forefront, searching for more clues.

The Penthouse Collection. Linden Court. Washington Street. Black Nissan with a white plate, blue band across the top. Cars on the side of the street, yellow or white plates. Easy Eddie's Fast Cash.

The bedside table lamp blinds me momentarily as I roll upright and light a cigarette. I sit still, for a long moment, the images churning.

My eyes fall on my telephone book jammed haphazardly under the bedside table. Pulling it out, I start flipping through the yellow pages, not really expecting anything, an exercise designed to give my hands something to do.

But...but...wait...Easy Eddie's Fast Cash, 17 Linden Court, Newburgh New York.

Newburgh. Less than forty miles from me.

The floor is cold under my bare feet, but I barely register it. Every hair on my neck is standing up, standing up like the hackles of a dog on the hunt.

I paw through the pile of papers on my kitchen table, pausing only to light another cigarette with shaking hands. My atlas peeks out from under the stack of bills and crap. I scoop it up, sending papers to the floor in a cascade, flipping open to the map of New York state, south.

Newburgh is due west of New Fairfield, Connecticut. I sit down at the table, drawing deeply on my cigarette, feeling the nicotine rush as I pore over the close up of Newburgh. I can't find Linden Court.

But I do find Washington Street. I fumble a pen out of the pile of junk and mark it, the line wavering on the map from shaking hands.

I scan the grid of roads that line this riverside town, a town caught in the rite of passage from past to present like mine is, yuppies to the north, poor people to the south, caught in a squeeze play of then and now, development and decay. I've been through Newburgh many times, through it without really seeing it. I close my eyes now and search my memory. Nothing.

Frustrated, I bang a fist on my thigh.

The clock over the stove reads 2:47. I stare out the window, overlooking the bare maple tree and my truck parked under it, a dark mound dappled in dim moonlight. My initial elation is gone, replaced by a sinking feeling. I'm no closer now than I was before I climbed into the car again. Craning my head back, I search for the edge of the moon, now barely visible along the roof of my trailer.

I have a name. I have his address. I know where he got at least some of the women from. I even knew how I killed them.

I didn't know where the bodies are.

A shudder worked its way down my spine at that. What I also didn't have was any shred of evidence, nothing physical to go to the police with, nothing I could drop in their laps and say, hey, check this out. You want this guy, right here.

Which meant I had to go get it.

But first, I had to find the bodies.

Chapter 47
Then

Snow squeaks and crunches under my boots, slipping and sliding me around. The kids yells pierce my ears, my brain chatters with their inside noise. I look around for Billy, but don't see him anyplace.

It's early, before classes start. Kids shout and race around as yellow buses trundle in and out of the driveway of the red brick school building.

I finally got Gramma to let me ride the bus in, something I have wanted to do since getting back HOME. This has been the first time I have been able to at least pretend I'm the same as them other kids, even if it's only for a little while. I stomp, spraying slush around, killing the world with my feet.

"Hey, it's the retard!" Red plastic boots, wet sneakers, in front of my face. I look up, wary, to see Darlene and Jimmy standing there. No Ricky. I haven't seen Ricky since coming back to school, I realize now. But I seen Darlene and Jimmy...a lot. This is the first time I've had them talk to me though. And I don't like it.

I go still, silent, staring at them. Darlene tosses her hair, elbowing Jimmy in the ribs. "Don't call him that! He's not a retard, are you Gerry?" She smiles, a prim little bow tie mouth smile. I look at her, aware of the waves coming off both of them. Jimmy, he hates me, has always hated me, more so now that he is afraid of me. With a start, I realize I am bigger than him, longer armed, heavier bodied. I could pound him into the ground if I wanted to.

Darlene, well she is confusing to me. She is somehow...interested in me, but also kinda scared of me. She wants something from me, something I can't figure out.

I stare at her with flat eyes and see annoyance flicker across her eyes, annoyance that makes her mouth go taut, her teeth showing slightly. She glares back at me with glittering eyes.

Beside her, Jimmy shifts uneasily, then plants his hands on his hips. Darlene speaks, breaking the weird silent standoff we have going on. "What's the matter, Gerry? Aren't you glad to see us again?" pink tongue tip flicks across her upper lip.

I shrug, I don't think I'm really glad, or sad, or anything. They're just...there.

"Told you he's a retard now." Jimmy, puffing out his chest, showing off. "He never was much of anything before, and now he's even less, aren'tcha retard?"

I say nothing, even as images from Jimmy flow across my brain, unwanted, unneeded. He's a gross little pig. I stare at him, disgusted when I realize what he's been doing, the hole he poked in the bathroom wall, how he watches his sister in there. Something in my face sets him off.

"Retard!" He shoves me, hard, making me stagger backwards in the slushy snow. I catch myself, feel the rage blooming, hot, sweet and red in my belly. I stare at him, unblinking, see his face redden as his own anger and...fear fight with each other. The fear calms me, soothes me. I hitch my backpack up again and smile, a flat smile, I know; I've seen it.

Darlene is frankly staring at me now, fascinated like you are when you find a spider. I say the first thing that comes to mind. "You should stop spying on your little sister when she goes to the bathroom. She's only five!"

Darlene gasps, and Jimmy's face goes white as the bell rings, signaling that it's time to go in. We stare at each other a beat longer, then I turn away and slowly join the stream of rushing bodies making their way up the low hill to the school.

"ASSHOLE! YOU'RE GONNA BE SORRY FOR THAT!" his voice breaks on the last word, squeaks.

I don't bother looking back as I trudge up the muddy slope.

Chapter 48
Now

The library is built of chunks of ancient river bottom, brown stone bleached tan by the years. Squat and long, it sits just off downtown, scraggly trees marching in a row down the sidewalk in front, faded posters dangling off the cork board inside the front doors. I've never been in here before.

A woman as faded as the posters signs me in and points me towards the kiosks I need, one of which sits empty on this Saturday afternoon. These kiosks don't hold books; they hold computers.

Clumsy, I go through the steps she walked me through, and the next 90 minutes are mine. My fingers fumble over the keyboard. This time, I change my search, to an entirely different state, to a single town in that state.

And this time, I start to get results.

I'm clumsy with Lexus Nexus, the service the washed out woman at the desk told me I wanted, but it starts to get easier. Slowly, fragments of information begin to appear.

"Body found in rail yard ruled a homicide." "Woman slain, left on riverbank." "Police grapple with disappearances, seek connection"

And on it goes. My thirty minutes passes, then my hour, then my hour and a half. I renew my time for another hour as the stories stack up.

They start in 1996 and continued through four months ago. I stare at the rows of text, my stomach sinking. All prostitutes. Well, all except one, the only one that got any press, a college student who disappeared while heading home from a date in 2004, a dark haired young woman with blue eyes, soft looking.

Bread soft.

A chill snaked up my spine as I realized I recognized her, recognized her from getting in the Nissan that night. Not a hooker at all, a college kid abducted to the wrong side of the tracks. Sweat started beading on my forehead as I printed out the story on her and added it to the growing stack.

In a story about a string of girls who were mysteriously gone, I spy two familiar faces, two women, well girls actually at only 19 and 21 respectively, girls whose deaths I witnessed, some girls whose bodies were as yet undiscovered. I scan the row of dead eyed faces in the story, wondering how many of them rode in a little red car before they died.

I think of Robert Blake and my belly churns with acid.

My time on the computer runs out again, and this time I let it. I can't stomach any more of this. Carefully I collect and fold my copies of the stories, tucking them into my coat pocket. Around me, lanky kids are plugged into the other computers, slouched in chairs, dull eyed, fingers flying over the keyboards, headphones on most of them.

None of them pays me any mind as I stand up, knees popping from the unaccustomed length of time spent in the chair. I make my way out to the lobby, sign out and leave, the woman behind the desk barely sparing me a glance.

Leaves kick and swirl down the sidewalk outside the library as I stop to get my bearings. I have names now, names to go with the faces, ages, photographs. But nothing besides my horrific psychic images to tie them to the car.

I stand for a moment on the sidewalk, debating walking back to the lot for my truck, or going the opposite way to the diner midway down the block. The diner wins.

Inside, the air is warmer, a sprinkling of people scattered throughout. I choose a seat at the end of the counter, away from the door, the booths, and unfold my printouts next to my coffee. My hand trembles slightly as I smooth them open, rereading the stories again. The coffee is stale, bitter. I wish it was whiskey instead, push the thought away with difficulty. The paper shivers in my hand.

The first girl I saw in the car, the one that exploded into my head when I was at the auction was Desiree Foster, age 19, from White Plains, New York. I study the lines of her face on the grainy black and white photo. Old far beyond her years, a hardness that came too early, she was last seen just under a year ago, in early December. I remember the cold air that stung when she climbed in the car. I scan the meager story, all too familiar in a depressing way; known drug addict, arrests for prostitution, a family who still searched for her back in White Plains, a middle class suburban family, the only reason anyone missed her now, the American dream gone bad. The tremor in my hand increases. I set the story down and unfold the next one.

This one is about bodies left like broken dolls in the grimy armpits of the town, at semi regular intervals. More photos of dead eyed girls, left in rail yards, alleyways, on the river front itself, broken and torn beyond repair. I see a hot-line number printed in the article, a net cast in desperation, or maybe apathy, searching for clues. The printout joins the others in the stack. Silently, the heavyset brunette reappears and sloshes more burnt coffee into my glass without being asked. I lift the cup to my lips, liquid spilling as I do so.

The girl with the bread soft body and blue eyes was Karen Wilson, a SUNY student who went out on a date and never came back to her dorm. Inexplicably, she was found on the riverbank south of Newburgh on a wet night last March, when slashing rain wavered between ice and water. Photos showed wet jacketed cops and EMT's lugging a shiny black form up the embankment, the photographers light reflected back at him from the body bag. One EMT is looking direct-ly into the camera, his face haggard, a thousand yard stare on it. It was bad, I would lay money on it remembering Robert Blake's rage at her.

Anger at him begins to awaken in me, a subtle white liq-uid running through my veins. My trembling hands start to still a bit.

The names and faces pile up. Dolores, Sunny, Leigh Ann, on and on they go. Probably not all of these women rode in the red car. Some of them likely found other ends, or simply left. But some of them climbed into that red Toyota for one last ride.

I wonder why he came back here again and again, why this one city on the bank of the Hudson when he had all of New York city as a happy hunting ground a few miles south. Something scratches at my memory, something about one of his holdings. I stare at the wall behind the counter seeing nothing. Was it Geotechnik? One of them mentioned a New York division, possibly over by the Hudson. I pull a pen from my jacket and scratch a note on the back of one of the sheets of paper. A connection finally?

I fold the sheets up again and stow them in my pocket, resolution crystallizing in my belly. *I'm going to nail you, you son of a bitch*, I whisper to myself.

My hands are completely still now.

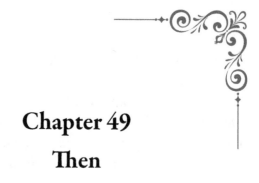

Chapter 49
Then

The garage where Gramma brought her station wagon is only three blocks away from us, two down and one over. I think of it a lot, especially when we go by it. I can hear the guy telling me, "Anytime, kid."

Cars fascinate me. I poke and prod through Gramma's, until she gets mad at me. I stare at the sleek shapes parked along the curbs, memorize the kinds, peer inside of them. I bug Gramma over and over to take me back to the garage where we were, but she won't do it.

"He didn't mean it, Gerry. He was being polite. Now stop asking me about it! Did you do your homework?"

Frustrated, I shrug. I don't have homework, rarely do, and when they do give it to us, I do mine before I leave the school. The special class I am in leaves me bored. I wonder why they insist I be there instead of the regular school.

On a damp but sunny day when winter was loosening its grip on the world, Gramma calls me from her doctor's office, where she is held up longer than she thought.

I'm home, have been there a while already, trying to ignore the faded screams in the house. Another hour or so, she tells me, you behave until I'm home, okay? I hear the tension in her voice as an idea blooms in my head. Solemnly, I swear I will be a model child. After telling me what to do several times, she reluctantly hangs up, unable to do anything differently at this point.

The phone no sooner hits the cradle and I'm across the room like a shot, yanking my coat from the hall closet, pausing to fumble at my pocket, making sure I have a house key. The front door snicks shut behind me, and a delicious sense of being BAD washes over me. My bike leans against the porch, a scarred up banana seated thing I cobbled together from two junk bikes I got at the dump. I throw a leg over it and shoot down the sidewalk.

The air is damp and fresh smelling, mud and water scents, different than the frozen arctic smells we have had for the past several months. I inhale deeply, remembering how surprised they were in the hospital when they realized I could smell, telling me how LUCKY that was, how most people with this kind of 'damaged frontal lobe' lose their sense of smell. At the time, I really didn't know or care about it. How lucky can you be to have what happened to me happen? But now, I realize that maybe, just maybe, I am lucky, sort of. I inhale deeply again, the air a delicious flavor.

I'm kinda nervous as I reach the two blocks down and start over. I've never gone this far alone, and certainly never without Gramma's approval.

I wonder if the guy will remember me, or if he will tell me to go away.

My feet slow on the pedals as the red painted building appears, two garage doors, one open, and two gas pumps out front. A winged horse is on a sign above it, a dirty plate glass window underneath. I can see someone in the bay where the door is open, beneath a car, a stream of oil dropping into a black funnel thing. I park my bike by the window and head for the garage door.

"Hey!" from behind me. Guiltily, I stop and whirl around, certain that Gramma came home and found me gone.

But no, it's a skinny old guy in a blue uniform who is coming out the door, bristle haired, black nails. "Where you going, kid? The air's over there." I realize he thinks I am here for my bicycle tires.

Tongue tied, I shake my head and look down at the ground, unable to think of a single thing to say. He stops and stares at me a moment. "Hey, I know you. You're Charlene's grandkid, ain't you? Are you supposed to be over here by yourself?"

I see the look in his eyes, feel the waves coming off him; this kid's not right, he's a retard, he's the one that got all messed up. That loosens the grip on my tongue finally.

"I'm not here for my bike. He said I could come by anytime." I jerked my thumb over my shoulder at the man who was rolling the funnel towards the doorway.

"Oh yeah?" He looks up at the other guy, who has just noticed me. "That right, Carl? You tell this kid here to come over whenever he wants?"

"Hey! It's the Master Mechanic!" He's reached the door now, wiping his hands on a red rag, grinning widely at me, the missing tooth a black nugget in his mouth.

"Hey." I smile back at him, some of my unsureness going away.

"He's ok, Dick. If'n he wants to come around, it's okay by me." I feel a sunny feeling coming from him, pleasant, kinda warm. I like him.

"So what you doing?" my eagerness shows as I peer up underneath the car.

He grins, pulls a cigarette out of his pocket and lights it. "Just finished up an oil change."

He walks over to the lift and grabs a lever. "Watch it. She's coming down." The lift hisses as the car, a Ford Pinto, he tells me, settles earthward.

I'm full of questions, peppering him mercilessly as he finishes that car and rolls another, a Dodge Dart, in to take its place. This one is in for a tune up, needing spark plugs, points and something called a condenser, plus adjusting the timing. I'm so lost in the procedure I don't realize that I've also lost something else: the time. It doesn't even occur to me until he says it's time to call it a day.

Startled, I look at the clock and realize with horror that three hours have gone by. The sun is fading, darkness creeping across the street at us.

Carl notices the look on my face. "What's wrong?" I can't answer at first, just look at the ground. He cocks his head to one side. "Uh oh...let me guess. Your Gram didn't know you was coming here, did she?" I shake my head no, miserable that I screwed it up so bad. He looks at me a beat longer. "Come on, G.L. I'll give you a ride home." G.L. The first person who ever called me that.

He has a dusty 12-year old truck, a 1959 Ford. In misery, I put my bicycle in the bed as he chokes the motor and coaxes it to life. "Aw come on, she won't be that mad." I can't answer at first, then I do.

"She's going to be really, really mad. She doesn't like me doing anything by myself."

"Big kid like you? You should be all over the place by yourself. I was your age, I was out from the time the street lamps went out to when they came back on." He glances at me; I feel the question coming off him. Strangely, it doesn't bother me from him.

I push my hair off my forehead, I wear it long in front to hide the scar. His eyes widen when he sees it, angry red and knotted. They tell me the bullet hit my head and went around it, over the bone instead of through it. They say it's cuz of the way Gramma was holding the gun, the way it was pointing. Billy Meeker says it's cuz my head is as hard as a rock.

Carl looks at it and his eyes widen. "Holy shit, kid! I knew you was hurt, but damn!" His eyes harden. I feel his thought then, hear it like he spoke it. *That fucking Donny Hopgood. I swear to God, I catch that bastard I'll take him apart myself.*

Startled, I can only stare at him. I've felt pity, felt discomfort, felt a lot of things, but never have I felt anyone who felt the same way towards HIM as I did. My second thought is, holy cow...I had forgotten HIS name. Donny Hopgood...I repeat it silently, three times, to make sure I don't forget it again. I almost ask Carl if he knew him, stopping only as I realize that he didn't say it out loud. I don't want him thinking I'm some sort of freak.

Gramma's house appears, light pouring from every window, the station wagon parked out front. Carl pulls up to the curb and gets out to help me get my bike out. The front door flies open, and Gramma is in it, yelling my name. I feel the waves off her, fear, anger, fear, then I am enveloped in her arms, briefly. A second later her hand snaps across my cheek, hard.

"Hey, hey, hey, hey Charlene! No! Don't hit him!" Carl has her upper arm, inserting himself between her and me, shielding me from her rage.

"Whadda mean, don't hit him? I told him not to go anyplace, and he couldn't wait to sneak out that door! I've been beside myself for the past two hours! I even called the police!"

Fear is gone now, leaving nothing but anger behind. I feel myself harden up. Carl glances over his shoulder at the other little houses that line the street. Lights are on in them, and I can see shapes in the window as people watch us. Carl sees it too.

"Come on, Charlene. Let's go inside and talk this over." He takes her elbow and guides her up the walkway to the front porch. To my astonishment, she goes with him meekly, her anger fading with each step. I roll my bike to the porch and trail in behind them, looking at my feet as I walk. This is gonna be bad. I stare at my feet and go numb.

Inside, the lights blaze from every corner, like she was keeping a monster out. She doesn't realize she's been keeping one in all this time. THWACK, I hear the first stab hit home. Screams float through my brain, brassy blood smell drifts across my nostrils. I breathe deeply, staring at nothing, willing myself to pull that blanket across my brain. I can see Carl talking to Gramma, talking all earnest like, looking at me from time to time with a bit of a funny look on his face. I just breathe and work really hard to block the sounds of HIM killing my mom again. Him...Donny Hopgood.

The silence breaks through where the noise doesn't. I raise my eyes to see both of them staring at me, Gramma all teary eyed, Carl with a kinda weird look on his face, like he can't figure me out or something.

"Gerry?" Carl breaks the silence. I look at him, feel the blanket slip away, screams echo through my head. "Uh...yeah?" A tear trickles down Gramma's cheek.

"I just said you should apologize to your Gramma for scaring her today. I guess I should have told her that I asked you to come work for me."

What? I blink at him. He stares intently at me. Waves come off him, washing over me, *C'mon kid, work with me here*...I blink again, nod and shrug. "I'm, um, I'm sorry Gramma." She sniffles, a loud wet sound, "Why didn't you *tell* me they were going to let you work there after school? I would have brought you over right away! I thought you wanted to go over there to pester them!"

Work? There? I make eye contact with Carl, who nods almost invisibly. "Yup." He says to her, "The day I met him I said to Dick, 'Dick, I think this kid is the one we've been looking for. We've needed someone to help sweep up and keep the place neatened up. Lord knows I'm not very good in that department!"

Work? Holy cow! I'm so stunned I can only stare at him. The screams and wet thwacking sounds are faint, background noise now. And he's talking to Gramma, talking, talking, charming her actually, I can see it from here.

She's putting a hand to her hair, smiling at him now, as he tells her how they want me there three days a week during the school week, and will have me more come summer. Maybe even teach me to pump gas, clean the windshields and check oil. And money! Holy cow, he's telling her they will start me $2.00 each day, just for a couple hours of work! Maybe more later, when I learn some more stuff, can do more. Money! We don't have much of that. I realize then that that was how he got her, how he talked her into it. A job! I can't believe I just got offered a job! With cars!

I feel something stinging in my eyes, something hot. Tears...wow...tears...huh. Maybe it's all gonna be okay after all. And now I know HIS name, and I'm gonna earn some money.

Then I'm gonna go find the son of a bitch.

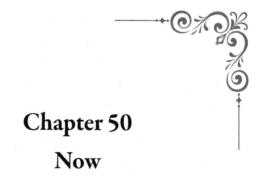

Chapter 50
Now

Bill's getting annoyed about the Toyota in the lot. It doesn't take much to get under his skin since the night I got shitfaced in his office.

Our chain link fenced lot isn't that big, and suddenly we have had an upswing in work as winter starts to slide down from Canada. All the bald tires and weakly firing batteries are rolling in now, along with the cars with marginal brakes and rotting exhaust systems. Being busy is good, keeps my hands and body going while my brain unravels the knot of how to nail Robert Blake's ass to the wall.

Bill keeps hounding me, bitching that the car is in the way, wanting me to move it from one side of the lot to the other every time he needs to bring another car in.

I send Howie out each time.

Maybe the third time I did that, Howie shuffles back in, something in his right hand. I look over at him as he stops by my toolbox. "This fell out of the visor." He drops it in the top of the box with a clink and plods away. Puzzled, I lay down the impact gun I was using and walk over to look at it.

It's a small silver cross with a lacy filigree on it. Without thinking, I pick it up.

"Please, mister, please! I got two girls, please! I'll do anything you want, anything you want, just please, please, don't hurt me! Nooo... please...please...nooooooooooo!"

My breath stops in my chest as the world around me grays out, my hand clenching on the cross so savagely it tears the skin on my palm.

"No! No! No! AIIIIIIEEEEEEEEEEEE! NO!" Fucking bitch, fucking bitch, fucking bitch, you're going into the fucking trunk you bitch, going into the fucking trunk and going into the fucking cellar, you bitch! You're gonna give me what I want, alright, you're gonna give it to me, you're mine now!"

I'm staggering backwards, the blood rushing from my head as my vision narrows down to a tunnel, roaring in my ears, Bill's face, white and scared, at the end of the tunnel, his lips moving, moving, moving. But no sound is coming out.

Blackness slides across his face and then there is nothing.

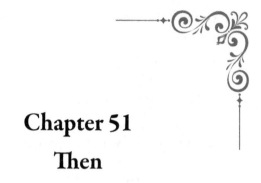

Chapter 51
Then

It's like my life went from really bad to really good, just like that. I'm working! Really, really working!

Every day, I suffer through school, impatient for the clock to get to three so that I can leave. Once I finally throw my leg over my bike and peddle down the sidewalk, everything falls off my shoulders, everything. I'm just Gerry again, not the weirdo or the retard. Just...Gerry. Or G.L., like my friend Carl calls me.

I'm gonna make sure I'm the best kid they ever had, the very best, so every day I grab the broom as soon as I get in and sweep up the office and shop, drag trash out to the dumpster, haul metal bits out to the pile out back. Then I get to hang over whatever Carl is working on and help him, hand him tools, pepper him with questions. He shows me the different wrenches and tools, teaches me how to unbolt things, and bolt them back on again. I work with a single minded concentration, the world sliding away until there's nothing left but cars and trucks in all their mystery, mystery that is gradually unraveling until they resemble puzzles instead.

Carl is patient with me, patient but kinda laughing at me too. On the third week, he says to me, "Kid, I think you're a natural born mechanic. You keep it up, you're gonna be good." My chest swells with pride at his words. I feel happiness in my belly.

Even Dick has gotten friendlier towards me once he sees how much I want to do this. He starts calling me G.L. too. I want to be here, every day. So I start showing up on days I don't have to. At first, Dick gets all tight, scared that he has to pay me for every day. I tell him I just want to work on the cars, and he relaxes again.

Gramma doesn't relax about it though. She starts fussing at me again, really fussing, telling me that I should be paying more attention to SCHOOL instead of the shop, how I should maybe play SPORTS after school one day a week instead. I can feel myself getting uptight inside when she starts talking like that.

I had been at the shop just about a month when Gramma announces to me one night that starting that Friday, I'm signed up to play baseball at school, and she doesn't want to hear any lip from me about it, that she knows how I will LIKE IT, and how GOOD IT WILL BE FOR ME to be with kids my own age more. I feel panic fluttering in my chest. I hate school, hate sports, don't want to hang around there where the only kid I kinda like is Billy. I don't want Carl and Dick to have to do everything alone, either. What if they find another boy?

We get in a huge fight about it. For once, Gramma is set on her way and her way only. In misery, I go to the shop the next afternoon and tell Carl and Dick what she did.

Carl just looks at me and lights a cigarette. I sniff the pungent smoke; I like that smell. Gramma doesn't smoke, but my mom used to. He cocks his head, a quizzical look at my expression. "Jesus Christ, G.L., you look like your best friend just died."

I hang my head a moment, mumbling, "I don't wanna do it. It's stupid."

Behind me, Dick tells me, "Kid, what's stupid is staying here five nights a week, that's what's stupid."

I look around at him, stung. "But, I LIKE it here."

He sighs, and pops open a can of beer, 'Schlitz' written on the side of it. I sniff again, catching a faint whiff of beer. His Adam's apple moves as he gulps in big swallows. Setting it down, he belches and wipes a hand across his mouth, smacking his lips.

"G.L., you got the rest of your life to spend in some shitty little shop. Right now is gonna be the only time you can do other stuff, like play baseball."

He pauses, takes another deep swallow. "I been thinking it prolly ain't good for you to be here every night anyway."

Carl shoots me a look at that, sees my face. "Hey, come on kid, it ain't like we're throwing you out or nothing. And besides, come summer, we was talking that we might want you here more full time anyway."

What? I swivel my head back and forth, eyes wide. Dick's nodding. "Yeah, me and Carl think that maybe you can be our gas jockey like we talked about. Now I can't pay you much..." he fixed a stern eye on me. "But we can start teaching you more about doing real mechanic stuff instead."

Carl says to me, "Who knows, maybe we can turn you in-to a top notch mechanic someday. So what d'ya think about that, huh?"

My head's spinning. Summer...full-time...mechanic work...I nod. I guess I can put up with Gramma's crappy baseball until then. I smile at them. "Okay. Deal."

I still am not too happy though, come that first Friday when the buses trundle away from the school without us on them, us ragtag kids running around like dummies on the baseball field, running laps, doing jumping jacks, stupid stuff like that.

'Nother reason I'm not too happy is that Darlene and Jimmy are here too. I haven't seen much of either of them at school since the day I made Jimmy so mad. They are in the upper class here at school, eighth grade for Darlene, sixth for Jimmy. I'm a full year behind him now, being as I got held back after getting hurt. But on the first day of practice, there they are, Darlene hanging out in the bleachers with that Tina Felder and Donna Phair. They're over there gig-gling and whispering to each other, while we run around like morons. Jimmy's got a bright red tee shirt on, a sweat vee down the back of it. I keep a wary eye on him as we 'warmup'.

Darlene sees me. I catch her looking at me more than once, her face all funny like, like she can't decide if she stepped in something or if she is interested in something. I feel a weird feeling in my belly every time I see her looking at me.

I catch Jimmy looking at me too. He just looks mad. I don't get a funny feeling about him; I just get a cold one. He hasn't forgotten what I said. And I haven't forgotten what I 'saw' him doing to his little sister. Once when we make eye contact, I just stare at him. He looks away first, his cheeks reddening. He's a coward.

I'm not so sure about this baseball stuff. Six weeks. That's how long I have to do this. It looms ahead of me, forever on the calendar.

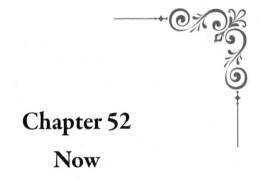

Chapter 52

Now

I feel like death warmed over. I'm sitting on the couch in Bill's office, the faint smell of my piss still there, my head cradled in my hands. Outside, I can hear the rattle and clang of Howie banging away at a Subaru. Bill sits in his chair, in silence. I can see his duct taped boots when I open my eyes a crack.

"You mind telling me what's going on?" He's already asked that, like three times. I haven't answered him any of those times. He's getting pissed. "Gerry. What the fuck is going on with you?"

I remain mute. There's a clink on the floor in front of me. "You had this in your hand. Howie said it was in your car. What the hell is going on with you and this fucking car?"

Cracking my eyes open, I see the cross gleaming on the dirty concrete floor. I flinch at the sight of it.

Bill's chair creaks as he stands. "Guess I'll just call the EMT's then. You're acting like you had a stroke or something." I hear the rattle of the phone coming out of the receiver.

Rage sparks in me, full blown red laced rage, red like blood and spit, boiling up, erupting up in a geyser. With a gurgling noise, I launch up off the couch, slapping the receiver out of Bill's hand, slamming it into the wall. He stares at me, wide brown eyes, shock etched on his face.

And fear.

That gets through the red fog, cuts through it like a cold knife blade. Bill doesn't deserve this, doesn't deserve my bullshit. The anger leaches away like air out of a ruptured tire, leaving me sagging.

I try to speak, mutter something unintelligible even to my own ears. I realize that Bill has shifted his stance slightly, his hand hovering above the right side desk drawer, above where he keeps his pistol. That makes me feel even worse.

I sit down, hanging my hands between my knees, trying to show him I won't harm him. He remains standing. "I'm sorry." Croaks out, except it sounds like, "Ahm sowwee"

It's like the experience has semi-paralyzed my vocal cords. For the first time I wonder if maybe I did have some sort of stroke. Then I see the cross again and a shudder crawls up my back.

"Gerry....what the hell is wrong?"

I shake my head in frustration. I can't explain this, not without telling him everything from day one. If I did that, he would make a phone call alright, to the loony bin.

He blew out a sigh, exasperated with me. I hear his desk drawer slide open, and I tense, thinking it's the gun. It isn't. It's a bottle of brandy. I suddenly crave it so bad my stomach clenches. He tilts the bottle, taking a deep swallow, then slides it into his pocket. I've rattled him. Bill isn't one to drink on the job.

"Okay. So you won't tell me what's going on. Okay, I get it. After all, we've only been friends and coworkers for over ten years now. I can see why you don't trust me. I get it, yup."

I close my eyes, frustrated. I can hear the growing anger in him, am powerless to do anything other than let it wash over me.

"Let's see, when everyone told me you were a head case and temperamental, I hired you because I believed in you. And for a long while, you earned that. But lately, Gerry, you've been testing my patience sorely. How can I trust you any longer after the way you've been behaving?"

He bent over, plucking the cross off the floor. "And do you mind telling me why you have jewelry in your possession with this girl's name on it?"

He turns the cross over, squinting slightly as he reads the back, "Leigh Ann. So who the hell is Leigh Ann?"

He drops it on the desktop. It lies there, a mute condemnation of me glinting in the dull silver.

"I don't like to get involved in your personal life, but if it's spilling over into my work life I will. And I surely don't need Amy storming in here on the warpath."

He snorted a laugh, sarcastic, angry. "Boy, you sure know how to pick 'em."

What the hell did he mean by that? I raised my head, squinting against the pain in my temples and stare at him. He stares back a moment, then lowers himself back into his chair. I notice he leaves access to the right side desk drawer handy.

I work my mouth, once, twice, and words finally come out, intelligible words. "What...the hell...are you talking...about?"

"Oh, so you CAN speak now." Anger sparks in his eyes. He pulls the flask out, takes another swallow, puts it back in his pocket. I stare at him, determined not to rise to the bait.

He laughs softly, rubs his right eye with a forefinger. I can see tension and exhaustion etched on his face. For the first time, I become aware of what kind of a toll this has taken on him. He looks at me, serious now, flint eyed. "She's fucking nuts, Gerry. In case you hadn't noticed."

"Why do you say that?" I'm only too aware of what it's like to get saddled with that description.

"With her family tree? Boy, if that didn't make you run, nothing would."

I stare at him, bewildered. He looks back at me a long moment, the expression on his face changing slowly. "Aw man....don't tell me you don't know?"

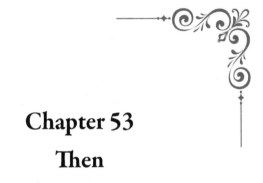

Chapter 53
Then

Spring is here, really and truly here now. Days are longer, sunlight like yellow white butter spreading across the field as we huff and puff through our stupid baseball practices. It seeps into the hallways during the day, making kids louder, teachers softer, and the air itself fresher and green. Everyone is happier, lighter almost.

Well, almost everyone.

Mr. Hawley is planning another camp out for his SPECIAL KIDS. I see the flyer tacked to the bulletin board, and it makes my stomach roll. I'm staring at it when Billy Meeker sidles over next to me. He studies it a moment, his lips moving as he sounds out the words. Then he laughs, a brittle barking sound.

"Hey, you signing up for that? Should be a good time!" Spit flecks fly from his lips, peppering the green paper announcement hanging on the wall, spreading the ink in wet droplets.

I stare at it silently, but an idea is starting to take place. Billy looks at me, hears me, says, "Oh man, come on! I was kidding, you big ox!"

I don't answer; my mind is rolling over and over, looking at the problem from all sides. I can still hear them, the kids he's carved himself into. I can't stand what he's done, what he's doing. Billy's right; no one will listen to us. But they would have to pay attention if we got evidence. I look at Billy.

He shakes his head, no, no, no, backing away. I feel anger, real anger, bubbling up. I grabbed his arm, hard, dragging him closer to me. "Listen up! If someone had done something, I wouldn't be all...all....messed up now. But no one did. And if someone had done anything for YOU, you wouldn't be all messed up neither. Do you want to just ignore what he's doing?"

"Yeah! Actually I DO!" Fear flickered through his eyes. I gave his arm a shake. "No you don't! You're just saying that! Look, you gave me a hard time about not going after...after...HIM. Well, I didn't although I should have. I can do something about THIS! And so can you!" I hissed in his ear.

He's trembling. I can feel it through his arm, the one I have a death grip on. His mind shuts down, closes me off. It pisses me off that he can do that so easily while I struggle with it still. I give his arm another shake.

"Don't be a pansy. Come on, we can stop him. You know we can." The trembling has gotten heavier, vibrating through his body. I stare at him, puzzled. He turns his face away from me, red blooming in his cheeks.

It hits me then. "Oh man....oh man....no." Billy wrenched his arm away then, bright spots on his face glowing now. "That's how you knew."

I feel bad for him suddenly, bad for screwed up little Billy Meeker. But he's shaking his head, no, no. "It's not, that's not..." he flounders, running out of breath, his eyes darting around the hall where groups of kids tromp past, laden with bags of books, bags of lunch, balls and gloves. We are going to have lunch outside today, an extended lunch and recess, a SPECIAL TREAT, being that it's Friday and almost spring.

Aware of the kids, I tug his arm. "Come on." We slip into the flow of chattering kids and head outside.

I inhale deeply as we reach the hill, the spot we usually go. Little kids are running and shrieking everywhere, older kids gabble like birds, seated on the greening grass, lunches strewn around them. Billy and I sit in silence a moment, a rock in the stream of kids.

I see Mr. Hawley then, across the field, playing referee to a kickball game, glowing against the newly minted green in his white and blue windbreaker. My anger spikes.

"Okay, Billy. Tell me what happened." He remains mute, looking at the ground. I jab him with my elbow. "What is it? I already know, you know."

He looks up at that. "No you don't!"

"Yes, I do. You went on one of them outings, didn't you? One of his campouts." He's shaking his head again, no.

I jab him again. "Sure you did. That's how you know, isn't it? What's wrong? You liked it?"

Mean, really mean sounding, even to my own ears. But Billy shakes his head slowly, and to my shock, a tear slides down his cheek. "No." his voice so soft I could barely hear him. "It wasn't me."

"Well who then?" I'm getting exasperated, this was worse than pulling teeth, getting him to tell me what was going on. Why let me know about this guy only to clam up?

"It wasn't me...it was my brother." He buried his face in his arms, folded across knees drawn to his skinny chest.

I stare at him, anger giving way to bewilderment. "But...but you don't have any brothers or nothing...you're an only child." An icy cold chill spiked through my chest at my own words.

Billy's reply was almost inaudible. "I used to have one..."

Chapter 54
Now

The river rolls by, gray glints and black swirls, specks of fallen leaves bobbing on the current. Cold is seeping in through the seams of my pants, the soles of my boots.

I ignore it. I'm seated on the picnic bench, alone in this riverside park under a lowering curtain of scudding clouds. My thumb caresses the cool glass of the bottle in my left pocket, the familiar, comforting shape and feel of it, unopened...for now.

Thoughts roll through my head, shapeless fragments, seemingly disconnected from each other. Bill, Amy, the red car, Robert Blake, HIM, Gramma, Billy Meeker, Darlene, Desiree, Leigh Ann, all of these disconnected fragments clamoring for my attention, to put them together in one piece, to make whole something torn asunder.

My punishment for failing so horribly at everything, everyone. My thumb caresses the smooth glass obsessively.

Across the slow rolling Hudson, I can see cars making their way along the road beside the river. Glints of color, red, silver, blue, barely visible as the sun sinks below the ridge behind me.

In the spring, I love this spot, poplar seeds blowing like snowflakes, green grass, boats on the river, the bridge just upstream arching gracefully over the water. Right now, I could be the last person on earth. Just me and the bits of trash blowing haphazardly across the parking lot, the wind sighing in the bare limbs of the trees. I wish I could say I've never felt this alone before, but I have.

Right before Amy came into my life.

My thumb rubbed circles on the glass.

Bill had told me, told me all he knew, all he heard, his own anger giving way to disbelief then sadness when he saw the incomprehension in my face. He hadn't wanted to tell me, you could see that clearly, but he had no choice by then. And as he talked, pieces fell into place, incidents and remarks, seemingly innocuous and confusing, suddenly became crystal clear. I can't begin to fathom the depth of the lies she's been telling me, the fabrications woven into a colorful life tapestry that resembles nothing of the truth.

She really was more screwed up than me.

I turned those thoughts over and over, as obsessively as I circled my thumb on the bottle. Raising my eyes slowly, I focused on the traffic threading through the gap in the trees to the entrance of the bridge on the far side and made a decision. Well, two of them actually.

I drew the flask out, caressed it lovingly, then raised it so the silky smooth, warm glass slid down my roughened cheek. Slowly, I stood up, my knees and back popping from sitting so long in the cold.

I walked down the frost roughened grass to where the edge of the water curled and rippled, smooth gray muscles against the shoreline. The seal on the bottle made a crackling sound as I unscrewed the cap.

I inhaled the intense aroma of the whiskey, Jack Daniels, my favorite, then said a silent prayer as I upended the bottle, my hand trembling as the amber liquid splashed into the currents, sweeping it towards Long Island Sound.

I had to grit my teeth to remain still long enough for the entire contents to empty out. A sadness, a profound one, gripped me when the bottle was empty.

I closed my eyes again, reciting another prayer, realizing as I did that I hadn't prayed in over thirty years now.

I wondered if it was too late for prayer.

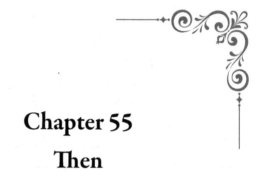

Chapter 55
Then

B illy doesn't want to do this. He really, really doesn't. But I make him. We march in to the principal's office, the foyer where his secretary, Mrs. Wells, sits, her desk piled with papers, the phone always at her ear as she talked with her sister in Florida, her friend down the street, her mother the next town over. Blue eyes take us in, widening slightly in surprise when she sees both of us standing there without a teacher escorting us. Bewilderment gives way to curiosity; cuts short her call to someone named Hazel. In a carefully bright voice, she says, "Why hello boys. What do you want?"

I feel Billy trembling. Afraid he will bolt, I open my mouth, me, big dumb silent Gerry the ox, and tell her, "We want to sign up for that camp out that Mr. Hawley's doin.'" Something crosses her face, a fleeting glimpse of unease. I can hear her then; hear her and realize she has a suspicion about what goes on at those camp outs. That makes me mad. If the adults know, why don't they DO something about it?

Billy is mute beside me. She flicks a look at him, and I hear her remember his brother, weird little thing, a couple years older than this one, gone darn near four years now, such a tragedy. She frowns a bit at his expression.

"Well...I don't know. This is a bit unusual. You see, the other children all had to get permission ahead of time and put their names on a list for these outings. You can't just...walk in and sign up like this."

Beside me, Billy finds his voice. "Why not?" I'm startled, surprised that he spoke up, doubly surprised to hear the hard edge in his voice. I snuck a look at him; his shivering has stopped; he wears a strangely intent look on his lopsided face.

Mrs. Wells doesn't have a ready answer, she stumbles over her own words. "Well, I mean...you can't just walk in and expect to be part of it when everyone else has worked so hard for the privilege....there's standards to be involved in something like this you know."

She means we're retards. And Mr. Hawley doesn't want retards on his SPECIAL TRIP. Anger begins to simmer in Billy. "Why do we hafta do anything different than them other kids?"

"Those other kids, Billy, not them..."

"I don't care! Fact is, we got just as much right as THOSE other kids! It says so, right on that flyer!"

She's getting mad now, mad and uneasy. "William Meeker, don't you tell me what you can and can't..."

"This camp out is open to all 5th to 7th grade boys. All children who want to participate in this camp out must sign up at the head office by Friday, May 14. You must have your name on the list by that date to go. The fee for this trip is

$2.00. Children are responsible for bringing their own sleeping bags, clothing, and fishing gear, if you have any."

Startled, I whip around to stare at Billy as he recites the entire flyer line for line, perfectly. He only looked at it for like twenty seconds.

If I'm surprised, Mrs. Wells is struck dumb. Her mouth moves, but no sound comes out. She stares at Billy like he grew two heads.

Billy keeps reciting; "Children will meet at the west school entrance after school on May 21 for transportation to the Dummer's Town Forest. Parents will provide transportation..."

"...to the forest, and back, returning at 3:00 p.m. on Sunday, May 23...." A baritone chimed in with Billy behind us, reciting line by line. Wide eyed, Billy stops mid word, and turns as do I.

Mr. Hawley finishes the sentence. "All are welcome on this team exercise and skill building trip. I hope to see you there." He smiles then, a thin lipped, greasy smile. "Let them sign up, Doris. The more, the merrier."

I can only stare at him, red spots floating in front of my eyes.

Beside me, Billy looks like he's going to be sick.

Chapter 56

Now

I stand in the deep shadows cast by an overgrown hedge, trying to make out details of the house that crouches behind it.

67 Stanton Way, New Fairfield, Connecticut.

It's stupid for me to be here, suicide, but here I am, as helpless to stay away as a moth can resist the flame. Acid burns in my belly. The desire for a drink is a white flame. My hands tremble from it.

The house is brick sided, white trimmed, conservative in its size and scope. The lawn is unremarkable, a few bushes denoting flower beds, trees with overgrown limbs hanging on the west and south sides, what looks like a privacy fence along the rear. It could be the home of some middle management type, with the requisite two kids and the PTA wife. Instead it houses the man who by most accounts is one of the biggest movers and shakers in this town.

A small two car detached garage sits to the east side of the home, a darker shadow, a shaft of light from the street light painting the facade. Like the house, it too is white trimmed brick with white garage doors, mullion windows lining the tops of the doors.

God, I wish I had a bottle right now.

I stare at the garage as the hedge pokes spiny fingers into my back, willing myself to get up the nerve to walk up the driveway and to the garage. It's late, or maybe early, the last light that was visible in the house extinguished an hour ago. But still, I hesitate. There's no going back once this line is crossed.

The decision is abruptly made for me as the low drone of an approaching motor is audible. With no time to overthink it, I leave the safety of the hedge and stride up the short drive, melting into the shadows on the far side of it, crouching behind a shaggy bush. Tires hiss as the sedan crawls by slowly, reflective tape on the sides winking in the streetlight.

The police. My stomach churns heavily as the car slowly passes, heart thumping hard in my chest. I wait, a minute, two, three and the silence returns. Somewhere several blocks away, a dog barks faintly. Traffic on the main road is faintly audible.

I straighten up, knees popping, glancing up at the side of the building. The white frames of two windows shimmer faintly against the darker brick. The house is alarmed, a fact the small octagonal sign in the driveway testifies to. I hope they neglected to alarm the garage.

I cup my hands around my face at the first window, scanning the interior. The metallic shapes of two cars can be seen, faint suggestion of lawn implements on the walls. Across from me I can see the shape of a pass door, on the side facing the house. Next to it, LCD lights glow; there's an alarm system in the garage too.

The lights glow green. No one set it tonight.

I cautiously cross around to the door, hoping against hope they left it open. No such luck. The knob stayed firmly rigid in my hand. I move back around to the far side and try the windows. Smooth vinyl replacement windows, they were locked. Except....as the cheap windows sometimes do, the rear one moved in its track ever so slightly, the frame not true. Gritting my teeth, I press the upper window in as I pry the lower one out...and the lock pops free. I freeze, waiting for an alarm even though the panel claims there isn't one set.

Silence. My own breathing loud in my ears, the dog barking someplace to the north. Vinyl hisses harshly as I slide the window up and pop the screen loose. The cold smells of cement, gas, new car and old lawn tools wafts through the opening. I slid my leg over and drop into the garage.

I'm lucky that Mr. Blake keeps a neat garage. My own garage, back when I had one, was a riot of stuff, lawnmowers, motorcycle, boxes of crap, stuff just piled and dumped, making a silent entry like this impossible. Here, I landed on clean, swept concrete, my eyes darting around as details revealed themselves. The new Camry sat on the left, the Matrix on the right. I cautiously move past the Matrix's flank, running my hand over the smooth metal, seeking something, anything. The exterior was mute.

I moved to the drivers' side and tugged the handle, hoping that I would get some luck. The handle stayed fast. Passenger's side, the same. Giving up, I look to the new Camry. The roof glinted faintly in the darkened building; new car smell emanated from it. Without much hope, I tugged on the door handle.

It opened with a smooth snick, the interior light flaring brightly in my eyes. Hastily, I pushed the door to, my heart pounding rapidly. Opening the door again, I press the button in the jamb, killing the light, my eyes taking in the shadowed interior. Empty, devoid of anything remotely personal. My stomach tremors and the desire for a drink roars over me, my vision momentarily narrowing. "Fuck it, Ger. Git 'er done."

I lower myself into the driver's seat.

Pulling the door to, I wait tensely as tendrils of sensation squirm around me. He's had this car for several months now, more than long enough for his own personality, thoughts and experiences to permeate it. I close my eyes as his psyche worms into my brain.

That God damned Lenny Carver. Stupid son of a bitch isn't fit to be the dog catcher let alone the Chief of Police. I can't believe he won't enforce a law that he has on his own books. Fuck him. I'll put a bug in Mayor Dean's ear, let him sort it all out. Tired of those God damned people hanging around in front of my buildings, dealing their dope and sucking off the government tit. Hope that Doug comes through on the Hill. I can use that defense contract, use it big time. Think I'll have James start lining up extra shifts now so I can be ready when it happens. Shit....forgot to stop at Stop N' Shop. Fuck it, she can get her own stuff. Doesn't she realize how much I have to do every day? Always worrying about Tim. Tim, Tim, Tim, the world revolves around Tim, ungrateful wretch. How the hell did I come up with such a lazy, ungrateful little shit like him? Jesus Christ.

Should have kept my dick in my pants. Should have taken up with Clarissa instead. Wonder how she is? Last I heard she was living over on the Island.

My eyes open as the waves of mundane assholeness wash over me. An asshole. Not a homicidal maniac. The vibes were different than what was in the little red Toyota. I would never buy a car from someone like this, I couldn't stomach the personality, but I wouldn't be ejected screaming from it either. Was he using the Matrix? Or did he have another little car stashed someplace else, one he used for his prowls? It had to be him, the car he used to own was too saturated with terror, immersed in blood and fear, straight from his ownership to the auction.

Bewilderment freezes my mind as a light from the house flares, sending a shaft of light through the window pane in the pass door. Taking a sharp breath, I tumble from the Camry, and scurry around the front of the car, the open window gaping hugely at me. A shadow of a person looms in the door as I throw myself through the frame, no time to close the window, no time, crouching, running down the side of the building, get away, get away, behind me the sound of the door clicking open, then silence. A soft exhalation, swearing, as the significance of the open window sinks in. Exterior lights on the corners of the garage explode into brilliance, illuminating the ground with a thousand watts of light, exposing me crouched along the foundation.

I leap up and run.

Chapter 57
Then

"Well what'aya ya gonna DO? You musta thought of SOMETHIN'!" I rub my face, irritated at Billy, at his insistent jabbering at me. "I told you, I'll figure it out. We got two weeks yet." Billy sticks out his lower lip at that, making him look even goofier than he normally looks. "You big dummy. You went and signed us up for this. Least you can do is figure out what you're gonna do."

"Me? What about you? You started all of this...this....shit." There. I said a bad word. It felt good. "Why'd you let me in on what he was doing anyway?"

Billy looks away from me, swings his leg up over the monkey bars we were playing on, hangs upside down and pretends to scratch his armpits. The other kids leave us alone when we are on these; Billy has a habit of blowing his nose in his hand and smearing it on the blue painted metal when they try to join us. It's really gross. I've had to grind his face into the dirt a coupla times for doing that.

He doesn't answer my question, just hangs there scratching, hooting like a demented monkey.

I'm no closer to knowing what to do than when I was the day we signed up. I just had a vague..feeling..that maybe if we went, I could catch him at it and do something about it, tell someone. There had to be other parents coming on this trip, right? How could he watch a dozen boys that were going to be spread throughout four cabins at the forest by himself?

But Billy doesn't think that's going to work. Even if there's parents everyplace there. "Unless they catch him themselves, no one will believe us. You watch. No one listens to a retard." He's making me mad with that talk.

I turn the problem over in my head obsessively the next few days, as I trudge through the chattering flock of kids in the hallway, as I unlock the door to our house, THWOCK, the first wet stab wound sounding even louder than before, even as I sweep the garage and follow Carl around, peppering him with questions. I lean on the fenders of Dodges and Chevys and listen to Carl describe what a distributor does as Mr. Hawley fondles his stack of Polaroid photos under the floorboards of his house.

Polaroid photos....

"Hello...G.L......earth to G.L." Startled, I break out of my trance to find Carl regarding me across the engine bay, concern in his eyes, worry in the psychic voice that muttered beneath our audible words. "What? I was listening."

I try to cover as I frantically go over what he was saying just now.

"Um." He straightens up, slowly wiping his hands on a rag as he regards me. "I asked if you wanted to take a break and have a soda."

"Oh, uh, yeah....sure." Phew, he wasn't going to ask me something I couldn't answer. I'm brimming inside as Carl pops open the soda machine and fishes out a grape soda for me, and a cream one for himself.

I figured out the problem.

We sit on rickety metal chairs in the sunlight streaming in the bay door and crack open our sodas. I take a long pull, closing my eyes as the fizziness hits my nose, aware of the heat on my face. I feel relief for the first time since I signed up for that trip, relief and new concern.

Because going on that trip is the last thing we should be doing.

Carl's voice breaks into my thoughts. "So, everything going okay at home?" I open my eyes, puzzled, "Yeah, yeah it's fine." He regards me thoughtfully a moment. "You wouldn't bullshit your wrenching buddy, now would you? You, uh, ain't seemed yourself the past couple of days."

For a crazy moment, I feel like telling him about Mr. Hawley and the problem we have, ask his advice. The thought fades quickly as I realize how weird it would all sound. I like Carl and Dick, love the garage. I don't want anything to change that. The urge passes as quickly as it came.

"Oh, um...yeah. It's just school and that stupid baseball Gramma signed me up for. I don't like it much." I actually like the game itself, it's the other kids and the endless running around training that I hate. And school is boring me to death now. I'm not sure why I need to be with the 'special' kids, but I don't ask why.

Carl takes a slug of his soda, his Adam's apple bobbing as he swallows. He burps, a rumbly deep one. I take another slug of my soda, then ask a question that's been hovering in my mind ever since I heard Carl say HIS name.

"Carl...can I ask you sumthin'?"

"Hmm? I don't reckon I've heard you ask if it was okay to ask me anything before." He winks at me, takes a swallow. I flush a little bit, aware of how many questions I throw at him when we are working on cars. "This is different...it's not about cars....it's about Donny Hopgood." My voice is almost inaudible to my own ears, as if HIS name paralyzes my vocal cords.

Carl's normally sunny expression darkens. He doesn't like this question, doesn't like it at all. But still.....don't I have the right to ask?

"Ah shit, kid. You shouldn't be wasting your time thinking about that...that....him"

"But no one will talk to me about him. Is..is he around here?"

Carl softens at that, looks at me with a sad expression. "Oh, uh...well I don't think so, I mean no one seems to know where he went. If he was around here, he'd be in jail, don't you worry about that."

I look down at the scuffed concrete floor, wondering how accurate that is. I kick my foot over it, ask him, "Where...where'd he come from anyway?" My early memories of him were just him suddenly there one night, there and never leaving again. I wonder if he would have gone back to wherever he came from.

I wonder if I could find him myself.

"That why you been moping around here the past couple days?"

"No...I told you, it's that stupid baseball stuff."

"It's not stupid, G.L. It's supposed to be fun. Hey, you're going on a camping trip from school too, right? See, you just gotta get out with those kids more and you'll have all kinds of fun."

I had told them about the camping trip once I was signed up for it, hoping they would tell me they needed me there on that weekend. But no such luck. Dick and Carl were acting like they were happy about it. I felt frustrated at Carl, he was steering me away from HIM, not being straight with me. I tried again. "Where did he come from Carl?"

He shook his head. "I don't rightly know. If he never comes back again though, it'll be okay by me." He dropped the pop top into his empty can and crumpled it. "Come on, G.L. We got work to do."

Annoyed, I crumple my can too and follow him back into the garage. He just lied to me, the first time I am aware of. I can hear him thinking about HIM, and how he came here from Pennsylvania, a place called Scranton. Carl thinks he's back there, back with his friends on the poor side of town. Probably beating up another little kid even as we don't speak about him.

Silently, I vow to stop him. Somehow.

Chapter 58
Now

B ill is silent as we emerge from the police station, the rays of the setting sun setting off daggers of pain in my head. Released to his custody, bail set and paid, my past record precluding any chance of release on my own recognizance.

I had made it two blocks down and one block over before running around a corner, smack into the headlights of the patrol car. I had no good reason for why I was running, nor for why I was in this neighborhood of McMansions in the first place.

It was a matter of minutes before I was being placed in the back of the cruiser. The call had come in while I sat in abject silence; attempted B&E, 67 Stanton Way. The cops had eyed me with deepened mistrust, before driving me over to the home of Mr. Robert F. Blake. Maniacal laughter had stuck in my throat as we stopped in the street. Someone was carving up women and leaving their bodies strewn like trash, yet I was the one sitting in the back of the patrol car.

A stout form that had to be Blake was pacing in the driveway, agitation clear to see, the trim silhouette of a police officer standing with him. They came over to the car, the cop shining a flashlight directly into my face, blinding me with a thousand watts. I blinked, and squinted, aware that I couldn't turn my face away.

"I think that's him. I only saw him for a second, but that looks like the same clothing and build."

Enough to earn a trip downtown.

We may have our ups and downs, but Bill is still the only one in my life that I could call for something like this. He arrived late afternoon, gray faced, angry, and bailed me out without comment. Now we returned to where I had parked my truck in relative silence, broken only by taut one word directions from me on where to turn.

My truck was unmolested, parked in the edge of the condo parking lot I had found last night. Bill puts his truck in park and kills the motor. "Well? You mind telling me what the fuck this was all about?"

What indeed? I owed Bill though, owed him some sort of explanation. The question was, if I told him the truth, would he believe me or would he send me packing? I looked across the seat at him, noticing the fresh lines around his eyes, the weariness in his face. From me.

"If I tell you what's happening, you're gonna think I'm nuts." I mutter.

He leans back in the seat and lights a cigarette. "So try me."

I do. With misgivings, I take a deep breath...and tell him everything.

Chapter 59

Then

F riday afternoon, stupid baseball again. The last game before we have our camping trip. We've been split up into
four teams, us kids. We compete against each other in two
games per night, rotating who we play against. I kinda like
some of it. I'm strong, so when I do connect with the ball, I
can really send it flying. The rest of it is a bunch of baloney,
from the too tight stained shirt I have to wear, to the other
kids and their mealy mouthed ways.

I'm thinking that if this is how the 'normal' kids are, I
don't wanna be in classes with them.

We play first, our green shirted team, the "Rangers"
against the blue shirted "Bucks". Kids run and scream, dust
puffing as the ball bounces shy of the glove and between the
legs of the outfielders, foul balls pop skyward. Still, somehow
the Bucks manage one more run home than we do, handing
us a loss. Our third one in a row.

Morosely, I take to the bench with the other kids. We're
all unhappy now. Bright red shirts file past us as the "Sox"
take the field, the yellow shirted "Flyers" their rival. Jimmy

struts past, twirling a bat jauntily, his red shirt glowing in the late day sun.

"You buncha losers." A sneer lifts his lip as he passes. Beside me, Johnny Johnstone looks like he's about to cry. I stiffen, anger coursing through me.

"Losers? You should talk, you creep."

Fury sparks in his eyes. "Gewwy Gewwy the wee-todd! Big man on the field! Too bad you can't find your own dick with a roadmap!"

I'm on my feet before I realize it, my voice booming out, "Oh yeah? At least I don't use my dick with my own sister!"

Jimmy's face pales, and he swings the bat back to take a shot at me. Gilbert Larkin stops him, grabbing his arm. "Jesus Jimmy, don't!" Around us the kids have drawn a collective breath, the potential of a fight lighting the fire inside of them. From the field, Mr. Davies, our coach, is yelling over to us, "Hey! What's going on over there? Boys, come on, get over here, now!"

Jimmy's face is a mask of rage as he is pulled out into the field by Gilbert. Beside me, Johnny releases a pent up breath, his face white. "Wow! What was that about?"

I don't answer, my own voice mute from frustration. We settle back into an uneasy silence as the Sox and Flyers take turns pounding runs home. Jimmy plays poorly, a source of small satisfaction to me. The four innings crawl past as the sun descends into an orange ball, mosquitoes emerging to feast on us.

The Sox manage two more runs than the Flyers, putting everyone out of their misery. The final game over, we vacate the bench and start collecting the gear, the responsibility of the losing teams. I stuff bats into a canvas sack and hoist it on my shoulder. Morosely, I trudge through the bottom of the bleachers, heading back into the school to deposit them in the equipment room.

The first blow comes from behind, a mean, sneaky sucker punch. Already off balance from the weight I carry, I stumble, sprawling to the ground, the bats spilling out of the bag in a heap. Motion and a weight hits me, hard, middle of the back, knees jamming into my kidneys as fists pound the back of my head. Dimly, I'm aware of kids yelling, noise, commotion, as a red rage descends upon me, Jimmy's psychic voice pounding in my head, *I'm gonna kill you, gonna kill you, you big fat fucking retard! I've wanted to do this for so long, I'm gonna fuck you up, fuck you up! I hate youhateyouhateyou...*

With a grunt, I heave myself up onto my hands and knees, Jimmy riding my back like a demented jockey, whipping his horse frantically. My ear rings and makes a popping sound as a blow lands solidly on it. I roar with pain, aware that the little prick is drumming his heels into my ribs, my side, and it hurts, it hurts, it hurts....

Donny Hopgood's face is a mask of feral pleasure as his arm raises and descends, the belt snapping across my bare butt, pain lancing through me. I twist, unable to flee, my hands tied firmly to the closet door, as he punishes me for taking a second bowl of cereal, gotta punish you, you won't learn no other way you fucking little prick, snap, the belt is liquid fire and I howl..

Jimmy is gone from my back now, flung across the dirt walkway like a ragdoll, his eyes suddenly wide with fear as he feels the power that came from me, his face dissolving as I descend upon him, the aluminum bat somehow in my hand

as I swing and swing, screaming echoing in my ear as Jimmy's
face turns to Donny's face, blood everywhere, then hands,
hands, and the weight of bodies grabbing me, dragging me
to the ground, trapping me in my rage driving me face first
to the blood soaked dust as the tears spring unbidden from
my eyes.

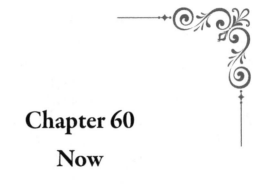

Chapter 60

Now

B ill is quiet for a long time after I finish. I sit looking at my knees, an odd sense of a weight lifted off my shoulders finally. I told him, told him everything, starting from way back through now. The dashboard clock shows that almost two hours have gone by since we stopped here, the first streetlights flickering on as we sit in silence.

The silence grows uncomfortable. Fidgeting, I finally look up at him. His face is a mask, he stares straight ahead over the steering wheel, the set of his jaw grim.

I can't stand it anymore. "So? Now do you see why I had such a hard time telling you anything? I bet you think I'm crazy, huh." A nervous laugh bubbles out. Surely he doesn't. Bill of all people knows me better than anyone, knows I wouldn't, couldn't make up something like this.

He doesn't answer me. Unease begins to ripple as he takes another cigarette from his almost depleted pack and lights it. I wait in tortured suspense. Surely Bill would believe what I tell him...

He turns to look at me finally, his eyes concerned, wary. His voice is careful as he says, "Gerry. I know you been through a lot, more than anyone I know, and I want you to know that I care. I know a man, down towards Poughkeep-sie I think you should talk to. He helped me out when I was getting divorced, and he did a fine job."

My throat closes up. He doesn't believe me. He thinks I'm losing it. I stare at him, mute with disappointment, mute with fear.

What if he's right?

"I'll give him a call tomorrow, see if you can get in sooner than later. I'll cover the first couple sessions, get you going." He eyes me, nervous, worried, his eyes showing what he can't voice.

"Jesus, Bill! I'm not making this up!" My voice is strained, taut. I can feel sweat breaking out on my forehead. I shouldn't have done this, shouldn't have done it...

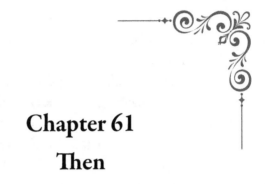

Chapter 61
Then

"Shouldn't have done it, shouldn't have done it..." I mutter the words to myself, over and over, a mantra, as I kneel in front of the little window in my upstairs room, banished there by a tear streaked Gramma, the police having just left. "Shouldn't have done it..." I bury my face in my folded arms, the window sill cool against my forehead. "Shouldn't have, shouldn't have..."

Jimmy was messed up, messed up bad, his teeth scattered across the dusty ground like kernels of corn, a bloody pulp where his nose used to be. It shocked me, shocked me out of my rage, scared me to death. The kids were screaming and wailing in my ear, one ear, the other one rang endlessly, still did. Mr. Davies took one look and almost barfed, his face white, jaws working. I quit struggling under the weight of the four kids who took me down, Gilbert Larkin sitting on my chest, blood spattered across his fear stricken face.

Jimmy's blood.

My breath hiccuped in my chest as I struggled to breathe under the weight of Gilbert, the weight of my shame. This was something like what HE would do. Tears burned in my eyes, tears, why tears? I hadn't cried 'cept once since coming home, now I felt like I was gonna start and not stop. I hiccuped for air again...

And saw Darlene. She had pushed her way up front of the kids, her skirt flapping above her colt like knees, white shirt streaked with dust. She stared raptly at Jimmy, crying on the ground, crying over the beating I gave him with an aluminum baseball bat, what the hell did I do? I shouldn't have done that, shouldn't have...her eyes were shining, intent, and her tongue popped out, a lizard like move, licking the air, tasting the blood in it. I swear to God, she looked excited, thrilled. I thought I was going to retch when she swung her eyes over and made eye contact with me.

In the mean twilight of my room, I settled back on my haunches and wrapped my arms around my knees rocking, moaning softly, ashamed of myself, of what I did, the psychic screams of my mother ringing in my head as HE crashed into her.

I moaned, ashamed because I had LIKED beating Jimmy, liked it a WHOLE LOT, as the bat thudded down, blood and gristle flying up from his nose, the crunch as his teeth exploded.

THWOCK! The first of the knife blows rained down on my mother, wet melon sounds of her flesh exploding, filling my one ear.

I saw Jimmy's little sister in his head, saw how she tried to stay away from him because she was scared of him, she didn't like how he touched her, didn't like the nasty games he made her play, and I pounded and pounded and pounded on him.

I heard one of the cops say I would have killed him if the kids hadn't yanked me off, would have pulverized him into a big, snotty grease smear right there. That scared me, scared me a lot. It was like someone had taken me over and run my body, making me do BAD THINGS. I rocked on the floor, hugging my knees to my chest as I heard footsteps out in the hallway. Gramma.

She opened the door but didn't come in right away. I felt her watching me, felt her worrying about me. She was afraid of me now. That filled me with even more shame. I buried my face deeper, willing her to just close the door, to leave me in peace.

Instead, she slowly entered the room. Rustling as she sat on the edge of the bed. She slowly started talking, then picked up speed, talking, talking, talking. About how much trouble I was in. About how the police were talking about sending me to juvenile hall. That I was going to be kicked out of school, expelled from baseball, barred from the camp out. I sat hugging myself as her screams from years ago vied with her voice now, my head filling to the point of explosion from the noise, the babble. I tried desperately to pull the curtain across my damaged frontal lobe, to at least still the psychic babble before I started screaming and couldn't stop.

I sat in silence, my face buried in my knees as she told me that she wouldn't let the police take me away, but that if there was ever a next time, she would. How she thought that maybe I had had a reason for what I had done, that Jimmy is a mean little bastard, but still, beating him half to death, well that wasn't gonna fly, not in this household. And how I was grounded, grounded for a month, maybe more. No swimming, no fun. No garage. I stiffened at that; my body stilled. And you gotta 'pologize, 'pologize to him and his family, maybe even do restitution for them, work for them this summer instead of at the garage. His daddy's gotta a farm over outskirts of the county, I'm hoping we can arrange for you to work for them, pick crops or something, if he's willing. Because Jimmy's dad could come after you, you know, make the judge send you up to juvenile anyway. Good Lord, how I wish I knew why you done what you done...

Finally she runs out of steam, beaten, drained. I sit mutely, willing her to leave. After a few moments of sitting there, sniffling occasionally, she does.

And then I wish she hadn't left me.

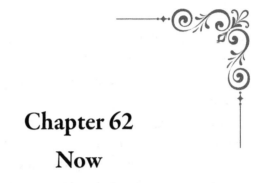

Chapter 62
Now

O nce, there was a time where for a brief, shining moment I thought everything would turn out ok, that I would get to be just a normal kid again, doing normal kid stuff, then growing up some, get myself a muscle car, maybe a Corvette Stingray, or a Camaro.

Then, maybe after screwing around for a few years, drinking Buds down by the river with my friends, or drag racing up old Route 9, I'd meet a girl and we'd do something silly like fall in love. Kids, hell maybe, I wouldn't say never or nothing. Such a fantasy. I should have tried to go on a trip to the moon. I'da had better luck.

Thing is, I'm not even sure when I felt like that. Maybe when I was hired over at the Carl and Dick's garage the year I was 11? Ironic how that was the same year everything began to fall apart.

I tip the bottle again, feeling the whiskey slide over my lips, the numbness creeping in now. Sighing, I cap the bottle clumsily, and tilt my head back to look at the sky through the streaked window in my bedroom. There's no moon tonight, just heavy gray clouds pressing down, as leaden as I feel.

"You fucking loser, Donahue, you pusshy." I laugh, a grating sound to my ears, and drink again. Fucking A. Fuck it. Everything was going down the shitter now. Good old Bill, thinks I'm a nutter, fuck me. Why did I open my mouth? I know better than that. Asshole. I could fuck up a wet dream.

A sodden giggle escapes at that, and I take another drink, clumsily, whiskey dribbling down my chin. I close my eyes and drink greedily. Fuck it. I just don't care anymore. I give up...such a loser. Why don't I just end it now, be done with it all? There's no reason for me to continue on. I can't do this; I just can't do this....

The contents of the medicine cabinet keep moving in front of me as I try to search through it for what I need, making it hard to close my hand around it. Finally, I do, then decide I need a drink to celebrate. The bottle is empty, so I pull out a second one, one I got for tomorrow, but fuck it, it must be tomorrow somewhere, right?

One drink leads to two then three, then...nothing.

Chapter 63
Then

"Man, you messed him up! That was really cool!" Billy's eyes shine as he bounces up and down on the balls of his feet, the way he does when he's really excited. I groan inside, excited is not the emotion I am feeling right now. I wish Billy would just shut up.

But he doesn't, of course he won't, this is Billy. He leaps and spins in a mock karate kick in my tiny bedroom, excitement in his every move. He kicks out like a retard, making, "Blam, blam, blam!" noises, like he's beating the crap out of Jimmy, and I am feeling sick. Anger starts to creep in, my fist curling.

He's dancing now, shadow boxing, his goofy narrow face alight, and I say to him, "'Course you know, I can't go next weekend." The camping trip.

It's like someone let the air out of him. He stuttersteps to a halt, the light burning out of his eyes. "What? Whadda ya mean, you can't go?"

I shrug. "Gramma grounded me. Grounded for a month, maybe longer."

"Aw...shit! No! I don't want to go without you!"

"You have to go. Nothing's gonna happen to you. Listen, maybe it's better this way. I told you I had a better plan. No, you go. I'll get what we need to bring him down."

"How you gonna do that?" He places bony fists on equally bony hips, narrow face pinched with mistrust. "You're grounded, you big dummy."

I just shrug. How much more trouble can I get in? Sneaking out for a few hours isn't going to change that. Maybe it would even make it better, if everyone sees what a monster Mr. Hawley is. I kick the carpet and stare blankly at the floor. Thwock! reverberates in my head.

Billy can hear it too. When he walked in the door, his face had paled and I could see him close down, close down hard and fast. Later when we was upstairs in my little bedroom, he asked me how I could stand to live here. I didn't have no good answer for him. I had to live someplace, didn't I?

Billy is quiet now, the maniacal light gone out of him. I'm expelled from school for a week, maybe the only reason Gramma let Billy come here today. I guess she thinks he had assignments from our retard class. I feel a laugh bubble up at that thought.

We stare at my graying, threadbare rug in silence a moment, as the weight of what is coming up presses down on us. I'm not sure, not sure at all this is going to work, but I can't change my mind now. Billy is scared, scared shitless, a fact he struggles to hide, struggles and fails. He told me what happened to his brother, and it's bad. Really bad. I wonder if I would be able to go on something like this if I had a brother who went through that. I don't know.

I do know that I can't sit back and let Mr. Hawley continue to do the things he's doing. Anger at him burns in my chest.

Beside me Billy sighs and kicks the carpet. "OK you dumb ox. How do we do this?"

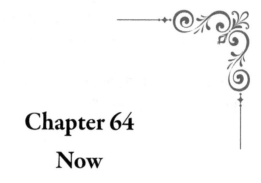

Chapter 64
Now

Sunlight scalds, piercing the dark tinted lenses that cover my red rimmed eyes. Heat bounces back off the sidewalk in this late season Indian summer, one last blast from the south that arrived on burning wings. I blink gratefully in the comparative darkness of the interior of the old library, cool air hitting my exposed skin. My left forearm itches under the makeshift bandage, I scratch under the edge absently.

I sign in for an hour on an aging machine in the carousel in the back. Dropping a dog eared notebook beside me, I log on and start to surf.

I search the web for an hour, then renew for a second one. This time, I search out Blake and everything to do with him and his family. There's an overabundance of information about him, less about his wife, and almost nothing about his son, Tim, the one I heard him thinking about that night. Only one photograph of the three together, taken some six years earlier. Blake trimmer, his wife less puffy faced, a sullen, gangly teenager stuffed into a tie and button down shirt, resentment visible in his every line.

Exhausting the electronic cache about his family life, I turn to his holdings as the second hour melts away and I creakily stand up to sign for a third one. A headache throbs mercilessly, the words jumping on the screen, yet I plow on grimly.

After all, it's not like I have anyplace else to be.

As the third hours closes, I finally relent and log out. The top three pages of my notebook are filled, notes and addresses scribbled in increasingly frenetic handwriting. Idly, I scratch the edge of the bandage again, exhausted beyond measure.

I decide that maybe I need some calories in me. My stomach flips and rolls at the thought.

I choose the same diner I went to the last time I was here, find an abundance of empty seats at the counter in this Indian summer mid-afternoon. A heavy blond takes my order, her eyes jumping away from my face, unease radiating off of her. Ignoring her, I pull my cell phone out and turn it back on.

The call log shows six missed calls. Two from Bill. Four from Amy. I close the phone and slip it into my pocket without listening to the messages.

A chipped plate lands in front of me containing my grilled cheese with tomato sandwich and a side of fries. I pull my notebook over and open it at my right elbow as I take the first greasy bite. My eyes wander back and forth, random bits of information jumping out at me. One piece prominent.

Geotechnik. Located about a mile from the river bank where three of the bodies were found. Blake's holding. Nineteen acres, one main building, three outbuildings, a three acre parking lot. Big bucks flowed through there, government contracts from federal level down to municipal ones. Blake active in the running of the day to day operations, there at least three times a week, maybe more.

A little Toyota Corolla would have been an economical commuter car.

I know it's him, despite the lack of horror in his new car. It couldn't have happened with that car yet, it's too new. But it will, it will and soon, too.

I puzzle over how anyone could slaughter someone in a car full of upholstered fabric and not leave DNA and blood traces everyplace. I remember the crackle of plastic when he jammed the girl, sweat beading as the memory flashes across my psyche.

Covers. He covered the seats, the floor, everything with covers to protect the interior. Some of them he started in the car and finished on trash strewn ground, blood running in rivulets down to meet the iron gray muscle of the river.

The river. It was important to him. None of the killings happened away from it, this I was sure of, as sure as I have ever been in my life. I couldn't explain it, but I knew.

I pushed away the partially eaten sandwich, my appetite gone now. The river. Son of a bitch, why hadn't I thought of this before? Before I went to Connecticut and put my ass in the line of fire? I couldn't go back there now, not without getting hauled off and locked away until I rotted. My appearance in court was in six days, circumstantial as the case was, I worried that with his power he would be strong enough to ram me into Somers for six months. To go back anywhere near where he lived would be suicide.

But I didn't need to. Because at least three days a week, he came here, to my territory.

The river...

Chapter 65

Then

Gramma is asleep at last, her snores echoing through the noisy little house. I hold my breath as I creep on cat feet through the living room, into the kitchen and the back door. Part of my grounding was having to stay inside at night, a bigger punishment than she knew.

The back door creaked softly as I pushed it open and stepped into the softly scented night, Gramma's snoring uninterrupted. I close it gently, feeling the latch take hold. My heart is pounding. Despite my brave face when I told Billy what I was going to do, I'm scared shitless at doing it.

The streets are alive with insects that buzz and flip in the street lights as I peddle through darkened neighborhoods as fast as I can. I don't have a watch, but it's gotta be late, most of the windows are dark now, cars parked in driveways with dew shining on them. I peddle harder.

Mr. Hawley's house is a white clapboarded thing, set on a corner lot a couple blocks from the center of town. I can see the spire of the Methodist church over the trees and wonder how God can turn a blind eye to the Mr. Hawley's of the world. Slowing to a halt, I scan his home for signs of life.

It stands dark and silent as a tomb. Gooseflesh pops up on my arms and legs. I don't want to go in there.

For lack of a better place, I drop my bike in the tall weeds that line the ditch that runs between the house and sidewalk and make my way on foot up the driveway. I feel like I'm exposed, naked, that there are hundreds of pairs of eyes watching my increasingly shaky path.

I pause at the base of the back steps and open up, way up, to try to feel Mr. Hawley, to see what he sees, what he does. A jumble of images flicker across my DAMAGED FRONTAL LOBE, the sensations like broken glass. My stomach curls and bile rises in my throat as some of his deepest thoughts crossed my fractured mind. My wavering resolve stiffens, and I concentrate fiercely on closing him out of my brain again.

He locks his back door, an odd thing to do in my opinion. No one I know locks their doors here. But the window over the back yard isn't locked. It stands open, a sliding screen in place, allowing fresh air to penetrate the stale house. It's a matter of seconds to remove it and slip over the sill, landing in an old fashioned dining room.

I've really crossed the line now.

I can see black patterns on the old fashioned wallpaper where dim light hits it. A peek into the linoleum clad kitchen shows the illumination is coming from a lamp left burning on the kitchen table. The house is empty of people. No psychic fluttering, no breathing breaks the heavy silence. I scan my surroundings, my eyes falling on a black rectangle off of the kitchen.

The back stairs.

Before I can think too much, I'm across the creaky floor and up the stairs, the treads noisy under my feet. A narrow hallway opens up, two rooms off one side, one off the other. Another door stands closed at the far end.

The attic.

Suddenly I'm unwilling, scared to take the ten steps down the hall, to pull that door open. Memories of the images in his brain strobe past me, and my bowels turn to water. I don't want to do this; I don't want to do this...

I cross the dusty smelling space and pull the door open. Steps yawn up into the total blackness of the attic. My knees quiver as I ascend.

Gramma's attic is a cluttered little place, hot in the summer, cold in the winter, with stuff jammed under the eaves and up to the rafters along the sides. There's Christmas decorations, my Mom's old stuff from when she was a little girl, bits of furniture and boxes of clothing. I go there sometimes to get away from the rest of the house, to let sensations of a different, happier time flow through me. It's a space scented with ancient, tinder dry wood, and splinters await bare feet of the unwary. I don't mind the heat or the cold up there, it's part of the experience.

Mr. Hawley's attic is nothing like that.

It has some of the same smell, but the narrow space stands mostly empty. Two small windows set in the peaks at either end let a little light from the streetlight in. I peer in the gloom, trying to make out what it is that I am seeing.

A dark shape over in the far window area reveals itself as a metal filing cabinet and a chair. Otherwise, the attic is empty, shadows filling the area where rafters meet the floor.

I turn around in the middle, unsure now. Nothing else suggests itself.

The filing cabinet yields nothing of interest. Papers, a jumble in the top drawer, maybe old bills from the size and feel. A couple of battered magazines in the bottom one. An ashtray on top, faint nicotine smell. A couple of notebooks, the writing indistinct in the darkness. I wonder how I am supposed to find what I came for, big dummy that I am, I didn't bring a flashlight with me. The images I had in my mind of this moment were lit with a psychic light. I look at the ashtray again, noticing a square laid in the edge of it.

I palm the rectangle and turn back around.

The blackness around me looks huge. My heart is thudding heavily, my ears ringing. Someplace in here, he keeps his stash. Dropping to my knees I begin to crawl towards the far window, tugging on every crack in the boards.

They stay in place, resistant to my pulling. Defeated, I sit back on my haunches and look back down the space towards the filing cabinet at the far end. There's only one way to find them, one way and I don't wanna do it, not here....but it's not like I have much choice.

Moaning softly, I allow the gray blanket I have pulled across my brain to slide back a bit

Smooth flesh, damn look at that little morsel, so hot and sweet to the touch. Oh how I relished that juicy little bit, how I would love to find another like him, that was one of my best yet. And here, here was another one, this one had such promise, such promise. Like a willing flower that opened up, way up to me, gave himself to me every time, I know he liked it as much as I did...oh my, the burning in my belly is strong again...there has to be another morsel from this latest adventure, another disciple...

I feel hotness on my cheeks, shame and fear mingled as I struggle to shove him OUT of my head, OUT! Splinters stab through my jeans as I fall on my knees next to the file cabinet and push, push hard on it, sliding it, shoving it sideways with a loud protest of metal on wood. My fingers scrabble blindly on the newly exposed floor, a sliver jams under my fingernail, unnoticed. The board sags on one corner, a searching fingertip tugs and it's gone, rising smoothly up, a black square of space beneath it showing something lighter in the middle, a square whiteness. I gingerly reach in and pull it out.

It's an old shoebox, the weight in it enough to suggest that something is in it, something bad. Holding my breath, I remove the lid. I can't see inside, not in the faint light from the street, so I search my front pocket for the square I removed from the ashtray earlier. It takes me a couple times to pull a match then light it, my hand shaking so hard I keep missing the striker. The flame snaps to life, shockingly bright in the blackness. Faces flicker before me, scared eyes, naked flesh, an impossible number. The match burns to my finger and I yelp as I shake it out. I strike another, quickly sifting through the stack. God help me, but I know two of the kids on top, the dark haired boy who is thinking about suicide and the sandy haired kid, the one who is a couple years ahead of me.

Again, my finger sizzles and I quickly shake the match out. I find the remaining one in the pack and strike it into life. I push a few more photos to the side.....

And Ricky stares up at me, black eyes miserable, white flesh startling in the wavering light of the match.

My breath leaves me with a whoosh and I sit down on the splintery floor suddenly. The match sputters against my finger, the light throwing shadows across Ricky's face, the faces of all the kids underneath and around him.

The pain of my burning flesh jolts me back. Yelping, I shake out the match and drop it in the ashtray. Darkness closes in, complete, menacing.

Blindly, I scoop a handful of photos out, and clumsily push them into my back pocket. With trembling hands, I put the lid back on and shove the box back into the hole. Replacing the board and the file cabinet are clumsily done, awkwardly, there's no way he won't notice that someone was in here.

I don't care. He's going to know before he gets home anyway.

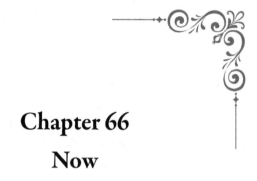

Chapter 66
Now

When she was ten, Amy came home one day to find her mom was gone. No warning, no notes, just a couple of empty drawers and a closet full of vacant hangers. She and her dad muddled along for a year or two, until his love affair with the bottle led to one too many nights away from home.

DSS came and collected her; a suitcase and a favorite stuffed bunny were all that left with her. For the next seven years she bounced from bad to worse, home after home, a stint in juvie when she acted out at 14, a stay in a psyche ward at 16 thanks to a foster parent who wanted her out of their home and life. At 18, suddenly deemed an adult, she was abruptly released from the system, for all intents and purposes an orphan. At least this was the version Amy gave me.

Nine years later, here she was, vibrant, attractive, successful. A licensed massage therapist for the past five years, she had strong hands and an even stronger will. I had been bowled over by her arrival into my life, bowled over and unquestioning of her, or her motives. Like why a 27-year old would want to be with a 45-year old? I never questioned it, not at all. Why would I? My ego saw to that.

Very few things in this world scare me anymore. How can they when the worst things in this world are the things that are in our heads?

But Amy, Amy has the power to scare me. And she was doing a fine job of that right now as I struggled to clear the cobwebs from my head, eyes still gritty with exhaustion borne sleep.

"Where the *fuck* were you?" hissed, her silhouette in the gloom of my bedroom disorienting. Sheets tangled around my legs, trapping me.

"Jesus, Amy. What the hell is this?" Night, full night pressed against the window; the clock read the early hours of the morning.

She circled to my side of the bed, rage flowing off of her, clenched fists and booze smell. I was suddenly completely awake. And afraid.

"Amy, knock it off. And back off!" She was near, so near I could feel the heat radiating from her. I reached over to the bedside table searching for my lamp. Her hand flashed, a thud and tinkle of glass as the lamp hit the floor. Anger began to flower in my belly, pushing aside the fear. Screw this.

She slammed me in the shoulder, knocking me against the headboard. "You *lied* to me! And you've been avoiding me! What are you hiding?"

"*I* lied to *you*? Oh, now that is rich! The Queen of Deception herself, crying that I lied to her."

She went still. "What are you talking about?"

"Oh, gee, I don't know, maybe it's because all you've ever told me about yourself is bullshit." I pushed myself upright finally, freeing my legs from the sheets.

She gathered herself back up. "You're acting like you're nuts, and yet you dare accuse me of lying? I'm not the one acting all secretive and suspicious! I can't find you anymore, you're never around, you never call me back. And now I find you got arrested in Connecticut? What the fuck have you been doing?"

Pain throbbed in my temples. I didn't need this, not now, maybe not ever. Looking at the outline of her, wild hair everywhere, booze smell sharp and haunting, I wonder why I ever thought I needed her in the first place. A tiredness crept into me that had nothing to do with sleep.

"Amy. You're drunk. Go home."

"Asshole!" Her arm flashed, a sharp slap and sting as her palm hit my cheek.

"Jesus!" I grabbed her hand as it rose again. She hissed, writhing against me, "You useless fucking loser! I hate you!" I wrenched her arm down around behind her, eliciting a yelp of pain.

"You're hurting me! Let me go, let me GO!"

My breath was ragged in my chest, burning, broken glass in my lungs. "I know about your family."

She went still. "Wha...wha...let go, dammit!"

"I KNOW about you, Amy. I *know*. You have a lot of nerve accusing me of lying when you hid who you really are from me all this time."

"You don't know shit, you motherfucker! Let me go, dammit!" She twisted around, her teeth finding my thumb and clamping down, my fingers released involuntarily.

"Ow! Son of a bitch!" I shook her roughly. She responded with amazing strength, twisting further and clawing at me with her freed hand. Her fingertips found purchase on the bandage on my left hand and ripped, tugged it loose. Pain splintered up my wrist as the fresh scabs tore open again. I pushed her away from me, hard, thrusting her towards the wall. She tumbled over and landed on the floor with a rattling thud.

For a moment, there is silence in the room. My ragged breathing, her hiccuping sounding breaths. Then the tempo changed, the hiccuping turning to full blown sobs, gaining in strength and intensity. I can't go to her, can't, won't. I roll off the bed, away from her and fumble on the wall for the overhead light switch.

She cringes in the glare of the incandescent bulb, her face red and tear streaked, swollen with booze, rage and pain. I stare down at her, wondering how I could have missed it, the naked clarity of what she was freezing me to the core.

"You lied to me, lied about everything in your life. How could you do that? How could you *do* that?"

She rolled away, towards the wall, drawing herself up into a ball, sobbing harder. I stare down at her, just tired, tired and worn out. I see red out of the corner of my eye, splashing on the carpet, trickling down from the reopened wound on my wrists, the raggedly carved word PUSSY angry red and swollen, red words overlaid on white ropy scars of words carved long ago.

I'm just so damn tired.

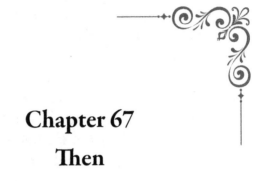

Chapter 67
Then

Dummer's Town State Forest is shaped kinda like a big L, with a pond and a swimming area at the end of the L, and then hooking around to a wider area where the cabins and trails are. Gramma lets me go there to swim sometimes, at the small pond in the base of the L. There's a bigger one up near the cabins where the kids are canoeing and fishing and stuff. I've never been up to that end of the park.

The swimming area isn't that hard of a ride for me, at least in the daylight. I've never attempted it at night before.

Fear and loathing tangle in my throat, fear and a sense that I'm too late, too late, so I pedal hard, hard, hard. I can hardly breathe; my throat is all weird and closed up.

The photos in my hip pocket burn.

Bats dart across the road, scaring me each time. Frogs peep and scream, deafening by the old swamp. Once I swear I see eyes flashing in the underbrush. I skitter my bike to the center of the road and pedal, pedal, pedal. I'm scared, maybe more scared than I've ever been before.

The park gate is closed when I get there, two moss covered stone pillars with a metal gate thing across. I push my bike around them, through the woods, and rejoin the cracked pavement on the other side. I start pedaling again, hard, hard, hard.

An unseen pothole catches the front wheel of my bike and launches me. I have a moment's sensation of air, then a crashing landing on the pavement, pain lancing up through a dozen new cuts and scrapes. I lie there in the darkness, panting. Slowly I stagger up off the pavement and pick up my bike. The front is wobbly now, the damage coursing up through my hands. I start pedaling again, slower, more cautiously, searching for darker spots that mean holes.

It takes forever just to reach the little pond. The cabins are way further back, further than I've ever gone. The night presses around me, sinister, evil, wanting to stop me, to send me back home. Gritting my teeth, I push on grimly. I'm too late, I'm too late. I don't know why I know this, but I do.

I see a dim light through the trees finally, after forever of riding, a small spark just as I'm think I'm never going to get there, and that I should just give up and try again in the morning. Panting now, I push harder, then I round one, then two corners and there they are. Four hulking shapes, a speck of light burning at the corner of one of them. The cabins.

There's a car parked in front of one of them. I see dim shapes here and there that turn into picnic tables and a couple of logs on the ground. Behind the cabins, a short distance away, I can see the lake, visible even on this moonless night. The air is chilly, heading towards cold, winter still a recent memory here. I stare at the cabins, unsure which one Billy would be in. Not the one with the car in front of it. I'm suddenly certain that is where Mr. Hawley is. My skin crawls at that thought.

"*Think*, you retard. Which one?" I stare at the buildings, slowly realizing that I need to do more than think. Carefully, I lay my bike on the ground and make my way towards the picnic table closest to me. I can smell burnt wood, recently doused, a firepit to my right. Touching the table, I allow my brain to open up, slip the gray blanket to one side...

Hey, gimme another S'more! Lookit that Johnny Reed, he's eatin' another one of them! That has to be the tenth one now! Ha ha, he's gonna get sick and puke on those things. Hey, we're all going fishing tomorrow morning. Bet I catch a big trout, like my dad does! Naw, you ain't catching nothing in here. Hey, retard, you bring a pole?

Billy's eyes are dark pools in the campfire light, Mr. Hawley's face is lit with a flickering light across the pit from him, fear, fear, such fear, from Billy, from the little sandy haired kid the next class up who sits in silence. The dumb ones, the Elliot brothers who sat at this table, are oblivious to the fear and undercurrents. They are in the middle cabin. Billy is in the end one, with the sandy haired kid and a black haired boy with acne scattered across his face.

My eyes pop open. The end cabin is dark, just a shape against the pond, big old pine trees pressing around it. Billy would hate it out here, hate it. He's here because of me. I wonder for a moment if we can both ride my bike back to town tonight, sneak him into my house. I don't want to leave him here another minute.

I hurry across the fire pit area, footfalls muffled by a dense covering of pine needles. The porch creaks as I cross it.

I hold my breath and ease the door open. Inside, I can hear breathing, regular, noisy from two people. Two.

The cabin is small, just an open space with two bunk beds and a small table and chairs in the middle. There's no bathroom, the outhouses at the edge of the clearing serve the whole campground. One bed is heaped with bags and gear, the bunk above occupied. The other bunk has the top one occupied and the lower one empty.

I can see a rumpled sleeping bag in it. Cautiously, I climb the ladder and peek over the edge of the top one. Noisy breathing, with some mumbling, a movement allows me to see a spotted cheek. Not Billy. Dropping back down, I tiptoe across the room to the other one and carefully climb up. I realize as I peer over the edge that I am only hearing one noisy breather now, not two. Wide scared eyes against the pillow, a bunched fist with a rock in it. The sandy haired kid, David something. We stare at each other a second, and I realize he's about to yell.

"Where's Billy?" I hiss softly.

"Who are you?" tremor in his voice.

"Gerry. I'm his friend. Where is he?" I hear the breath whoosh out of him.

"I thought...I thought..."

"That I was Mr. Hawley, I know."

He looked at me sharply. "How do *you* know about that?"

There's not enough time to tell him, so I ask again, "Is Billy staying here with you guys?"

He sat up slowly. From the other bunk came a rattling snore. "Yeah. He's sleeping in the bottom bunk over there." Where the bag lies empty.

"Well he's not there now. Where would he have gone?"

David sat up and peered over the edge of his bunk. "I dunno. He was there when we went to bed. Maybe he's taking a leak or something?"

Or something. Mr. Hawley. As he says it, he grimaces, fear evident again. "I didn't want to go on this, but my dad insisted." He swallowed noisily.

Anger coursed through me. "Why doesn't anyone *do* something about it? Everyone knows but no one *does* anything!"

The breathing across the room stuttered as my voice rose. I froze, unwilling to have more kids know I was here. The rattling breaths resume.

"Look. Don't say anything to anyone about me being here, okay? I need to find Billy. Where would he be?"

"There's not a lot of places to go. The lake? The other cabins? The fire pit?"

Slowly, I back down the ladder. David sits up, swinging his legs over the side. "No!" I hiss.

"Why not? I'll help you look for him." He doesn't want to be left alone here. I can feel his fear.

"No...you haveta stay here, in case, in case he comes back. If he does, tell him I'm looking for him, okay? And remember, don't tell anyone else you saw me here, ok? No matter what, don't say a word!"

He nods slowly, reluctantly. I drop back to the ground and head for the cabin door. Behind me, the black haired kid snores again.

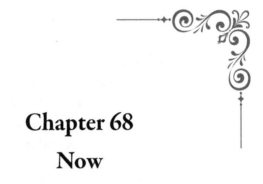

Chapter 68
Now

I stared at the huge building as I slowly rolled by on the service road, gray blocks and red trim, narrow glass block windows, a parking lot with a scattering of cars. Geotechnik. Biggest employer on this side of town, maybe in the area.

Facts rattled through my brain as I eased the F150 along the chain link fence. Government contracts fortified it through the recession, new inventions in geo technology propelling them to the forefront in the past five years. Money flowed, flowed like water through this place. If you needed to find anything underground, this was your place. If you needed it extracted, this was your place. No mineral or substance could hide from the revolutionary ground penetrating systems they designed and sold, an MRI for the earth they said.

Money. Cubic yards of it. Enough money to fund an entire city for a year, maybe more. Owned and run by a man who drove a shit box compact car, who trawled for hookers on the water's edge. Who satisfied his gnawing hunger with massive doses of arterial blood.

No Toyota Camry's with Connecticut plates graced the lot.

I turn around at the end of the service road and drove back slowly, aware of the black eyes of cameras located at the corners of the buildings, at the gates and intersections in the parking lot. An uneasy feeling crawled down my spine, my foot goosed the throttle up, pushing past the cold gray monolith faster, getting away from it. I turned down the next side street and traveled back down a short hill, where the oily surface of the river glinted through leafless trees. The river. A common thread in this bloody saga.

I pull into a parking lot next to a rundown marina, the motor ticking over in the sudden stillness. Across the river, traffic hisses on the roadway, audible even at this distance. Here, I'm lost in a sudden cocoon of silence, an uneasy crawling stillness that sends chills down my arms. I become aware of the rhythmic slapping of water against the hulls of two motorboats that bob in the current, a lonely refrain. Whispers of past ghosts flutter in my ears, a murmuring soundtrack to the beating of my heart against my ribcage. Without realizing it, I am out of my truck, a dozen yards away. The edge of the parking lot is a black edged sword against the slow rolling gray muscle of the river.

Here. Right here. Late one night, when the rain slashed down hard, a downpour, her eyes huge in the dash lights, dilated pupils from the crack cocaine she was ingesting, here she offered up her innermost secrets, secrets that disappointed yet again. Here. Right over there her blood dripped black and shiny onto rain slicked pavement, swirling, expanding, dissipating in the rain in a crimson tide, swept away to the waiting arms of the Atlantic Ocean at last. Cartilage cracked against the knife, an oh so satisfying feeling and sound, the excitement, the thrill of being this **bold**, *this* brassy, *doing it* right *here in the wide open, swept over me, oh how wonderful, how freeing that was.*

Weeds crunched under my feet, the water swept past mere feet away, somehow I was all the way across the lot, at the river's edge, the siren call of the water pulling me in, calling me, just give yourself to me, my love, and everything will be okay again, everything will be right, come to me. Come to me...come...to...me....

"Hey!"

I stop, water swirling around my right foot, the one in the edge of the river's current, bewildered, rudely awakened from my dream. "Hey!" again, from my left. Blinking slowly, I turn my head, surprised there's no rain, no darkness, just low gray clouds, and a skinny guy with a cap who is standing next to one of the floats they've hauled out of the river. "Where you going? There ain't no docks out there now."

I look at my foot in the water and pull it out, my breathing ragged. I fumble for my pocket, pulling a cigarette out of a battered pack with a hand that is shaking too much. "I know. I'm just stopping to have a cigarette." I tell him in a voice that isn't mine, not mine, can't be, it's too high, too shaky. The old guy, he is old I guess, he looks sunken in and sunbaked, just stares at me for a long moment before shaking his head and turning back to a tractor that sits behind him, unnoticed until now. With a last suspicious look at me, he fires up the motor and backs around. I can see the look on his face, hear the words in his head.

Trouble, that guy there is trouble, mark my word.

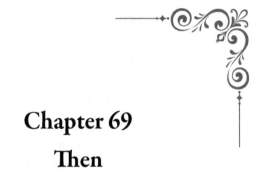

Chapter 69
Then

"Please be out here you dummy." My whisper sounds shockingly loud to me in the noisy dark. A mosquito lands on my cheek, biting, hungry. I swipe it away and two more show up to take her place. I'm crouched outside the last cabin, scanning the clearing, hoping against hope that I see the retard come out of one of the outhouses.

But of course he doesn't.

I eye the remaining cabins, loathe to search them. Where the heck could he be? My eye falls on the first cabin, the one with the car in front of it. The cabin Mr. Hawley is probably in. My stomach clenches. If he's in any of the cabins, it has to be that one. Has to be.

I rise slowly, and creep along the side of the buildings, bent over like a soldier. More mosquitoes find my face and arms, high pitched buzzing jarring in my ears. I ignore the little bloodsuckers. The rough wood of the first cabin is under my hand at last, the sagging step beneath my feet. I ease up onto the porch and listen.

Silence. Complete silence. Grimacing, I allow the tattered blanket that barely covers my brain to slide away just a little bit, just a bit. I have to know...

Nothing. No noise in my head. Bewildered, I open my eyes. Faint echoes of people who have spent time in this building rattle around the edges, like a far off radio playing. But nothing louder, more immediate. What the heck? Straightening up, I push the door open, not bothering to hide myself. I can see outlines of two bunk bed sets, like in the first cabin.

Finding a lamp, I turn it on.

The room is empty. Gear is piled on the upper bunks, poles, back pack, stuff like that. A lower bunk is made up, sleeping bag, pillow, but unused. Turning around slowly, I see a blue and white coat hung on the back of a chair. Mr. Hawley's windbreaker.

He came in here, but he didn't spend any time in here, no more than it took to leave his stuff. That thought chills me to the bone.

David Something's voice in my head, *"There's not a lot of places to go. The lake? The other cabins? The firepit?"*

The lake. I snap the light off again and stand still for a long moment, waiting for my eyes to adjust. Able to see again, I peer through the window at the water, shimmering with a faint inner light. Gramma once said that lakes and ponds capture the light from stars, that if you can stare into them when it's really quiet and still, you can see stars, even in the daylight. I wonder of that is the source of the faint but definite light that pulses out of the water now.

You're too late, you're too late, you're too late. The words send me hurtling out the door, no pretense of silence now. My feet slap on the dirt path down to the water's edge, running blindly, panicked, too late, too late.

Water laps on the packed mud shore softly, hungrily. Canoes lie overturned, in a ragged row, a circle of tree stumps sits around another fire pit. I trip over one stump, landing heavily on the mud, feel it soaking through the knees of my jeans. Scrambling up, I spin one way, then the other. Nothing. Fear beats in my ribs. "Billy!" I hiss his name. Silence, lapping water. Left or right? I go right.

Mud, more mud, then ragged bushes scratching my cheek. I scramble on, calling Billy's name periodically. I'm met with silence. Finally I stop, panting. Turning, I hustle back the way I came, back to the firepit and canoes on the edge of the lake. I continue past them this time, clambering over the rocks that jumble the edge of the lake. Somewhere nearby, an owl hoots, startling me with its voice. A large boulder juts out into the water's edge, towering over my head. I clamber up the side of it, to the slanted top.

Water laps softly below me. I can just see the outline of the shore ahead of me, a ragged cove lined with drooping tree limbs. Something is lying on the edge of the water, still, small, maybe a log, must be a log, has to be a log...

I leap from the top of the boulder and sprint, mud slipping and splashing under my feet.

He's so still, so small, he hardly looks like a boy anymore, like a dummy, he's just so darn small. I'm gasping, sobbing as I roll him over, his skin already cooling under my hands, his dark eyes flat and staring, jaw slack. Sobbing, sobbing, I did this, I made him come here, I killed him. I grab his shoulders, shaking, shaking, "Wake up you dummy, wake UP!"

His head lolls around, loose and slack, his once hyper-active brain cooling, quieting. Images flash across me, his fear, no terror, as Mr. Hawley pushes him down onto the muddy ground, his pants trapping his ankle, the pain, oh the pain, the red hot shards of pain in his gut as Mr. Hawley pounds himself into him, ripping him open, shredding him, no, no, no, no! Merciless pounding grinding his face into the mud, choking him. A strong hand at the back of his neck, pushing his face all the way into the water and holding him, holding him as he bucked and flailed against the water filling his lungs, the water stilling his heart and brain, stilling him....

"Oh my God! What have you DONE?" I'm sobbing into Billy's scrawny chest as the words boom out over my head, a flashlight cutting across my face. Squinting, I see a tall shape flanked by several shorter ones. Mr. Hawley...with the rest of the kids. I see David staring at me, his eyes huge, face white, as Mr. Hawley yells again, "What did you DO to Billy?"

"I didn't do it! I didn't do it! I just got down here and found him like this! You did this! YOU did it!" My eyes swiveled, trapped. "David, tell him! Tell him how you just saw me up in the cabins looking for Billy! I didn't do this!"

David turns whiter, his throat working noisily. He looked at Mr. Hawley, whose face was hidden in shadows, then back at me. The rest of the kids were dead silent, scared out of their minds.

David swallows at last, his voice catching. "I didn't see nothing. I was asleep." His eyes miserable.

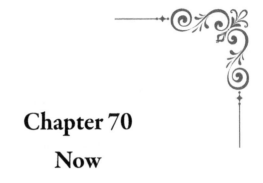

Chapter 70

Now

The Toyota Camry is here again. I find a spot off to one side of the building where I can sit in the brush and watch the lot. The bushes conceal me for the most part, a wild tangle that ends at the sterile neatness of the property Geotechnik sits on. I spy the roof of Blake's car among the thinning ranks of employee vehicles. This is the second time I've seen his car there since I started coming.

The last rays of the sun are slanting across the river, already hidden by the slope to the west that looms behind me. Lights flickered on in the parking lot twenty minutes ago, casting pools that create a stepping stone pattern across the vast lot. One by one, the other cars have exited, from a rush at five to a trickle over the past hour. Only a handful remain.

Including the Toyota.

I stay where I am as the minutes, then hours creep past, my legs cramping, my back protesting. The wind has a cutting edge to it, dry leaves rattling though the bare branches of the bushes I am crouched under. I furtively smoke a cigarette, cupping my hand around the end to hide the glow and wait.

It's late, real late, when I finally see a figure leaving the back door of the building, a stocky, short figure that moves with a purposeful gait. I draw a breath sharply, rising to my knees as I see him. I scramble down the slope towards my truck as he reaches his car, losing sight of him as I reach the parking lot. My hand has a tremor as I twist the key in the ignition, the motor coughing to life.

I wait, a minute, then two, then three. No Toyota. He has to come by me. This is the only route out of Geotechnik.

Ten minutes goes by. No Toyota. Making a decision, I drop the truck in gear and pull out, turning up past the complex again. I can see the parking lot, a half dozen cars left illuminated in the stepping stone pools of light.

The Toyota is gone.

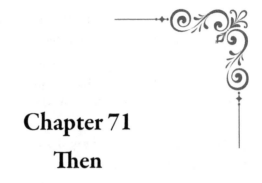

Chapter 71
Then

Everything looks so much different now; smaller, kinda grungy. I stare across Main Street, my face as flat as the concrete beneath my feet, flat and lifeless. There's Dom's Marketplace, where Gramma did her shopping, the glass store front looking half the size I remembered. And over there, that was Quinn's Deli and Butcher shop, where the pieces of dead beef cows could be seen hanging in the back on Thursdays, blood spattered men and women hacking off cuts of meat for housewives. It looks dingy, tired. The movie theater is boarded up now; Gramma said they closed last winter.

I lean against the rough brick of the electric company's office and light a cigarette. Inside I can see Gramma doling out wrinkled bills, she herself so much smaller and beaten down. Because of me.

I lower my head, letting my hair fall over my eyes as a Ford sedan cruises by slowly, the driver eying me with frank disgust. Mr. Fairline, his daughter Lisa was, or used to be, the same grade as me. I been getting a lot of that since I got home, the stares, the whispers. Four years later and somehow everything and nothing has changed.

Gramma emerges finally, carefully tucking her receipt in her bag. I fall in beside her wordlessly. I tower over her now, hulk over her, something she doesn't like. I can't help it though.

She can still talk a lot, my gosh she can talk. And talk she does, enough for her and me. Freed from the worry of making nice, I say nothing, my mind wandering as we head back down the street.

It's late August now, and kids all over town are getting ready to go back to school. Except me. I'm just past my sixteenth birthday, the day I was released from juvenile detention, "juvie" as the kids called it, and there's no more school for me. The school wouldn't have me for one thing. I wouldn't go back there for another. I don't even want to be in this stupid town, where everyone is pointing and staring at me, but I don't have any place else to go. So I duck my head and let my hair fall across my face so no one can see my eyes too clear. And Gramma talks, and talks, and talks.

We climb into her station wagon, the same one I used to sleep in, and she cranks the starter. And cranks it. The motor coughs and coughs, dourly refusing to fire up. She slaps the steering wheel finally. "Well, goldarnitall!" And bursts into tears.

I'm ashamed, more ashamed than I was when I was tried and convicted by my peers in that instant they found me with Billy's body, tried and sent up to juvie without benefit of a trial. "It's best this way," they whispered to Gramma.

"Those pictures he had; this boy needs help. Professional help."

They claimed it was because I was chronically disobedient. They claimed it was because I had "anger issues". No one could prove I killed Billy, but they couldn't disprove it either. And the pictures, well my trap for Mr. Hawley trapped me instead.

And so here I was, days out of juvie with Gramma bawling like a little kid because the car wouldn't start, bawling in front of a dozen people who stared...and wouldn't help her.

I climbed out of the car, crossed around to her side and opened the hood. Memories of those times in Carl's company flooded me as the simple scent of grease and oil hit my nose. Oh how I had loved that time in the garage. Tears of my own prickled for an instant, blinked away. I eyed the motor, replaying the images I had of everything to do with the starting system of the car, and began to wiggle wires. The third one I touched had more movement than I thought it should. I wiggled and pressed it back into its seat.

"Gram, try it now." She wiped her face with a tissue and turned the ignition. It cranked once, twice, then caught. I felt a stab of satisfaction, coupled with a fresh burst of mourning. For Billy. For the loss of the garage. For me.

I get back into the car in silence. Gramma sat silent too, uncharacteristic for her, the rough idling of the engine the only noise.

"Well." She finally says. "Well." And runs out of words. She puts the car in drive and pulls away from the curb. We head downtown instead of toward the little run down house we call home. I look at her but say nothing. I don't really care much what she does.

I recognize the streets though, the turns, the intersections, and my heart drops when I realize she's heading to the garage, to Carl and Dick's place. "No." my lips move, but no sound comes out. I haven't seen them since before that last baseball game, my last words to Carl being that I would be back to work the next day. Over four years ago now. "No." I whisper this time. Gramma either doesn't hear it or doesn't care.

The garage looks smaller too, the winged horse in need of paint. I duck my head low; hair covering my eyes and stay in the car as Gramma gets out and goes inside. Through the open garage door I can see the shape of some guy working under a Pontiac. I can't tell if it's Carl or not. A skinny brown haired kid comes out, lugging a trash can, his face screwed up in disgust at the smell.

My old job.

I slide lower down in the seat. Gramma's in the office a long time. I think about just getting out, leaving, walking home, but I can't, not with the open door and the brown haired kid, who is sweeping the garage now, his movements slow and bored.

Motion catches my eye, the office door opening, Gramma in it, talking, talking to someone behind her, turned to face them. They emerge from the dim interior, eyes on the car, on me. It's Carl.

He looks almost the same, maybe a bit skinnier, a little less hair. He's wiping his hands on a rag as he slowly walks over to the car, Gramma talking, talking away at him. His eyes are on me though. I try to sink further into the seat, to disappear. Carl's going to turn on me too, and I can't take it anymore, just can't take it...

"G.L., you wanna pop the hood for me?" Like nothing ever happened and he just saw me yesterday. Blinking, I reach across the seat and tug the hood lever.

"Why'ncha come out here and show me what you did?" Silently, I open the door and climb out. I'm almost as tall as he is now, a weird feeling. I don't speak, I just point at the wire in question. "Huh." He fiddles a moment. "I think the connection to the starter is gone. What do you think, G.L.?"

"I...uh...yeah...I mean..."

He flicks a look at me. "Well? Yes or no? Come on now, I taught you better than that." His voice...warm. Welcoming.

"Yuh...yeah. I think it needs to be soldered. I think she might need to get the starter rebuilt too. It's been sounding kinda weak."

"That's better." He ducks under the hood, examining the starter again. "I think you're right, G.L." He straightens up, wincing as he does so. "So when do you think you can drop it off?" to Gramma.

I'm looking at the garage as he talks to her, at the mechanic who comes into view finally. It's not Dick, it's some guy with greased back black hair, muscular forearms and a mustache. Frowning, I look over at Carl, who catches me looking at him. "Where's Dick?"

A shadow crosses his face. "He had a heart attack about a year and a half ago now. Sold out and moved after that. I'm the sole owner of this fine establishment now."

Oh. I glance at the guy and the kid inside, then look back down at the ground. I realize with a start that Carl's talking to me again, "So think you can bring her car over for me tomorrow morning?"

"I, uh, I...I can't drive." I'm embarrassed now. That wasn't one of the things they taught you in juvie.

Now it's Carl's turn to flush. "Oh, shoot, I mean, sure, sorry, I ah, just assumed." Gramma jumps in then, jumps in hard. "Well maybe you can't drive right now, but I plan to teach you. We'll start soon as I get my car fixed."

I hadn't expected that. Irritation mixed with gratitude and shame in me. Carl saw something in my face, smiled at Gramma and touched my shoulder. "Hey, look I got a Pontiac out back I can use, teach him on something that it don't matter if it gets beat on. Don't want to be too rough with your old gal here." He caressed the hood as he closed it gently.

I'm bewildered at the turn of events. Carl was actually offering to do something with me? Didn't he know I was the no good kid, the one who everyone said killed little Billy, didn't he know it?

He turned to face me square, his eyes level. "G.L., you're welcome here anytime. Anytime, kid."

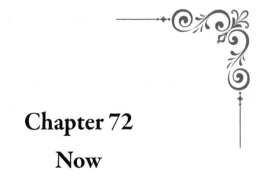

Chapter 72
Now

The lot is almost empty now. Two Fords and a Hyundai remain parked along the front row, dew clouding the windshields. The Toyota's spot is empty. The chain link fence is cold under my hand as I lean into it and scan the lot. How the hell did that happen? This was the only entrance and exit from the place.

For regular people, maybe. I realize as I think that that this is no 'regular' person, this is Mr. Robert F. Blake, owner and psychopath. Blake would operate by a different set of rules.

Blake would have access to the keys to the emergency exit, the gate that backs onto the quiet street along the backside of the building. A gate that doesn't seem to have a camera guarding it like the front one does. Frustration boiled in me as I realized my mistake.

Too late, too late, too late...

Streets were dark and still at this hour, a few houses showing flickering blue light from television sets. I twist and turn through the ragged little neighborhood, trying to decipher which way he took from the plant. Nothing comes to me.

An hour passes, then two, and finally I quit searching. A needle in the haystack, finding a plain Toyota in such a large area. I finally pull over, in a commuter parking lot and give up, sagging with defeat and exhaustion.

I dread the news tomorrow.

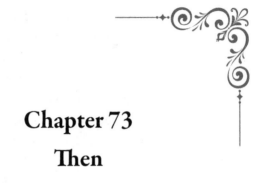

Chapter 73
Then

H E was out there someplace. As summer wound down
and fall came in on a shower of dead leaves and frost-
ed glass, my brooding over HIM began to grow into an obsession. Maybe 'cuz I didn't have enough to do, and didn't
have no friends to do much with, or maybe it was 'cuz for the
first time in years my mind wasn't filled with so many other
things; the whack and thwack of my mom dying faded into
background noise. School was long gone, the other kids
strange, distant creatures to me when glimpsed on the side-
walks or around town.

The only thing I had going on was going over to Carl's a
little bit again. He seemed okay with me, he didn't ever tell
me no, but I could see the people's looks when I was there,
the tension in Carl's shoulders as he faced them with me in
the background leaning over an engine bay. So I took to only going over for a couple of hours at a time. Carl didn't say
anything about it, but I think he was relieved that he didn't
have to face down everyone in town.

I was left with a lot of time to brood.

Mr. Hawley was gone. They said he picked up and moved away, summer after I was sent away. I overheard Gramma telling Nancy Becker that he was up around Albany area, she thought. I filed him away in my damaged brain for later; a squirrel hiding a nut for an upcoming winter's day.

Gramma wouldn't tell me a thing about Donny Hopgood, my piece of crap stepfather. Not a thing. I finally stopped asking her.

I spent a lot of time wandering around town on yet another cobbled together bicycle exploring and thinking.

In early September, I rode my bicycle down East Street, past my old school, feeling gangly and awkward, propelled by an impulse I couldn't name or stop. The yard was empty on that sun bright morning, kids all inside bored out of their minds. I pedaled slowly past the ball fields, the bleachers where Jimmy jumped me empty and small looking in the flat sunlight. A memory of Billy surfaced suddenly, released from the depths of where I had locked him up, his narrow face and goofy grin slamming me in the middle of my chest, as substantial as a physical blow.

I heard his voice, a psychic echo in my head, vibrating off my brain, as he turned and considered me carefully, finding me lacking. "So why doncha go find him, you pussy?" he whispered. "How hard can it be to find one piece of crud like HIM?"

"How?" my lips moved as I wobbled on the rickety bike, eyes suddenly stinging and blurry.

"How?"

Billy's gamine face slowly dissolved as I passed under the shadows of the oak trees at the corner.

"You already know how, you big dummy."

Chapter 74
Now

It takes three days before they find her. I read the article on line in the dusty carousel of the library, a place I've come to spend more time at than anyplace else lately. Carmelita Mendoza, 24, found discarded like a used wrapper, her body small, diminished, violated, dead of multiple stab wounds. They found her under the shadow of a derelict mill, a scant half block from the river.

The pixels swim as my stomach rolls slowly. Anger bubbles up, acidic and hot. He's there, right there, and I need to stop him.

The Toyota hasn't been back since that night. I've taken to haunting the area surrounding Geotechnik, looking for the car, for any sign of Mr. Robert F. Blake. And yet he remains stubbornly absent.

About two or three days after I find the article about Carmelita, I run across a Blake's name in a society column, of all places.

"Charity Cruise nets Big Fish"
By Dorothea Parker for the Tribune.

Summer may be long gone for those of us stuck here on the Island, but for a few local philanthropists the heat lingers. On Saturday, the Holiday Empress returned to New York after a week-long cruise to Bermuda. Among her lucky passengers were a number of local luminaries who paid dearly for five star accommodations, all in the name of charity.

Holiday Cruise Lines of America donated their proceeds from the passengers, who paid a reported $10,000 each for the event. Among those who dined on lobster and danced under a full moon while docked in Hamilton was the CEO of Lumalife Enterprises Roger Shelburne, with his wife Melissa, actress Petrovia Janseen, New Fairfield philanthropist and businessman Robert Blake and his wife, Tina Blake, nee Cumberford of Cumberford Banking, John Hart of Metrowest and his wife Patricia Martin-Hart. The event netted a reported $100,000 plus for the Jenny Hanniford Cancer Foundation of SNY.

Attendees participated in events such as a celebrity auction and high stakes roulette, with all proceeds going to the Foundation. The guests wore brilliant smiles as they disembarked, sporting freshly tanned cheeks and glowing from the satisfaction of helping those who are afflicted with breast cancer.

Disembarked Saturday from a week long cruise? Bewildered, I flip back through my stack of print outs. The Toyota was at Geotechnik on Monday, Carmelita's body found on Thursday. Blake disembarks from the Holiday Empress on Saturday. A weeklong cruise...he should have been in Bermuda by Monday.

So how was his car in the lot at Geotechnik?

Sweat beaded on my face as I considered this. Could I have been stupid enough to have watched the wrong car?

Even as it crossed my mind, I knew it wasn't so. That was THE Toyota. I was sure of it.

Dead sure.

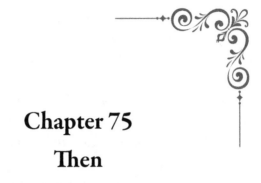

Chapter 75
Then

I hate this. Gramma talks, talks, talks as I sit there dumb as a stump. I have to do this, but I don't want to. It's like I'm spying on her while she's taking a bath or something. That thought brings fresh heat to my face, and I duck my head lower, actually feeling a little bit sick at the thought. We're sitting at the table in the kitchen, mac 'n cheese and burgers cooling on my plate, my stomach in no shape for greasy food. Across from me, Gramma rattles and rustles, telling about people I don't know or care about, anything to fill the silence between us. She's nervous about me being there, scared a little. I can't blame her I guess, although it pisses me off some too. I mean, shouldn't she know me better than that?

I hear Billy's voice again, a grating whisper dragging across my brain, "Go on, you retard. What are ya waitin' for?"

I dip my head a bit lower and drag the tattered cloth back from my brain a bit, seeking, searching...

Good Lord, this boy just never says anything anymore. Maybe if I tell him about Judy Draper's daughter, he'll be interested. How I wish I'd listened to him about the baseball. That rotten little Jimmy Hodges. He's a bad one, mark my words. I can't believe Gerry's at all like that no good Donny. He was just a stepfather anyway, there's no blood there. Damnit, I warned her about him too. Look at what came of that. My land, how I miss her still.

Sweat beaded my forehead as I listened to Gramma's thoughts, painfully aware that this was wrong, that it was trespassing, but unable to stop now. Come on, Gramma, tell me about HIM, come on...

Donny Hopgood, my land, why can't I get him out of my head? I sure hope he never shows his face around here again. I asked Timmy Page over at the Police station to keep an ear open for me, and to let me know if he comes back again. Damn that no good son of a bitch for that! Bad enough he takes my daughter, why did he try to take my grandson too? Oh, if I ever get my hands on him...how I wish I'd hit him that night instead of Gerry. Gerry will never forgive me for that, hasn't, I can feel it, I can't ever make this right, ever...

I glance up at her from under my hair, seeing as if for the first time the lines on her face, the stress and age. Lines that weren't there four years ago. I feel an almost overwhelming rush of guilt, a sense of how badly I've screwed up, and it almost paralyzes me. What a screwup I am, what a total screwup...

....from Scranton, and I damn sure hope he's back there. Dirty bastard anyway. I need to check in with Mark, see if he's collected anything more for the box. This isn't over, mark my words...I get ahold of that rotten son of a bitch, I'll make sure he disappears, mark my words. He'll be gone.

Box? What box? Her thoughts are a confusing jumble, words, words, words, battering my damaged brain, a rainstorm of words and images. Now that I'm in her head, I'm having a hard time getting out of it again, but I need to, need to bad. I can't handle hearing her inside and out, her endless stream of noise in my ears echoing in my head, a jarring medley of noise, noise, noise...

I'm standing now, unaware that I even moved, her face looking up at me, momentarily still, watery eyes through smudged glasses, a prickle of fear across her face before she can stop it, echoing in my head. I'm ashamed, ashamed she would even feel that with me, and unable to stop it, to change it, although I want to.

Instead, I mumble, "I gotta take a leak." and head to the bathroom, my brain fizzing, gray heat and nausea as she calls after me, "I have to use the bathroom, not 'I gotta take a leak'. You know better than that, Gerry!"

Chapter 76
Now

Amy's left me alone in a sullen silence for a week now. Not so Bill. He glares at me in my kitchen, pissed, frustrated, and I look away, ignoring him. I haven't gone in to work since he turned on me in the truck. His sympathy for me is fading, fast.

Glasses litter my table; the ashtray overflows. I know he can see the clothing strewn across the floor of my tiny bedroom. Truth be told, I simply don't care anymore. And it pisses me off that he looks at the stuff on the counters and judges, without seeing what the truth is. The glasses, the residue on the bottom is Coca Cola. None of them contain booze. But he doesn't see that. He judges me, judges me and finds me lacking. So I shut him out. I can't have Bill, Amy or anyone around me, not right now. Eventually, he gets frustrated enough to leave. I can't even tell you what he has said in the twenty minutes he was here.

The silence is deafening in its relief.

The door has barely snicked shut before I'm up off the chair, moving, moving, snagging a sweatshirt off the couch, keys off the counter, vaguely aware that I smell funky, sour.

The air is cold across my face, winter is really coming now, the light fleeing before the arctic mass that creeps closer day by day. I'm off again, off to Geotechnik, to my many hiding spots where I can wait and watch. It ticks in my head, an obsession now, worse than finding HIM ever was.

I've found three different places to do surveillance on the building, and I shift them around so no one wises up to my presence. I don't dare go to his house in Connecticut now, my initial hearing made it clear that I was to remain far away from Blake and his family. The judge released me on personal recognizance, much to the dismay of Blake's lawyer. Fact is, except for my juvenile record and a couple of DUI's, I have no violent past. So I play it smart and stay far away from his home turf.

Good thing Geotechnik is in mine.

I park beside the VFW this time, a full lot with voices booming out the door. The sunlight is fleeing rapidly, leaves skate across the narrow road as I follow the cracked sidewalk up the hill. Reaching the low knoll with the gnarled apple tree and tangle of brush, I duck into it and crabwalk to the other side, following a barely discernible path I've worn over the past couple of weeks. Peering down into the parking lot, I check the spots reserved for the big wheels in the company.

The Toyota is there.

My heart pounds in my ears, momentarily deafening me. I realize my hands are quivering again, dancing of their own volition. I pat my right front pocket, feeling the square through the fabric, and swallow. Below me, the lights in the lot are starting to blip on, the sensors in the darker areas coming on first. I need to hurry.

My knees protest as I crawl over the ragged chain link fence, the weak point in their security. I know there are cameras at strategic intervals, my cap is pulled low to cover my face. I'm banking on them being placed to face out, not in, and I walk casually like I belong.

Frissons of energy, nervous energy, spike up my spine the closer I get to the Toyota, the building looming overhead, dark, flat fronted and flat roofed. I jump as a light two rows over buzzes and flickers to life. I have to hurry, hurry...the fender is slick under my palm, my stomach coiling at the feel, almost reptilian, not the smooth glossy feeling you normally get on a car, this was something darker, evil.

My joints pop as I crouch down momentarily, as if I dropped something, the square plastic case clenched in my hand, thrust up into the inner wheel well, past the plastic inner fender, contact with the hard magnet against the subframe with a click. Then I straighten, intending to head on towards the building as if I belong, when suddenly a stray tendril sneaks in past my defenses.

Thwock! Thowk! Thowk! Fucking bitch! Fucking dirty bitch, stick that nasty bitch! Scream all you want baby, daddy's home!

Gray spots dance in front of my eyes as I yank my hand off the car like it was toxic to the touch. No doubt, no doubt at all in my mind, none. I'm going to get you; I'm going to get you...

Chapter 77

Then

Donny Hopgood, aka HIM, aka my step father, well, common-law stepfather I had learned, was a walking piece of trash from Scranton, PA who had the great misfortune of coming to our area when he was on the run from his no good friends in PA.

My mom was a beautiful but weak woman, who was waitressing when she met him, down at Denny B's Bar and Grill. The monster had covered himself with a sparkling front, all flattery and greasy charm. Already well into drinking herself, mom fell for it. And him. By the time she found out what he was really like, we were living in the battered apartment I remembered.

A master manipulator, he had started supplying her with drugs to go with the booze, pills mostly, Quaalude's, Valium, shit like that.

Gramma had a box stashed under an old quilt in her closet, a box I hadn't known existed. Inside were old clippings she had saved from those dark, tormented years, clippings about the attack on her and me, and the subsequent hunt for him, clippings that dwindled until about a year ago, when a fresh batch joined the yellowed ones. He had popped up again, this time suspected of killing a clerk in a robbery gone bad.

The new set of clippings were from a town some fifty miles from us, midway between here and Scranton, PA. The police had not been able to find him, yet again. The clippings had petered out after some six months. I wondered how Gramma had come to have newspaper stories from so far away, wondered who was getting them for her.

My hands trembled as I looked at the papers. I needed a cigarette, needed one bad. Carefully, I replaced the clippings and buried them back under the quilt.

Outside, I swung a leg over my bike, considering where to go. I wanted to go to the garage, where Carl had finally made good on his promise to teach me to drive. This stupid bike I was on was for pussies, little kids, and I was no longer any kind of kid. I itched to put a car together for myself, maybe a muscle car, something with huge horse power and lots of torque. Something I could use to leave this shitty town once and for all.

I was lost in thought, sitting on the bike but not moving, not aware of the car until it stopped alongside the sidewalk I was on, driver's window cranking down. Belatedly I came out of my fog, my brain still swirling about HIM, aware that the car that idled at the curb was a green Plymouth Barracuda, the motor rumbling, a soundtrack to my fantasy, the lines of the fenders mesmerizing.

"Hey, Gerry! What'cha you doing?" I looked up at the driver and my heart sank. It was Darlene.

She tossed her hair over her shoulder, a smirk on pouty lips as I sat on my piece of shit bicycle, pinning me with her eyes. If I could have crawled under the porch right then, I would have.

I mumbled "Nothin'" unintelligibly, hoping, praying she would leave. She didn't. She turned off the motor instead.

"I've seen you around a coupla times, I waved but you looked right through me. What's the matter? Are you mad at me or something?"

Heat flushed through my face. I dipped my chin down, long hair falling over my eyes. Why won't she just leave? She eyed me for a long time in silence, then, "You know, that Jimmy turned out to be a real asshole. He's over in Medford now. His dad split from his mom about a year ago, and she moved, took the little turd with her." She rummaged around in the console of the car, found a cigarette pack and pulled one out. She offered the pack to me. I shrugged, still mute, but took it, surprised to see her smoking. She lit hers then offered me the match. I leaned forward and ignited mine, huffing the smoke greedily.

She continued, apparently unconcerned by my lack of conversation. "Anyway, we all thought he had it coming when you popped him like that." She picked a piece of invisible tobacco off her tongue, smoke dribbling from her nose. "He'd been such a turd that year, pretty much everyone hated him."

"Oh yeah?" my voice had returned as my discomfort eased. I frowned at her, remembering what I had "seen" between the two of them, Jimmy exploring her with his sticky hands. "I thought you two were an item."

"Ha! Uh, no. Although he wanted to be. But I prefer someone more mature than him." Her eyes tracked over me, slowly, intrusively. I felt a shudder work through my growing fascination. I looked at the junction of her neck and chest, aware of the freckled skin visible in the collar of her chambray shirt.

"So what do you think of my car?" her change of direction caught me flat footed. "Huh? Oh, yeah, nice. This your dad's?" I looked away from her, eying the car hungrily.

"It was, but he gave it to me last spring for my 18th birthday." She smiled, coolly confident. "Come 'mere. Check it out." And patted the seat next to her.

My stomach clenched. I wanted to climb in that car, wanted to check it out in the worst way, wanted to drive it, but my inner sense was screaming at me don't get in with her, don't, don't, don't.

I found myself laying my bike down on the sidewalk and cautiously coming around to the passenger side to peer in. She thumped a hand on the seat again, impatient. "Come on. Don't just stand there. Get in!"

I looked at her face, searching for her intent, pulled the tattered gray cloth back a hair from my damaged frontal lobe, searching for her intent, listening.... *Oh come on Ger, just get in with me, please? I've been looking for you for weeks...*

What the heck? Startled, I looked at her closer, noticed the colt like lines were gone, replaced by the long, leggy lines of a young woman. I thought I didn't like her much, but maybe it was time to change my opinion of her.

I opened the passenger side door and dropped into the vinyl bucket seat.

Chapter 78
Now

The laptop is clumsy for me, with its touchpad and no mouse. I struggle with the commands to open the right program.

I've moved from the VFW to the parking lot of the supermarket near the center of the town, anonymity found in proximity of so many vehicles, even at this slowly latening hour.

I hold my breath as I finally open the program, feeling that it was going to fail even though I had tested it out before coming here. The map came on, brightening my face with the light. A blinking dot appeared in the lower left side of it.

I let my breath out with a whoosh. It was working.

I shift down in the seat, resting the battered plastic case against my lap, a case that held much of my rapidly dwindling funds. Some of the hours spent in the library had been in search of a program just like this, something discrete that could track for me and let me know every move the car made. And now, now it was show time.

Unfortunately, there was an awful lot of hurry up and wait involved next.

I started dozing a bit around midnight, despite keeping a wary eye open for the cops. Around 12:55, the light on the screen started to move.

Adrenaline jolted me awake, wide awake. I watched, tremors coursing through me, as the light crept through the lot then out the back gate where it picked up speed. It turned left, up the hill, away from the river, and crossed through several blocks of a sleeping neighborhood. As I watched, it made a series of turns then joined a main thoroughfare, heading right into the downtown section, then through it, to the north end, the seedy district.

This was it; he was hunting!

I looked at the dash clock, 1:15 now, time flying, the prey getting too far away now, over three miles away. I needed to be closer to the action. I fired up the truck and pulled out of the lot.

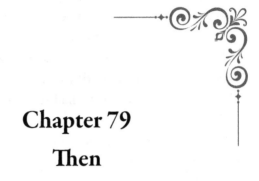

Chapter 79
Then

Darlene was talking as she drove, her hair flying around her face from the open window. I listened with half an ear, my focus on the sleek interior of the 'Cuda, still uncomfortable at being this close to her. She didn't seem to mind my silence much, she just talked and talked. Must be a girl thing, the amount of words they had to use.

We rumbled toward the edge of the town; Carl's garage visible a block over as she accelerated through the last stop sign heading towards the open farmland by the river. I snuck a peek at her, all legs and confidence, driving with one hand on the wheel, the other laid across the window. I feel big and clunky next to her, weird.

She hammers the throttle as we straighten out, and the big 318 responds, pushing me back in my seat. I felt a silly grin creeping across my face as she took a corner at speed, the back end kicking out, pebbles pinging off the under-carriage, then another, faster, bigger sliding turn. Trees and fields whip by, blue sky and bright air. Too soon, we are slowing, decelerating as she sedately makes the turn into the dirt lot down near the Oxbow lake, the boaters and fishermen absent on this mid-week afternoon.

"So what do ya think?" She was grinning at me, a big grin, different from her usual smirk. I grinned back at her, suddenly liking her, wondering why I hadn't all these years.

"That was wild!"

"You wanna try it?" She sat up, reaching for the door handle.

Would I? Holy moly, would I ever, but..."Darlene, I don't have a license yet." Just a half dozen driving lessons from Carl was all.

"So what? Just don't get caught. C'mon!" She was already out of the door. I popped mine open and followed suit.

I dropped into the driver's seat; my mouth suddenly dry. Hot dog, this was some kind of car! I smoothed the wheel under a sweaty palm as she slammed her door and crossed her legs. She was wearing jeans that draped and accentuated her legs, making them even more intriguing by hiding the skin like they did. I could see delicate feet in sandals peeking out, the nails brightly colored. I swallowed, my throat as dry as my mouth.

She was looking at me, a little smile playing around her lips. Breaking eye contact, I looked back at the dash. It was an automatic, a good thing being as I hadn't mastered a stick shift yet. Tentatively, I dropped the lever into D and wheeled it around in the lot, pointing it out towards the open road. Power rumbled under my foot and butt, an intoxicating feeling. Suddenly confident, I swung it north and punched it.

The 'Cuda was a Thoroughbred. Trees, river, fields flashed by as I laid on the power, the surface changing from dirt to pavement, then gravel. Beside me, Darlene laughed. She lit another cigarette for me, lighting it with cupped hand before leaning over to place it between my lips. I felt a surge in my low belly at her touch on my lips.

I had no idea why I had disliked her all these years.

"You look like James Dean now!" Her hair was whipping across her eyes, glints of brown through the tangle. I smiled at her, my cigarette held jauntily on one side of my mouth, laying an arm along the window as my comfort with the car increased.

I swore I was going to buy my own 'Cuda someday.

We roar through the outer edges of the county, dust from the dirt roads boiling around the car. All too soon, we were back by the river, gritty and laughing as I slow the car to a halt. I had never felt like that in my life, never. Reluctantly I parked, the ticking of the motor loud in the stillness of late afternoon along the water.

She sighed, a contented sound. "God, fast cars make me horny."

I froze, suddenly tongue tied, scared to say anything. Did she really just say that? She looked over at me and laughed, hitting my arm, "I'm just kidding. C'mon, lighten up!" I felt heat rising in my face, embarrassed suddenly at what a dummy I was sometimes. But geeze...I didn't think girls said stuff like that.

She was out of the car now, stretching, her small breasts pushing up against the fabric of her shirt as she did so. I was transfixed by the skin at the vee of her neck, where her throat disappeared into her shirt. Slowly, I opened the car door and climbed out to join her.

She was leaning against the hood, half seated on the bumper. She gave me a sly smile as I joined her. "You want a drink? I have something in my bag."

I was suddenly aware of my dust dry mouth, a drink sounded like just what I needed right then. She went back to the car and pulled her pocketbook out of the back. A small brown flask appeared from the depths of it. That kind of drink, not the pop I was looking for. I frowned as she opened it and took a long swallow.

"Ah, I was hoping for a drink, not that. I'm thirsty."

"Well drink this. It's liquid. Go on! Take it!" Her eyes glittered.

I took the bottle, slippery in my fingers and slowly put it to my nose. A sharp tang bit me, warning me. I started to pull it away from my face. Darlene's eyes never left me.

"What's the matter? Aren't you a man yet? Come on, drink up!"

I didn't want her thinking I was a pussy, not after driving her car like that, and I really kind of liked her now. I put the bottle to my lips and took a large swallow.

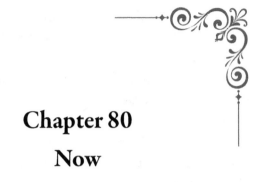

Chapter 80
Now

It was hard to drive with the big laptop open on the seat next to me. Twice I lost satellite signal and had to stop, the second time for almost thirty minutes. My gut twisted when I finally picked up the light again, finding it in a small raggedy community park that paralleled the river, maybe ten miles from me now. It was stationary.

I abandoned the side streets I had been creeping down and picked up the main route down the waterway. At this hour of the night, no one was out. A quarter moon hung low in the eastern sky; few houses showed lights. The neighborhoods shifted from large lots with old apple trees to derelict Mom & Pop stores, a brightly lit Shell station and firehouse before plunging back into the darkness that only fields and woods can make.

I pushed the Ford up to 75, the fastest I could go on this winding roadway, flecks of light exploding up from the reflective paint marks laid along the edges and middle. I flashed on another drive in a car with a big motor, flying through the dark in Darlene's Barracuda. I pushed that thought away hurriedly.

The park sign loomed to the left of me, the river lost in sight through the tangle of trees and brush that lined the banks, a black morass of naked, thorny branches, uninviting, evil, whispers in my lizard brain saying, "Go away. Now. Just leave before it's too late."

I slowed the truck to a crawl, extinguishing the lights, and crept along the outskirts searching for a roadway in. There; a darker rectangle in the murk, leading into the heart of the thicket.

The sky was black, stone black, even the slightest light extinguished by low hung clouds, clouds that swallowed up the light from the nearby town, relentlessly dark, tomb still and silent. My reluctance to enter the park rose another notch.

I stopped on the curb, some twenty feet from the entrance, unsure, no, unwilling, about my next move. Sweat beaded on my forehead. I woke up the laptop again, squinting as a blast of light hit my face. The spot glowed brightly, maybe a quarter of a mile from where I was parked. The park was ill defined in the map, just a green square marked out, a gray line traversing it to the river's edge.

A drop of sweat rolled off my cheek and landed on the keyboard.

Chapter 81
Then

The alcohol traced a fiery path down my throat, momentarily making my eyes tear up. I struggled not to cough, to look cool and mature. I hand the bottle back over to her. She watches me, amusement visible in her eyes as she took the slippery bottle back, expertly throwing a huge slug down her throat. No tears there. She handed it back to me.

The second slug was smoother, the third smoother still, full, flavorful. Lava burned in my belly, some of the weight I carried on my back started sliding off, slowly falling away. My hands stilled, the tremors that had threatened fading away along with my unease around her.

Why hadn't I liked her all these years? I eyed her now, hyper aware of her breasts pushing against the fabric of her shirt, points just visible where her nipples created mini tents. Dang...I reached for the bottle and took another pull.

"Hey, easy now!" She was laughing, reaching for the bottle. "We won't have any for later if you drink it all now." She removed it from my hand. Dumbly, I stared at her.

She slipped the flask back into her bag, bending into the window, a shapely, long legged rear end on view. My heart thumped an extra beat as the fire in my belly shifted lower.

She straightened up, stretching again, pushing her breasts out against the fabric as the ends of her shirt rose higher, revealing smooth flesh that disappeared into her skin tight jeans. Dimly, I realized that she was doing this deliberately, that she was displaying herself to me. Her psychic voice, the one I struggled to keep out of my cluttered brain was working its way in, calling, calling. I wasn't able to push it away, dimly wondered why as the alcohol buzzed up my neck and set fire to my cheeks.

Come on big boy. I know you want it. Give it to me.

Discomfort warred with my growing arousal, a desire that scared me. This wasn't how I pictured this happening, not this. I wasn't really sure how I pictured it, had entertained vague thoughts of finding a girl who was pretty, the two of us riding in my car, wind in her hair. But, wasn't that what had just happened? Except it wasn't really right, it was her car, her calling the shots. Not that that was a bad thing, was it?

She walked around the front of the car, back to the driver's side as I stood there tongue tied.

"Come on. Get in."

I open the passenger side door and climb unsteadily into the seat.

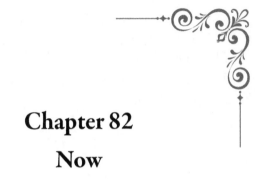

Chapter 82

Now

Feathery branches wove a lace ceiling over my head as I slowly shuffle stepped into the blackness, aged macadam uneven beneath my feet. The faintest light from the quarter moon illuminated the tips of the low trees I passed underneath, the ground beneath them devoid of light. I stop several times, straining to hear. Whispers, faint traffic sounds, then as I drew closer, water noises.

My gut curls into a tight knot as sweat trickles down my temples, leaving cold streaks in the chilly night air.

The road bends to the left, and faint light bloomed in front of me, light from distant houses reflecting off moving water, pinpoints of illumination shockingly bright on the shore line across from me. I stare at those for a moment, suddenly aware of people so close, sleeping peacefully, maybe still up watching television, as I creep through a tangle of trees to stop a killer.

A noise cuts through my reverie. I crouched lower and strain to hear. Water noises. Traffic hissing. And there, a glint of reflected light across the hood of a little car, parked deep in the shadows on the right of the lot. Another faint noise comes from it, a groan.

I felt in my pockets for my knife, a sorry weapon, but all I had. I crouched lower, my feet suddenly sure and silent, and head towards the car.

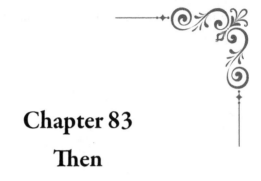

Chapter 83
Then

Oh my God! My hand closed around the naked flesh of her breast, her mouth crushed under mine, leg flung over my back, my rock hard erection pressing into her jean clad groin. Oh God!

We were in the back of the 'Cuda, sprawled across the enormous rear seat, parked under some weeping willows down along the edge of the field fronting the river, Darlene having guided the car down a bumpy farm track almost hidden in the weeds. Alcohol buzzed fiercely in my brain as her shirt was raised, revealing the hidden smooth freckled flesh I had been fantasizing about. My mouth joined my hand, closing around the pale mound of flesh as she groaned.

She took my hand, guiding it where she wanted it as she unbuckled my jeans, sliding them off of me expertly, my tremors back, oh God...

Dimly, I wondered why she seemed to know so much, why she wasn't more innocent than this. I decided I didn't care. Jeans puddled around my ankles, hers slid off one leg, my flesh super-heated as she grasped me firmly, pulling me into the hot, moist depths between her legs, oh God, oh God....

Chapter 84
Now

Another noise from the car, a moan, and my feet pick up speed, stealth going away now. The light from the river shows the outline of it, motion briefly visible inside, steamed over windows, more moans, and I am there, there, ripping the door open, blinding myself with the interior light as it floods across my face, across the faces of the two women in the back seat, naked from the waist down, a head framed by bent legs, wide scared eyes above the moisture smeared across her face as she struggles upright, a scream from the owner of the other pair of wide eyes at the sight of me, disheveled, a knife held firmly in my hand.

Stunned, I can only stare at the lovers for a moment before the one scream becomes two, with one reaching for something, reaching, fumbling, and then I am running, running, as a motor roars into life on the other side of the lot, and the dark shape of a small car accelerates away from the black hole it resided in, lights off, straight at me, straight at me, then gone, up the roadway, me running behind it as fast as I can, the screams of the women still ringing in my ears.

Shit. Shit. Shit.

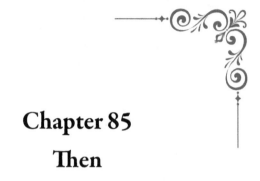

Chapter 85

Then

Suddenly my life was a lot more interesting than it had been. Darlene was on fire, insatiable, and we got together almost every day. Fields, tree lines, parking lots, the number of places where she took me grew and grew.

The number of things she did to me grew too.

The first time was kind of a mess. I came almost immediately, as soon as I had sunk fully into her. She had simply laughed and taken my hand, showing me what she wanted me to do to her.

From hands, she started teaching me what to do with my mouth. And then she showed me what she could do with her mouth.

I couldn't think. I couldn't worry about anything else except seeing her again and again, especially as my skills grew and I became able to hang on longer and longer. I wanted, needed to prove to her that I was a man now, not a little kid. Nothing else mattered. Nothing.

On a Wednesday, about a month after we started fooling around, on a day she wasn't gonna be around, I pedaled over to Carl's. I was fidgety, horny, needed something to distract me. He was working when I got there, underneath a big old boat of an Impala, a stream of oil throwing dark glints as it cascaded into the oil barrel underneath the car.

I said hi, and he pointed me towards a Pinto, sitting in the lot with the exhaust system hanging down on the ground. I happily got it in on the lift and started taking the old exhaust off.

Carl appeared at my shoulder, his eyes troubled, far away. "Hey, G.L., let's take a break and grab ourselves a pop."

I was a bit taken aback at that, I hadn't hardly gotten started and he wanted to take a break? Still, this was Carl, and I would do anything he asked me to, so I nodded and wiped my hands off on a rag and followed him. He pulled two sodas from the cooler, a Coke for me, a Root Beer for him, and headed into the office instead of out front like we usually did. It crossed my mind that he maybe didn't want people seeing me out there with him.

My new found good mood began to wither a little bit.

The office was piled with papers, the fog of years of cigarettes permeating every surface in there. I sat down in the rickety roller chair and began spinning it. Carl pulled his creaky wooden office chair out from behind the desk and shoved some papers aside so he could set his soda down. He still looked somber, troubled.

I cracked my pop and took a slug, wishing it had the fiery rum Darlene liked in the sugary drink. I really like that stuff now, so much so I had taken to getting the odd bottle myself whenever I could talk Denny Holmes into buying one for me when he was heading into the liquor store. Denny was a drunk and would pretty much do anything for a couple bucks, a fact we under aged kids were finding out. Only a few months until I was eighteen and finally legal anyway. I waited for that date with impatience.

Carl lit a cigarette, handed me the pack and settled back in his chair. I waited, knowing that something was up.

"So, Ger, how's it going these days?" All awkward like, like he didn't see me every week. I just shrugged. "S'ok I guess."

"You been looking for work?"

I scowled. That was a sore subject for me. No one in this piss ant town was going to hire me and he knew that. Even he wouldn't hire me, although, to be fair, it was because he had no money.

I didn't bother answering. He knew better'n that.

"I was thinking that maybe I would talk to my friend Jon over in Red Hook, see if he had something open. You would like working there. He does a lot of imported stuff."

Red Hook? That was a good thirty miles away. At that moment, the last thing I wanted to do was be thirty miles away, especially if it meant Darlene was here and I wasn't. I didn't respond, just lowered my chin and took a drag off my cigarette.

He took another hit, setting the bottle down carefully. The silence stretched. Without looking at me he said, "So...I been hearing you're spending a lot of time with Louie's daughter, Darlene."

Hearing that come out of his mouth startled me. As far as I knew, we had been pretty careful about being seen a lot together. I scowled a little bit. "Who told you that?"

"Pert near everyone who knows her has mentioned it." He was looking at me now, his expression dead serious.

I felt a burst of an odd pride mixed with a bit of guilt over what we were doing. So I was getting laid? What of it? I looked at Carl, shrugged and smirked. "Guess you caught me then." Man to man like.

Except he didn't smile back. He had a serious, almost scared look. "Ger, you're playing with fire. I don't know or want to know what you been doing with her but stop, stop right now and I mean today."

"What? Why? It's no one's business what Darlene and I do."

"Well, let me enlighten you, Ger. There's more people involved than just you. And if you don't quit, things are going to get really unpleasant. Just...trust me on this one. Find another girlfriend, find a real girlfriend instead of that....her."

"Why? What's wrong with Darlene? She's been really good to me. I ain't ditching her."

Carl's lips tightened and he was silent for a moment. Then, "Ok. Ok. Have you at least been using birth control?"

My cheeks flamed, hearing that come out of his mouth. Birth control? Why the hell was he telling me about birth control? My discomfort increased as I realized that no one had ever talked to me about it. Oh sure, I heard other kids talking about it when I was in school. And Darlene had said not to worry about anything, so I took her word for it. Truth be told, other than rubbers and pills, I really didn't know anything about birth control. I guessed she was using pills, because I sure as hell hadn't been wearing any rubbers. I felt the heat in my face increase. Carl watched me silently.

"Ger....you do know how to protect yourself, right?"

"Sure." I mumbled into my pop bottle.

"Good. Because you ain't an exclusive with her, if you catch my drift. And anyone she's with is gonna be the same as if you slept with them too."

What? I stared at him across the cluttered desk. He looked away, setting his empty root beer bottle down.

"I got somethin' else to tell you too..."

Chapter 86
Now

Stupid, stupid, stupid, stupid! I watched the dot speed away as the Toyota flew up 9W, the screams of the two women still ringing in my ears. Stupid! I never looked, never thought there would be two cars in the lot at that hour, never ever even thought about it. Stupid!

My breath rattled in my chest as I struggled to dampen my growing panic. I was crouched in my truck, tucked in alongside a row of cars and trucks lining the street in the center of a tiny hamlet, some five miles south of the park. The dot was now about ten miles south of me, moving along at a good clip. I watched the green light as it traveled down 9W. Go back to the park? Or start tracking the car? Where was she? Or had there even been a she this time? Was he still hunting, or was there a body carved into lumpy flesh lying on the ground over there?

A police car rocketed past heading north, red and blue lights strobing, silent except for engine whine, the wind from it rocking my truck. A second one followed a moment later.

S.L. FUNK

That decided that. With shaking hands, I turned the key in the ignition and pulled the truck away from the curb, heading south.

Chapter 87

Then

For once, my thoughts weren't Darlene, Darlene, Darlene. My thoughts were crazy, jumbled as I pedaled my bicycle back home as fast as my legs could go. Gramma, Gramma, Gramma, did she know? Would she tell me if she knew? Did she know?

Anger bubbled in me, hot and sticky. When was everyone gonna stop treating me like a kid? If it hadn't been for Carl telling me about who Tom Mosely had seen night before last, I'd be going along all fat dumb and happy. Unguarded.

She knew. I could tell as soon as I walked into the kitchen. She knew; she knew and she was sick about it. Her face looked gray and drawn. I stood in the doorway, filling it, staring at her. She looked up at me, looking old, scared, tiny. Her mouth moved, then with unaccustomed solemnity, "Gerry. I got something to tell you. Sit down." She swallowed noisily, gestured towards the battered Formica kitchen table.

I stayed standing, looking at her, seeing her for the first time in a long time, seeing how aged and fragile she was becoming. She had always been this noisy powerhouse in my life, noisy and protective of me. I had resented her for a long time for it, resented the ways she tried to protect me, the ways she tried to shield me. I realized now as I looked at her that I was it in her life, her everything, her only family now. Anger melted away, leaving behind a strange feeling. Responsibility. Responsibility and anger at myself for being stupid for so long.

I didn't sit. I just looked at her and said, "I know. He's here again. Here." And there wasn't a damn thing the police were going to do about it either, that I was sure of. HE was like smoke, dissipating the moment a breath hit him.

She looked up at me, tears glittering in her eyes. Her shoulders sagged in around herself, frail wings curled around her birdlike body. She opened her mouth, closed it, then, "I won't let him do anything to you! I won't!" a drop spilled over the edge, she wiped it away hurriedly.

I didn't answer. I stepped forward and wrapped my arms around her, holding her against me, aware of the fluttering in her chest, the bony knobs on her shoulders. She hiccuped once, then tears flowed. I held her, held her, pressed my cheek against her head, mumbled to her. "Gramma, it's alright, it's alright. He ain't gonna do anything to us, I guarantee it."

"Isn't, Gerry, not ain't." Gramma, always on autopilot with my grammar. Instead of anger, I felt a laugh, building inside, bubbling up. It snuck out and I giggled, snorted into her thin hair. She snuffled for a moment, then it trickled out of her too, laughter, mixed with tears, her face buried against my chest.

I whispered into her rose scented scalp, "He's not going to do anything to us, not now, not ever. You can trust me on that, Gramma."

Chapter 88
Now

The light moved steadily south, at a fast clip along the river, heading towards 84 and the Newburgh bridge, his escape road back into Connecticut. I pushed the old truck along as fast as I dared, wary of police, terrified of losing my one chance at the son of a bitch. Then, he slowed, slowed and turned off, off on a spur of a road that crossed by trailer parks and open fields of stubble, dropping down to a boat launch across the river from where the Vanderbilt's built their mansions along the shore of the Hudson. I knew the road, knew it from days of fishing and drinking in my younger years. It would be a lonely stretch. I pushed the throttle harder as the light slowed then became stationary.

Right along the banks of the river.

Five minutes, seven minutes, the truck rocked and whined, lonely clusters of houses and trailer parks flashing past, punctuated by neon from gas station canopies. The light stayed put. Eleven minutes out, as I closed in on the final two miles to the intersection, it moved again, moved quickly back up the road, rejoining 9W and speeding south again, south towards the interstate. I saw street signs glowing in my headlights, the intersection where he had just been, as he sped away, a good three miles south, moving fast. Go, stop, go, stop, my foot wavered over the pedal, the truck slowing almost of its own volition. With a muttered curse, I yanked the wheel at the last minute, sending the Ford careening left into the side road, rear wheels slipping as traction left them. Rocks pinged off the undercarriage as I slammed into the turn. The truck shuddered, then straightened, gathering speed again.

Lone lights pierced the darkness as I slowed, searching for the road, newly built McMansions vying with an aging trailer park, the denser darkness of fields and woods between them. A swath of road to the right, the spur that led to the river's edge. A glance at the computer screen confirmed it, even as it showed the light slowing and turning off 9W, off onto 44, the Mid-Hudson not the Newburgh bridge his route. I swore. I hadn't seen that coming, hadn't seen it at all.

The truck had slowed again, slowed almost to a halt. Dread began to creep up my spine as I stared at the blackness that my headlights burrowed through. I swore the night felt suddenly alive, pulsating, a giant beating heart full of evil. I didn't want to go down this road, no sir, not at all.

A tiny pond broke the blackness to my right, water glinting like blood, dark diamonds dancing across the surface. I fumbled, then switched the lights off, feeling too exposed. Ahead of me, the dark tunnel of the narrow road widened into the dark black pool of a parking lot. The computer screen bathed my face in white fire. Flinching, momentarily blinded, I pushed the lid shut, and rolled the truck to a stop in a broad half turn, killing the motor.

Silence. Blackness so complete it was like sensory depri-
vation. I rolled my window down, cold air slapping the side
of my suddenly sweating face. My eyes adjusted slowly; my
ears quicker. Noise, faint noise, traffic hiss from somewhere,
faint and intrusive. Almost inaudible noises from the river
now, a burble of water as it tumbled around an unseen ob-
struction. My eyes could make out water, water and faint
pinpricks of light across the river where the road ended at the
oily surface of the Hudson.

My heart hammered triple time in my chest, raggedly,
leaving me gasping for air like I had run a hundred yards. I
swallowed, shockingly loud in the smelly cab of my Ford. I
stunk, stunk of sweat, stunk of fear.

The wind hissed faintly through dead leaves hanging on
the oak trees that lined one side of the lot, trees I remembered drinking beer under as I packed up my fishing gear. A
hundred million years ago.

I fumbled for the interior light switch, rolling it down
to the off position before I opened the door. The cold sliced,
welcoming. The sense of wrongness sliced, terrifying. I stood
on wobbly legs and thought about giving up, just giving up
and driving away, never doing anything more with this, just
finally packing my stuff and leaving, leaving for good. An image of a cabin on the flank of the mountain beckoned, mocking me in its surreal coloring. "You'll never be here," it whispered. "You're too much of a pussy to ever come here."

I carefully closed the door, the snick loud in the silence,
my hammering heart louder.

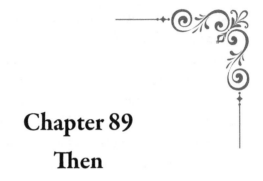

Chapter 89
Then

Red Alert. I once read a book about how soldiers were on Red Alert. I thought I knew what that meant, but I didn't, not really, not until now. Gramma and I, we were on Red Alert now.

We talked that night, really talked, until the light was long gone from the sky. She told me things I never knew. I told her things she didn't know I knew. She wiped her eyes until they were red and swollen, but she couldn't wipe away the iron in them, the determination. I looked at this noisy old lady I thought I knew, in awe. I wondered what she was like as a young woman, what she went through when Grampa died, and then her only child.

And now, she was in danger of losing everything. The weight of that lay heavy on my shoulders. We were on high alert now. And I was in hunting mode, but I couldn't tell her that.

Darlene came by a couple days after that night. I hadn't realized until I saw her sitting in the 'Cuda at the curb in the flat light of the morning that she hadn't come around, hadn't called. Oddly, I hadn't even noticed. A week ago, I'da been climbing the walls. Now, I just looked at her.

Her face looked puffy; a cold sore dimpled her upper lip. I felt flat; this wasn't the time or place for her. Carl's words from a couple days ago, damn, just a couple days ago, floated through my head. Time for that later I guessed.

"Gerry! Aren't you glad to see me?" Petulant, a hint of a whine in her voice. I was tinkering with Gramma's car, doing an impromptu tuneup for her. Unspoken between us, we wanted the car running right in case we had to rely on it getting us out of the way.

Or getting me to him. I had gotten my permit last week, a license to hunt to my way of thinking. I wiped my hands on the rag and closed the hood gently. "Hey." I said finally, the only thing I could think of.

"Hey? That's all you can say to me is 'hey'?"

I shook my head, tongue tied and clumsy suddenly, awkward. "Nah, I mean, no. What's up, Darlene?"

She cocked her head and looked at me for a moment. "I've had a bad couple days, Ger. I need to talk about it." She looked rough, wearing a man's button down shirt untucked over torn jeans and untied sneakers. Like she threw on the closest things she could find to wear. I looked back at the house. Gramma was home today, home and fussing over some bread in the kitchen. She liked to bake when she was upset. We had a cupboard full of freshly baked things now. "I dunno, Darlene, my Gramma's home. I shouldn't leave her alone."

"What, that never stopped you before? Don't you want to talk to me?" And she burst into tears.

Oh holy moly! Darlene crying wasn't something I had ever seen before, ever wanted to see before. "Oh hey, hey, hey, come on. No, don't cry." I had crossed around to the driver's side window, crouched down, rubbing her hair. I realized it wasn't her usual shiny mane. Instead it lay lifeless, oily like she hadn't showered recently. I felt kinda sick at the feel. She wiped her nose on her sleeve, snot glistening like a pearl. "Gerry, we really, really need to go for a ride."

Trapped. I was trapped, the deer in the headlights. I couldn't say no, didn't want to say yes. What I said was, "Lemme tell Gramma I'm going out for a bit."

Ten minutes later, Gramma's voice still ringing in my ears, I clattered down the rickety front steps and crossed the sidewalk to the car. Darlene's tears had dried away, leaving a sullen look behind. She fired up the car, the motor cutting through my deepening dread, the heavy throb of the 318 singing to me even through the pain. She shifted into drive and jerked away from the curb.

She didn't say anything, nothing at all as we criss crossed the streets in my neighborhood, heading towards the outskirts. She drove past the side of Carl's garage, eyes straight ahead as the 'Cuda rumbled past. I thought I saw motion through the office window, like someone looking out the window at us. I felt redness spreading up my cheeks as the memory of that conversation prickled at me. I said nothing too, nothing back at her to break the increasingly awkward silence that lay between us.

About three miles outside of town, she swung down a rutted dirt track, a track I had only learned about recently thanks to her, a track that had led to hours of fevered exploration of the hidden places on her body, the hidden places in my soul. Despite the way she was acting, I felt a stirring in my groin as flashes of memory erupted. I reached over and put a hand on her knee. She didn't shake it off, but she didn't take it and place it on her crotch either. She just ignored it.

Willow branches scraped the roof of the car as she guided it in under cover. Daylight was muted under here, the cloudy light turning gray from the drooping branches. I smelled the sharp tang of dried leaves and grass; a last burst of summer swathed the land.

She cut the motor and sat silently, fiddling with her shirttails. I patted her knee. "Darlene. What is it?" She sniffled a bit, picked at her torn jeans. "You know I really like you, Ger."

"Yeah, I like you too." I felt a foreboding feeling. She wiped her nose again, sitting up. "Well, what I'm about to say is gonna be really, really hard because I like you."

My stomach sagged. Gritting my teeth, I stayed silent and waited for it. I felt her swirling around outside my brain, swirling and needy. I struggled to keep the curtain firmly drawn. I didn't want to hear what was coming; of that I was certain.

She drew a breath, a hiccuping one. "Gerry. I'm in trouble."

"What did you do? Trouble with who?"

"Oh Jesus..." She threw her head back against the seat back, eyes closed. "Are you really this dumb or are you just giving me a hard time?" She groaned, grabbing a fistful of her hair and pulled on it, hard. Bewildered, stung by her dumb remark, all I could do was stare at her, mute.

"Gerry...I'm IN TROUBLE! I'm pregnant! You knocked me up!"

Pregnant? What? I stared at her, my jaw dropping. Pregnant? Holy...holy shit. Pregnant? An image in my mind suddenly, blue eyes looking up at me over a toothless grin, my daughter's tiny fist closing around my finger. Pregnant? Wow...

"Darlene, are you sure? I thought...I thought....but you said you were on the pill...I mean...this isn't a false alarm is it?"

"Of course I'm sure! I haven't had my period for seven weeks now, and this morning I started throwing up! How much surer do I have to be?"

Pregnant...wow. Wow. That was gonna change everything. It didn't scare me like I thought it would. In fact...it was kinda cool. I flashed on the reactions from Gramma, her parents and friends, pushed them away. How would we afford it? Maybe we could go to Red Hook together, I could work for Jon and we could live in an apartment of our own just...the three of us. Pregnant...a weird feeling began rising in my chest, a poignant, full feeling.

I slid across the seat to be closer to her, hooking an arm around her neck and pulling her into my chest. She sobbed as she leaned into me, sobbed and clutched my shirt with both hands. Pregnancy made chicks weird, I'd been told, all those hormones and stuff. No wonder she looked so ragged. I had to take care of her. I rocked her back and forth gently as she sobbed.

"Darlene, listen, it's okay. We'll be okay. I can get us a place over in Red Hook, we can have our own place. I can work for this guy, I know he'll pay me, pay me good. We can raise our baby alright, don't worry about a thing..."

She stiffened in my arms, pushed away from me, shaking her head, no, no, no. "Are you crazy? I'm not having any baby! I'm only 19! I don't WANT this baby! No, you have to give me money so I can get it taken care of. My friend Sheila told me about this place over in Poughkeepsie, you don't need your parent's permission, they can just take care of it, but it's $200 and I need to do it now..."

There was a dull roaring sound in my head, like the ocean rumbling up on a gravel beach. She couldn't be serious, couldn't be, this was our baby, MY baby, she couldn't be serious that she was going to just throw it away like a discarded cigarette butt. My grip on the curtain in my brain began to slip, the fabric sliding back, her chatter filling my head...

I can't BELIEVE this retard thinks I'm keeping this fucking kid! Damn, damn, damn, I didn't think he would want this, thought he would just give me the money, just give me the MONEY damnit because Jimmy sure as shit doesn't have any, and I'm already in the second trimester, damn it all, if I wait any fucking longer I'm going to have to head down to the city to get it done...shit..shit...should have done this sooner..come on dummy!

I recoiled from her, my stomach rolling with acid as my conversation with Carl echoed in my head, *"Ger, you're playing with fire. I don't know or want to know what you been doing with her but stop, stop right now and I mean today."*

"What? Why? It's no one's business what Darlene and I do."

"Well, let me enlighten you, Ger. There's more people involved than just you. And if you don't quit, things are going to get really unpleasant. Just...trust me on this one. Find another girlfriend, find a real girlfriend instead of that....her."

Jimmy...holy shit, what was happening here? I stared at her, cold, chilled to the core, wanting desperately for something I knew in my heart didn't exist even now. My daughter's blue eyes were gone, replaced with Jimmy's brown ones. "I can't do this." Four of the hardest words I ever uttered.

"What do you mean, you can't do this? You HAVE to do this! Gerry, I can't have a kid at 19! My life will be OVER! I swear to God, if you don't help me, I'm gonna kill myself!"

I cringed at her words, cringed at the blood in them, yet felt a heaviness. I had struggled to not die when I was barely old enough to be a kid not a baby, and she was talking about killing herself because of a baby?

"Well, what about putting it up for adoption then?" I couldn't let go of those blue eyes and toothless grin. Gramma would help me take care of her. She had to be mine, had to be. "What about you have her and I take her?"

"Are you out of your FREAKING MIND? Do you think I would give you a freaking baby like it's a...it's a...puppy or something? Gerry, you wouldn't know the first thing about taking care of a baby! No!" She was shaking her head now, resolved, sure of herself. "No. It has to be this way. It's for the best."

I stared at her for a long moment. "No."

"What do you mean, no? You HAVE to help me out! You're the one got me in trouble!"

"Well, I'm not so sure about that." Color flared in her pale cheeks.

"Gerry...I...you...what the hell are you saying?"

"Jimmy. That's what I'm saying. Jimmy's smack in the middle of all of this, isn't he?"

"You...ASSHOLE!" Her hand was a blur, the crack loud in the car as a stinging sensation burned across my mouth. I caught her hand as she drew it back again. She kicked at me, screaming unintelligibly, her rage overflowing, roaring in around my guard, knocking me down with her angst.

I can't believe you're doing this! I hate your guts! I hate you hate you,hateyouhateyouhateyou! I wish you had died! I wish he blew your brains out! I can't believe I screwed you all month! Damn you, damn you, damn you!

And a pair of blue eyes with a toothless grin stared up from me from the bottom of a whirlpool, relentlessly getting sucked to the bottom of an unfathomable lake, never to be seen again. A piece of my heart went with her.

Chapter 90
Now

I waited for my eyes to adjust as fully as they could to the dense darkness. The river gurgle grew louder, then fainter. Pinpricks of light waved through naked branches across the river. Leaves rattled past, kicked up by a puff of wind, shockingly loud. I scanned the boat ramp.

Pavement, dappled with holes, led down to the oily surface of the water. No cars this time, no darker shapes under the trees, no movement, nothing. Just me and my nightmare.

To my right, about thirty feet away were the oak trees that lined the lot, two battered picnic tables underneath them darker shapes against the wood line. Across from where I stood, low bushes with scraggly trees that separated a sand filled creek from the boat launch. I slowly edged away from the truck. The hair on the back of my neck prickled, electric nerve endings sparking. Damn, it was dark here.

A vision of the dot racing away filled my head again, you're too late, leave here, go after him, don't stay here. I wavered, halting about mid ramp. Water gurgled. Leaves rattled. And something else...not a sound, a smell. I sniffed the air like a dog, seeking it, turning to track it, to place it. Somewhere behind me on 9W a car hissed past.

I had never felt so alone in my life.

Slowly, I moved again, one step, two, trying to catch the elusive odor. Nothing. River stink and body odor. The water rolled right ahead of me now, light refracting off the surface like a thousand black diamonds. I scanned the edge of the pavement, another time, another body of water imprinted on my brain, sure that I was going to see a small bundle lying there.

The pavement was empty.

Slowly, methodically, I covered the right side of the lot, then the left, peering hard at the shadows for a darker one, for anything that was out of place. Nothing.

The truck's skin was cool under my hand as I stopped next to it again. I drew a deep breath, then another. The desire, no, need, for something sharp and alcoholic burned through me so fiercely for a moment that my knees went weak. I stayed still, stone still, breathing rapidly as I waited for the moment to pass. That smell again, stronger now, familiar yet unidentified. I needed a cigarette.

Leaning against the quarter panel on the passenger's side of the truck, facing the ragged line of oak trees, I fumbled one out and put it to my lips. A book of matches came to the surface of my pocket grudgingly, and I struck the sulpher tip against the strip. A brilliant flare of light, white and yellow, blinding me as it illuminated the immediate area around me, the truck body, the ground, the hand that protruded from beneath my vehicle, black fluid glistening on the palm.

I yelled and leapt away, my heart triple hammering in my chest, oh my God, oh my God....the match had landed on the ground, still lit, the feeble light it cast reflecting on black nails, fingers curled in to the palm, a slender arm disappearing into the shadows under the truck. My knees shook violently.

Oh my God...I stared at the hand as the match burned out, leaving the after image in my retinas. Oh my God...

My hands shook so badly I couldn't get the key in the ignition. Once, twice, on the third try it finally seated itself. The motor roared to life, the starter grinding as I held the key too long, noise, noise, noise, shocking and disorienting, oh my God! I grabbed the lever...drive? Reverse? A jerk forward, then I changed my mind, put it in reverse. I couldn't, wouldn't drive over that fragile arm, oh God!

Cranking the wheels towards the driver's side, I slowly edged the truck backwards, in a taut turn. No thumps came from under the tires. A darker bundle appeared in front of me, dark and wet looking. Trembling, I put the truck in park and turned the parking lights on.

She wasn't more than a kid, at least I don't think she was. I could see her face, smooth and slack looking, her mouth open as if in surprise. She lay on her back, her left arm outstretched, her right folded haphazardly across what was left of her midsection. Bile bubbled up in my throat as I realized that I was looking at what was supposed to be hidden inside of her, great loops of guts spilling out of her belly in an untidy pile, the puddle of black liquid around her framing her like a negative image of a Virgin Mary.

My knees gave out finally, I sank to the ground hands flat on the pebbled surface. Images, impressions, battled with my brain, sending snake like tendrils inside, no, no, no, I don't want this, no!

No, no, no, please mister, no! Oh God, oh God, if you let me go I'll promise to never run away again, please mister, no, I'll do anything you want, no, no, NO NO NO! Oh God, why did you desert me? NOOOOOOOOOOOOOOOOOO......

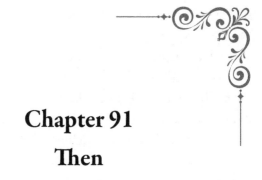

Chapter 91
Then

It was a long walk back to town from where she had pushed me out of the car underneath the weeping willow trees. I had simply stood there and watched as she bounced away up the rutted track, the car jerking and wallowing, a grief I hadn't known I could possess rising up in my chest.

Not for Darlene.

Finally, my feet began to move, almost of their own volition, left, right, left. I trudged up the dusty track to the gravel road, turned left and started walking.

I stared at the ground as I marched along, left foot, right foot, puffs of dust. Twice I lit cigarettes, the pack miserably close to empty now. My gut was empty, stone cold. I relished the lack of feeling, reveled in it. I was going to go to Red Hook, gonna go, take that job and start a new life, maybe get trained as a factory mechanic, move to a bigger city, work in a dealership. I would finally buy myself a muscle car, maybe a Camaro.

Not a Barracuda. Never a Barracuda now.

My head was hanging, hair low over my eyes, lost in my head when I realized that there was a vehicle slowing alongside me, the first one since I had started walking an eon ago. I looked up warily, a blue Ford pickup truck, window rolled down, black haired arm over the door.

Dale. Carl's mechanic, black eyes over a dark scraggly mustache, mocking light in them. My stomach flipped. He didn't like me, didn't like me at all, and I didn't like him either. He was...oily, always watching when I was there, always looked like he was gonna say something smart.

"Hey, kid. What the hell you doing out here?" a smirk.

"Nothing." I mumbled, looking down at my chest. What the heck could I say? I was still a good six miles outside town. I kept walking.

"Hey! Look, you want a ride, or are you into some kind of health kick here?"

My feet slowed to a halt. A ride would make things a lot easier, but I wasn't keen on getting in the truck with him. Still....Gramma was alone, and I was already late.

"Okay. Thanks." I crossed around to the passenger's side and crawled into the cab. It smelled of cigars and booze, sharp, old. Dale looked at me again, amusement evident in his expression, and shifted the column lever into first. He was dressed for work, DALE written in block letters on the stained gray shirt Carl had for his mechanic's uniforms. I realized it was lunch time, that Dale went home for lunch every day. I hadn't realized he lived out this side of town.

I looked out the window at the abandoned, overgrown apple orchards as the truck picked up speed, grief again threatening to well up inside of me. I shoved it down.

He stuck a cigar in his mouth and lit it, the clouds of acrid smoke blowing over my face, making my eyes water. At least, I told myself that was why there was so much moisture in them suddenly. I waved it away and looked out the window again.

"So. What happened? You and your girlfriend have a tiff or something?" he chortled. "Kid, you better learn that no woman should get the upper hand, ever. They're all bitches." He blew a cloud of stinky smoke out, secure in himself.

I glanced at him, couldn't think of a thing to say. Undeterred, he went on, taking my silence for rapt interest. "You get yourself a bitch, you keep her on a short leash. Your first mistake was picking one that has more than you. Shit, boy. You been looking like a joke, hanging all over that little piece of work." He chuckled, mean sounding. "Although, at least she been letting you drive that car some. Hoo wah! Pussy and a 'Cuda. Well, guess I can't fault you too much for that part." He looked over at me, where I sat in a growing rage. He smirked, black mustache twitching. "Looks like maybe you two had some kind of falling out huh?"

"Shut up." My voice finally scratched out past the growing lump in my throat.

He laughed. "Shut up? Shit, maybe I should have said something sooner, before you found yourself walking back to town. Listen up, boy. I'm gonna tell you something important here. Women are bitches. Got it? They're just good for two things: a piece of ass and to keep your house clean. They step outta line, you put them back in. Your mistake, well one of them that is, was you didn't backhand that little shit the first time she got smart with you. Trust me, one good pop and they listen up but good." He took a deep hit on his cigar, coils of moldy smoke filling the cab. "Your other mistake was taking up with the town whore." My jaw clenched, painfully.

He looked over at me, amusement evident. "Yup, me an' Carl been watching you now for a month. Hell, the whole town has. That girl spreads her legs easier'n cream cheese, you catch my drift. Sure hope you been using industrial strength rubbers on her."

We were still about three miles outside of town now, back on the paved roads that offered faster access and more traffic. I could hitchhike from here. "Let me out here." I said through stiff lips.

He just laughed. "Oh come on, kid. Don't get all twisted up on me. Shit, I'm just tryin' to give you some friendly advice here." He stubbed the cigar, the tires hummed on the pavement. Ahead of us, on the right a small honky tonk bar came into view, a handful of cars on this Thursday afternoon.

As I stared resolutely out the window, a scrawny man climbed out of an old Ford LTD, gray, greasy hair in a knot on his neck, a rolling limp evident in his walk. He paused to light a cigarette as we rocked past, dust blowing out from under the Ford, and our eyes met. Mean, small piggish eyes. Eyes I recognized, knew well.

HIS eyes.

Chapter 92
Now

Sunlight crawled reluctantly over the low hill, shrouded in shredded clouds as I lay sleepless, shivering. The bed was cold, cold to the core, freezing me to the bone. No matter how many blankets I pulled over me, I couldn't warm up. My teeth chattered relentlessly.

Finally, I gave up, rolling upright, a wave of nausea sending me running for the bathroom, a race that I lost scant inches from the toilet. My vomit splashed across the linoleum, I dry heaved on the floor until there was nothing left but pain and fear.

The longest four hours of my life.

I barely remembered how I got home, how I managed to drive here, to get inside, into my bed. My clothing lay in a heap on the bedroom floor. I kicked it aside as I staggered back into my bedroom, looking for something warm to wrap around my shivering torso.

The jeans had black stains on the knees, black and red. More dry heaves threatened.

I wasn't drunk, that was the hell of it, wasn't drunk, wasn't hung over, although I desperately wished I was. I wished I was dead right now, dead and buried, no longer subject to this living hell I was buried in. Dead....she rose in my vision again, unable to stop her, her slack face with her lips in an 'o' of surprise, her fingers curled in towards her palm, her guts...

I remembered leaving, leaving in a hurry, leaving like the fires of hell were burning on my door. It was pure luck I hadn't run into a cop anyplace, pure luck. I'd'a been in deep shit.

At some point, mere miles from home, I remembered the laptop, the tracking device. I pulled over at the Gas N'Go, my eyes burning at the sickly light from the station's canopy and fumbled the computer up off the floor and into my lap. Dimly, I had wondered if it was damaged during the flight away, away, away, nothing mattered but getting as much distance between...her...and me as I could.

It hadn't been. The battery was almost gone, a scant line showing in the icon, but it fired up, fired up and turned the tracking program on. I looked in the map that showed, the one that went out east of Poughkeepsie. No blinking light.

My hands shook so much it took me three tries before I could re-center the map to include Connecticut. And there it was. Stationary, green dot pulsing, 67 Stanton Way, New Fairfield. My stomach heaved thinking of him climbing into bed beside his puffy faced blonde society wife, his hands still warm from pulling her intestines through the hole in her belly. Maybe he had sex with his wife then, turned on by his night's activity.

An image rose unbidden, of a threesome from hell, him, her and his disemboweled lover all tangled in a heap on a bed piled high in stinking guts.

I flung the truck door open and vomited all over the parking lot.

I wrapped a blanket around me, shivering like I had a fever, my face hot and bright feeling. On shaking legs I left the bedroom and made my way to the tiny living room where my couch groaned under piles of newspapers and take out boxes. I shoved a stack to the floor and sagged down in a corner, hugging myself against the chills that racked me, closed my eyes against the painful light.

The batteries. The batteries, they would last maybe two weeks according to the information included on the insert, a fact that hadn't seemed important at the time because I had assumed that I'd only need it for a night.

The police. Shit. I needed to tell them, needed to warn them about the Toyota. Even now, someone, maybe an early morning walker with their dog, was going to walk down that macadam roadway and end up in hell. I needed to tell them so they could get their forensics people on it, get the prints from the Toyota's tires to match up with the tire tracks at the side of the road, get his DNA to match against the spit that speckled her face from his rage. My eyes opened. Tracks. DNA. A fragmented memory, a cigarette flying from my mouth, bloody knees on my jeans, my truck tires inches from the lifeless bundle, a bundle swathed in blood. The ceiling over my head was a blur as I stared through it. Oh my God...how could I have been so stupid?

I had to get him now, had to. Before they came to get me.

Chapter 93
Then

I was breathing heavily as I jogged the last hundred feet back to the honky tonk. Dale had been a jerk, refusing to stop and let me out until we were back at Carl's. He'd smirked as I took off at a fast jog, back the way we'd just come. "Forget somethin'?" A weasley laugh followed. I ignored him; I was already on Red Alert, gotta get back there now, now, NOW!

A mile and a half in, it occurred to me I should have gone the three blocks home and taken the car. I should have a plan, some kind of strategy, a way to take him down. My mind was blank, filled with a white wall of noise. I kept jogging.

The place looked sad and dreary on this mid-week mid-afternoon, dreary and hard. One story, a ragged hand painted sign 'The Joint' in fading red paint, dirty single windows lining the front, roof line sagging and flaking. There were a half dozen cars in the front lot, none younger than ten years old.

The LTD was still there.

I crossed the warped porch to the metal lined door and tugged it open, releasing a blast of cigarette and beer scented stale air. Inside I paused, blinded at the transition from sunny afternoon to perpetual twilight.

Shades were drawn in front of all of the windows, neon light in blue and red behind the bar, an elaborate lamp with a team of Clydesdales overhead. The clack and clatter of pool balls came from the other side of the room where two skinny guys in work clothes banged balls around in a bored fashion.

Two more people sat in front of the bar, turning to look at me as I entered the room. The bartender was a guy I recognized from Carl's place, Mitch, Mitch Slocum. He did a double take when he saw me, a frown appearing. "Hey G.L. Whadda want? You eighteen yet? 'Cuz if'n you ain't, you cain't stay here."

I glanced at the people at the bar, a tired looking woman and a slack faced man, both of them leaning close and murmuring to each other again. The pools balls started clacking as one of the men racked up a new set. I cautiously crossed over to the bar, a wary eye on the others and beckoned Mitch over. He set down the beer glass he was drying with a scowl but came over.

"Look kid, I like you and all, but I know you ain't eighteen yet."

I shook my head, still having trouble catching my breath. "No, no, that's not it, I don't want anything to drink." A lie, at that moment the desire was fierce, sharp. I looked around again. "There was this guy I saw coming in here, older guy, long hair in a ponytail, limping. He still here?"

Mitch's face hardened. "What do ya want with him? You don't want him for nothin'. Besides, he ain't even here anymore." A lie. I could FEEL him there suddenly.

I looked at Mitch steadily. Something in my face made him pull back a step, nervous suddenly. His hands darted around, picking up and setting down a coaster, straightening an already straight ashtray. "Look, G.L. If you ain't eighteen, you can't be here. Period. Now either gimme some ID or git gone." He jabbed his chin towards the door. "Nothin' personal."

"Where is he?" A cold fire I hadn't known I had was burning in my belly, burning bright and hot. The light in the room began to pulse around the edges. "Where is he?"

"I told ya, he ain't even here." His voice raised, the people at the bar looking over at us, curiosity on her face, blank stare on his.

I heard a toilet flush, somewhere down a dim hallway behind the pool table, an opening I hadn't seen before. I looked past Mitch's face as he paled fractionally. Behind the grubby guy in canvas jeans banging striped balls into the pockets of the table, a form appeared, rolling limp, greasy hair, cigarette hanging from his lip.

I stared at him, mesmerized, a white rage crystallizing into something worse, something harder. He didn't see me, not at first, then he felt my stare, felt the intensity and raised piggy eyes to bear on me, red rimmed nasty glaring eyes. I recognized him, recognized him through the years, through the layers of alcohol and grime that coated his soul, recognized the man who killed my mom and tried his best to kill a six-year old kid. My rage was so far beyond rage now it wasn't even recognizable anymore.

He stared at me, scowled, a scar tracing his chin on the left side, a scar I remembered when it was fresh. I straightened slowly, waiting for him to react, to call me by name, to try to kill me again, come on you dirtball. This is no six-year old kid.

He pulled the cigarette out of his mouth and spit on the barroom floor. "The fuck you lookin' at, kid?"

He had no idea who I was.

Chapter 94
Now

A week and a half gone by since the night from hell, gone in a blur as my psychic fever morphed into a real one. Days of hallucinogenic haze, reality blurred with fever. Blood red flashes in my brain, silver knife cutting through skin, arterial blood pumping blackly across the ground. Knocking at my door sometime during it. Knocking, knocking, my fevered heart straining to burst.

On the third night, or maybe it was the fourth, the fever broke. I was weak, weaker than I could ever remember, chilled to the core now, skinny sticky and smelly. Hot water sluiced over me as I sat on the floor of the shower, too weak to stand, lathering up again and again.I couldn't scrub myself clean. Sobbing, I leaned my head against the wall as the water lost its heat.

My body had needs I couldn't ignore. Hunger returned, pushing through the sloshing sea in my gut. Swaying on my feet, I picked through crumpled bills in my nightstand, decided maybe I had enough to eat. My cash was getting perilously low now.

Opening the back door, I stared at familiar settings that looked so alien, squinting in the bright daylight. A piece of paper waved in the breeze, tucked under the windshield wiper. Cautiously, I approached it, yellow lined, scraggly handwriting, Bill's writing. 'Call me. It's important.'

I crumpled the paper up and tossed it in the passenger side footwell.

The diner looked old and tired on this almost winter afternoon. Some eggs, an English muffin and coffee returned my stomach to something resembling normal. No sausage. Not enough in the jar for that.

Dropping my meager collection of bills on the counter, I left the diner and headed towards the library. The dim interior was soothing to my still burning eyes. At the battered carousel I reluctantly faced the screen. Some part of me, the before Gerry wanted me to get up and leave, not turn the computer on, maybe if I never saw it in print, it would cease to exist. Maybe leave and finally head to Colorado, look for that mountain with the quaking aspen and the tiny cabin lost in the foothills.

My trembling fingers punched in a search engine and the terms to define what it was I sought. Hit after hit surfaced.

Missing Teen Turns Up Dead
Runaway Found Brutally Murdered
Sad end to Amber Alert as Allison McKinley's body found
17-year old Runaway Found Murdered
Oh shit.

Twenty minutes later, the breakfast I'd indulged in threatened to come back up as I closed the program out. Poor Allison. Just a kid, a screwed up kid who ran away after being grounded, never to be seen again. Last seen walking down Mt. Washington Avenue in her hometown of Sadieville. Five miles from Geotechnik.

While I had watched the light moving, he had found her, found her and terrorized her, fled with her from one riverside park to another as I pursued him. If I had checked the lot closer before settling on the wrong car, maybe, just maybe I could have changed the ending to this story. Her ending was messy, rage fueled, thrust out onto the pavement as he landed on her and gutted her alive like a butcher, no time to linger and enjoy it, gut and run. He knew, knew he was being pursued, knew and reacted with rage.

My head throbbed on my damaged frontal lobe. Why didn't I use it that night? Why didn't I open up in that first lot and feel him out?

I knew the answer, an answer that shamed me even as I acknowledged it. I was afraid, afraid to feel him, afraid to be drawn into his swirling cesspool of a mind. I was a pussy, a scared ass little pantywaist. Shame filled me was a blackness, a dour, sour feeling.

I returned to the pages and scrolled through again morosely. A headline caught my eye, one I had missed the first time around.

Cops Have New Lead In Case

New York State Police state that they have what they term are "credible new leads" in the case of the murdered women found along the banks of the Hudson over the past year. A source close to the investigation told the Chronicle that evidence left at the scene of the latest murder, that of 17-year old Allison McKinley, has investigators searching for a light truck. Author-

ities said that tire prints left in the blood at the scene gave a clear tread and wear pattern consistent with a pick-up truck. Those same prints were also found some twenty miles upriver where two women were terrorized by a knife wielding man earlier in the evening. A composite sketch made from the description given by the women has been distributed to authorities...

My heart thudded in my ears. The women, the lovers. I had forgotten about them, forgotten that I had stood there, framed in the door of their car, the light washing over my face as I stared at them in dumb surprise. Bloody tire tracks...my stomach rolled over. Oh God. You big, dumb ox.

Chapter 95
Then

"The fuck you looking at, kid?" No idea who I was. I could see it in his eyes. Confusion warred with rage; of all the times I had seen this in my head, lived it in my mind, this was not one of the scenes that played across the stage of my imagination, this indifference, this sneering contempt for a stranger, dismissed as a kid.

A kid.

I wasn't a kid any longer, hadn't been one for a long time now, especially after today. My soul felt as old as Methuselah, an ancient one trapped in the fresh skinned body of a youth. No idea who I was...How was that even possible?

Mitch laid his hand on my shoulder, "G.L. You better go."

I shrugged it off. HE curled his lip at me, and slowly roll stepped his way around the pool table, back over to the other side of the bar where a half full glass of beer sat. I kept my eyes on him, unblinking.

Mitch shook my arm again. "Gerry, you hear me? It's time for you to go, son. Now."

At the sound of my name, HE looked up at me, a flicker of something crossing his face, crossing then gone. I narrowed my eyes at him as the door to the outside opened, momentarily blinding me with a burst of sunlight. A slender man silhouetted in the light stepped into the murk closing the door behind him. Beside me, Mitch looked over my shoulder at him.

Carl.

I was frozen in place, frozen, every detail of HIM burning into my eyeballs, to be remembered forever, new details laid over old ones. The greasy hair longer than I remembered. The limp he hadn't had eleven years ago. The old scar I did remember, the pockmarked skin I didn't.

A tremor was starting up my arms as I felt him, felt him probing around my head, poking into my brain. I let the fabric slide away from my damaged frontal lobe, the lobe HE caused to be damaged...

The fuck this big ox staring at me like that? Jesus Christ, he don't let up, I'm gonna gut him. Maybe I should anyway, don't like this kid, he's fucking weird. Staring at me like that, I don't like it, don't like it at all. Do I know this shithead? Fuck, I shouldn't have come back here. Once I get ahold of Richie and get a load, I ain't coming back. Shithole town never done me no good anyway. What the FUCK is wrong with this fucking kid? Son of a bitch needs someone to teach him some manners, gotta stay cool, Donnio, stay cool, get your shit and get out, even if you do want to kick the shit out of this lummox..

Carl was at my side, his hand on my shoulder, his voice low and strained, "G.L. Come on, son."

No, no, no, this was my time, my time to get this son of a bitch. My throat closed around frozen words. Carl tightened his grip. "G.L. Come on. We got work to do."

The door opened again, another blast of light, another man shape silhouetted in it, this one bigger, beer bellied, worn work boots clunking on the wooden floor. Oblivious to the frozen tableau in front of the bar, he called over to Mitch as he made his way around the bar. To HIM.

"Hey Slim. Set me up and bring my friend a refill."

He lowered his ample buttocks onto the empty stool to HIS left. Richie. Richie Curtis. He had a Chevy Monza that he brought in from time to time, a red one. Carl thought he was lazy, never said it, but I knew. Always had money, never had a job.

He lived two blocks from Gramma and me.

Once I get ahold of Richie and get a load, I ain't coming back...fuck this town. Never did like it here.

Carl tugged me towards the door. I followed him on numb feet.

Chapter 96
Now

I'm screwed, I'm screwed, I'm oh so screwed. The phrases chant in my brain, like a metronome, lightning flashes of memories flickering, illuminating things unnoticed until too late. My head pounds like a bass drum.

I'm screwed. My tire tracks at the scene.

My face on the flyer the police are distributing (although the women messed up my nose; my nose wasn't nearly that big...was it?)

My cigarette butt dropped into her blood, dropped with my calling card of spittle flecked all over the butt.

Oh I am screwed. I tried, I tried to call, tried to tell them. My fingers went numb every time I dialed the number.

In the end I gave up. They wouldn't believe me anyway, why would they? Hell, I wouldn't even believe me and I lived it, I was there.

Blake had to be laughing, had to be. He had me backed into a corner. He slid under the radar while I hid from everyone, from Bill, from Amy, from everyone.

Blake stayed away from Geotechnik. A week passed, then two. On a Thursday night, the blinking light stuttered out.

I was feverish. I had to catch him, had to stop him, had to show the police Blake drenched in blood, and scream, "There! There, see? It's him, not me! Arrest him!"

But I couldn't do a damn thing. Bill kept calling and calling, left notes on my truck, pounded on my door. Finally, after about a week, week and a half, he stopped.

My truck. My truck was poison. I couldn't use my truck, couldn't.

The red car started buzzing in my brain, buzzing, buzzing. I had to get it, had to use it, had to have it. It was locked up in Bill's yard.

I fingered my key ring, the gold tone key that unlocked the gate to the yard. Would it still work? Could I do it? I had to. I couldn't drive that truck back there, couldn't, wouldn't. But could I actually drive the Toyota?

On a Saturday night when the air was wet with the promise of the first snowfall, I drove the Ford over to Bill's lot. The air was heavy, weighted with that peculiar feel you get when clouds laden with moisture are boiling up from the south, the temperatures hovering around freezing. Sweat steamed off my neck as I grasped the chain wrapping the two gates together, prickles of unease crawling up my spine. It won't open, it won't, Bill must have changed the lock by now.

Of course the lock snicked open smoothly. Sudden tears prickled across my eyes. Damn you Bill, you still trust me, damn it! Flashes of memories send jagged spikes of pain through me; Bill talking to me every time he saw me when I worked at Frankie's, Bill offering to buy me lunch when I was working here, Bill taking me to the races with him. Bill giving me days off when the flashbacks got too bad, days when I couldn't see around the hugeness of what had happened to me. Quiet support, always there, always willing to listen.

Which made his doubt in me hurt even worse.

The cars and trucks were blurry shapes in the dark lot, blurred from the moisture that threatened to overflow, the wetness caused by the cold November wind that creased my eyes. Or so I told myself.

I drove the Ford inside, closing the gate behind me, and carefully made my way through the crowded little space. I saw a number of cars that hadn't been here a couple weeks ago, customer cars most of them, more than usual. Stacking up because he was short-handed. Guilt stabbed sharp and hot. I shoved it aside. Focus. Focus. Save yourself first, then worry about trying set it right again. If that was even possible now.

The little red car had been moved, put way in back by the dumpster. I hoped for a crazy moment that it was blocked in, but of course not, it would never be inaccessible to me now would it? It wanted me to climb inside of it.

My stomach heaved. I should have sent that thing to the crusher, maybe I still would. When this was all over.

The red car sat, a silent, menacing slippery stack of steel and plastic. My brain processed this, my knowledge knew this was nothing more than a mass produced economy car from Japan, a popular model for its efficiency and ease of accessibility. My lizard brain told me differently. It was evil, wrong in ways I couldn't begin to fathom. My gut clenched.

I didn't want to get in it, didn't want to...

Chapter 97
Then

The house was gray and tired looking, just a small Sears kit that had been erected in the thirties, and then ignored. White paint long ago lost to the dingy, gray sheen of time and apathy. A chain link fence cut the front yard off from the lumpy concrete sidewalk, kid's toys, probably some scavenged from the dump littered the front. A saggy front porch bracketed a splintery looking door, about as welcoming as a lost tooth.

The Monza was parked in the overgrown driveway. No LTD.

I pedaled my bike past it, wound tight with the effort of appearing casual, my brain buzzing with a white noise. HE was here, HE was nearby. And HE had no idea who I was.

I turn right onto my own street again and stop under the old Sycamore tree that heaves the sidewalk.

Now what? He has to show up. Tilting my head back, I scan the sky, where the evening stars are starting to gleam. In the houses the first lights are coming on. A late season mosquito hones in hungrily, drawn by its encroaching death. I slapped it away. A memory lances me: another night spent slapping mosquitoes while crouched by the lake, Billy's slack face in the faint light. A shudder crawls up my spine.

I need to wait for him, somewhere, ambush him. The kid's toys flash through my head, I push it away. I can't think about that, I won't. The overgrown bushes along the driveway, those would cover me, at least enough so he would not be alerted. Another mosquito zeroed in on my face.

I push my bike into the hedge in front of the Hanson's yard. The streetlight a few houses up flickered on, a metallic hum preceding the light. I felt like I was the only person left on earth alive, like everyone else had died from some awful disease.

A bubble of rage swelled in my chest. HE was responsible for this; HE had killed me a thousand times over despite my surviving that night. Faces flicked in front of me; my Mom, Billy, Gramma, Carl, all of the people who had cared about me, even just a little bit, all of them damaged because of HIS actions. The bubble grew, pressing against my lungs, making it hard to breathe. Come on, you son of a bitch. Let's go.

I walked, no, stalked down the street, fists clenched. The Monza was a dark lump, branches from the driveway pressed up against the passenger side. I crouch walked into the cavern they made against the car and pressed myself up against the trunks to wait. I could wait all night if I had to.

As it turned out, I only had to wait a little while before the LTD lumbered into the driveway, throwing yellow beams of light across the Monza, me safe and unseen in my black cocoon.

My rage had crystallized into a white, ice cold block in my chest. I fingered the blade I had slipped into my pocket before leaving; Grampa's blade, slippery sharp after all these years still.

He pushed the car door open with a creak; a skinny shape levering himself out. I could smell him from here, cigarettes, foul clothing. My thigh muscles tensed as I readied myself.

The back door of the house opened, spilling light across the driveway, Richie Curtis's fat frame partially filling the doorway.

"'Bout fucking time you got here. I was about to start drinking your beer."

"Now you just leave my God damned beer alone, you ox. Got here quick as I could."

Both of them sounded about half drunk.

"Well come on. I ain't got all night. Nancy and the kids are out at some school thing, they're gonna be back in an hour or so."

HIS skinny form passed in front of Curtis's larger one and both men disappeared into the house.

An hour. I settled back down to wait again. Mosquitoes tormented me, humming in my ears, my face. Every hum reminded me of Billy, of how I failed him, of how I had been waiting all of my life for this moment.

Time crawled past. I heard a noise, faint, far away, a thudding sound, maybe a yell. I stiffened, listening. It didn't come again.

After an eternity, the back door opened again, a slight figure clutching something slipping through it.

Alone.

I didn't hesitate. I didn't think. I rose from the hedge in one smooth move and crossed around the Monza to intercept him.

Chapter 98

Now

Pools of light dot the parking lot at Geotechnik. I'm sitting in the car, parked in a slot near where Blake's car normally sits. It's there. Of course it is.

I have no idea how I got here.

Minutes tick by. My eyes track the lot in a slow-motion metronome, tick, tock. Moisture seeps under my palms, resting on the wheel. I lift my left hand slowly. Blood drips off of it, a molasses slow rainfall. I replace the palm, dreamily, unconcerned. Flashes, heat lighting in my brain keep flickering.

Her face, mouth open and screaming...Blood, blood, so much blood, so pretty...Screams reverberating in my head, music, music, drowning my own screams...Her soft puffy coat with her hard body underneath, surprise in her deadened eyes as the blade carves through the down...

Dreamily, the images play across my brain. Someplace deep inside, the place where Gerry is still alive and sane, he's screaming, screaming for my attention, begging to be freed from this horrid car, these memories that aren't his, can't be his, won't be his.

I tell him to shut up. That Gerry can't do this.

The images aren't bothering me, not at all. In fact....I kind of like them. Oh, but that has to be wrong, wrong, I know it. But I don't care. Warm, silky sensations flutter across my belly. I stare at the facade of the building, aware that I am waiting for Blake, tell myself I need to stay and wait, to not just drive away and make memories of my own.

Inside, Gerry screams louder.

I raise a palm again, look disinterestedly at the carvings all up and down my forearm, across the palm. Words, scratched there during the struggle with Gerry as we sat in the car together, waves, of emotion, fear, lust, pain, rolling over us. He carved at me, cutting fiercely with the car key, trying to send me away.

I knew I had to do this though. He couldn't, wouldn't; he was a pussy.

I wiped the blood onto the knees of my jeans. Wouldn't do to have anything warn Blake, now would it. Slowly, I opened the door and eased out into the lot, aware of the security that patrolled on a regular basis, of the cameras, that pointed at most corners of the lot, although not here.

Blake made sure of that.

His current car sat a mere twenty feet from where I had put the old one, half hidden behind a mini-van. Dreamily, I fingered the kit of lock picking tools I carried. He wouldn't see it, couldn't. His entire being would be consumed with hunting tonight.

I could feel him.

Gerry was a wimp, blocking all of the senses and feelings like he did. Not like me. I welcomed them, relished them.

I crossed around behind the Camry Blake owned now, trailed a fingertip along the quarter panel. Sensations jolted into me, sweeping across like fireworks.

Oh yes, he was going hunting tonight. And he didn't know it yet, but he was going to have some company.

Chapter 99

Then

"Who is it?" He stopped ten feet from me, a shape in the darkness. Waves of uncertainty, fear even, rolled off of him. I filled his path, huge with my hatred, invincible, ready to fulfill my destiny. I didn't answer him.

He moved a little, peering at me. "What the hell? What the fuck you want? Richie ain't here." My vision adjusted, showing me the side of his face, his rumpled clothing.

"I'm not looking for Richie. I'm looking for you." I stepped into the light from the window.

"You again?" I felt him relax fractionally. "What the fuck's your problem, kid?" Cockiness returned to his voice.

"You are, actually. You have been for a long time."

His eyes glittered. "Oh really? So where have we met before? Because you ain't exactly ringing no bells for me."

"That's because the last time you saw me was the night you killed my mom."

He froze. Then, "No shit. You're that little faggot kid she had. I thought you got your head blown off, by her mom. Ha!" He cackled, an impossible noise. My chest froze.

"That was rich, her mother blowing your head off. Shit! Saved me the trouble! You were nothing but a little shithead loser then, and you ain't changed, not one bit. Fucking bitch." He spat suddenly, explosively loud in the pregnant silence.

"Get the fuck outta my way. I got things to do, places to go. Count your blessings I ain't got time for you tonight."

I launched myself at him. He grunted in surprise as I hit him. I wasn't a tiny little kid anymore, far from it. Hatred and rage made me huge, huge, huge, invincible.

He hit the ground beneath me in a whump of smelly clothing, grunting as he twisted underneath me. I started pounding at him, pounding, white hot noise in my ears.

My fist connected, once, twice, then hit the ground as he twisted, impossibly wiggly, impossibly quick moving out of my range, twisting under me, a sharp knee slamming into my ribs, knocking the breath from me.

Suddenly, I was too big, too much of an ox, unable to pin him down in his wire quick moves.

He slithered his lower body out from under me, slipping free to kick with skinny legs, heels driving into me.

I roared with pain, fear beginning to lance the fog, struggling to regain control, control that was rapidly sliding away from me as he slid ever further free, now an arm, incredibly strong pinning mine, foul breath in my face, grappling with me...The knife was sudden and shocking in the darkness, a sudden flash of light as the glare from the kitchen washed over it.

I screamed, high and breathless in the suppurating darkness, then...blackness.

Chapter 100

Now

Amy came to see me. She was all hardness and angles, high cheekbones and smoky dark eyes. I looked at her silently, wondering why I never questioned why someone like her, so wild, so young, would take up with me.

She sat perched on the edge of the hard chair, reflections on the glass obscuring part of her face.

I wondered what possessed me to agree to this. Most people were uncomfortable. Most people looked around at the barren walls, at anything except me. I think they thought it was a great idea until they actually got here.

She didn't seem uncomfortable, not at all. She looked at ease, at home here, staring directly at me, her expression part pity and part anger. I felt a glimmer of discomfort.

She lifted the receiver. "You never did tell me how you knew."

No "Hello", no "I'm sorry", no, not Amy. Straight to the point.

I swallowed, a dry crackling sound to my ears.

"Does it matter?"

"Who told you?"

I shrugged.

Her eyes narrowed. "It doesn't matter. I already know anyway."

"Your coming into Bill's wasn't an accident, was it? You knew I was there."

She laughed softly. "Give the man a dollar. Congratulations, maybe you aren't as dumb as you look."

I looked her straight in the eye. "Why? Why did you do this?"

"Why not? Mom never wanted me. Just seeing if maybe my Dad did....right 'Dad'?"

I looked at her, wondering who I could have missed the clues, not seen the cheekbones, the same slant to her nose, even the same wild streak her mother, Darlene, had possessed. An image rose unbidden, a tiny wrinkled face with blue, blue eyes, eyes like I had.

Sadness washed over me as I stared into her smoky brown eyes, the exact same shade of eyes that her real dad Jimmy had.

She was defiant even as the tears threatened, bravado in the face of emotional catastrophe.

"So how did you like it "Dad"? Huh? Did you get your rocks off, screwing me? How was I? Better than Mom?"

I slowly hung the receiver up and gestured to the guard to take me back. I could see the rage streaking across her face, hear her screaming at me through the glass as the matron on the other side came to intercede.

"Huh? Did you like screwing me too, Daddy? Did you? *DID YOU*?"

Chapter 101
Now

We build our own prisons with the rubble of the lives we tear apart, brick by brick, stones laid so quietly you can't even hear the first ones chinking into place.

I fought and fought, tearing at the world with my bare hands. I was determined to free myself from the pain and misery that chased me, never realizing that the blue skies of freedom I thought I had glimpsed was actually the smoke from the embers of the bridges that burned all around me.

The smallest stones make walls if piled high enough. My words to Dean the night he drove me home, my tire prints in the dirt, hiding from the world, searching on line for murdered women, the lovers in the parking lot, obsessively stalking Robert F. Blake, stones falling ching, ching ching into a wall that slowly rose as I pushed on, oblivious to what I was building.

The walls towered over me now, stout, impervious, trapping me here forever, for the rest of my natural life.

I stare through the small opening, the dirty glass revealing the lines of two or three cars in the parking lot below, my entire view of the world. The Toyota is gone now.

But I am still here.

The demon I chased through the New York woods wasn't the demon I thought it was, no, not at all. He was a monster, no doubt about it. And he won't kill another woman again, I saw to that even as I fell short in saving her, his last victim, Shelly Copea.

I was too late, too late once more, too late in freeing myself from the trunk of the car, stupid, stupid, stupid, didn't think he would strike as fast and viciously as he did, her life bleeding away even as I wrenched the door open and launched at him, Timothy Blake, Robert F. Blake's son, gangly teenaged lines still visible in his angry face.

I ripped the knife from him and turned it on him, tearing his own life from him even as lights washed over me as a spectator arrived just in time for the ghoulish dance we engaged in, convinced someplace in my brain that I was in the right but of course I wasn't, not by a long shot.

The police were deaf to me, the papers tried and convicted me, and in the end the jury wouldn't listen to me either. They found me guilty of both of their deaths, Blake and Shelly portrayed as lovers caught in the wrong place at the wrong time, me a demented stalker with a vendetta.

I won't be guilty for Timothy Blake's death, no never for that. He was a personal dragon I had to slay, my demon who haunted my sleep. I'm glad he's gone, relieved, worth it even if it has cost me my own life.

Shelly still haunts me though.

Maybe I deserve these endless days watching a sliver of parking lot through the narrow window. Locked up for deaths I didn't cause is probably just punishment for the one

I did cause, the unsolved slaying of Donny Hopgood in the driveway of the sad little gray house 28 years ago, another demon laid to rest. Inside the shotgun shack, Richie lay face down in a puddle of his own fluids, the noise I'd heard just before HE came outside.

Gramma had watched every story, listened to every radio broadcast about it, a tight faced hope visible. When the newspaper showed a photo of the knife police found outside the home, Grampa's knife, she had looked at it for a long, long time in silence, before carefully tearing the article to shreds. She never spoke a word about it to me in the last five years of her life, not a peep.

I suffered, tongue tied, unable to give voice to the words I needed to say to her, trapped in my own mire.

And now, now, I'm stuck here all because of a little red car with a nickel's worth of road measles.

But there is a sort of cosmic humor, a karmic poetic-ness about all of this.

Because, you see, inside these block walls, wearing an orange suit like mine is my old friend, Mr. Hawley, incarcerated finally for his continuing crimes against countless boys. Brought down by his own computer, betrayed by the place where he thought he was secure.

The dark hair is gone, replaced by thin white strands now, and he's bent over like he broke in half at some point. But it's him, oh yes, it is him.

He will face me one day, one last time, and when he does, he will face more than just me, he will see Billy too. And he will know. It will be the last thing he ever knows.

My laters are all gone now. And I have all the time in the world to wait.

———⟨∾⟩———

APRIL 1, 2020

Don't miss out!

Visit the website below and you can sign up to receive emails whenever S.L. Funk publishes a new book. There's no charge and no obligation.

https://books2read.com/r/B-A-QIAK-NRVDB

BOOKS 2 READ

Connecting independent readers to independent writers.

About the Author

Stephanie Funk is a former journalist and editor living in western MA with her husband Edward. A long time auto racer with Sports Car Club of America and a neophyte motorcycle racer of vintage machines with the United States Classic Racing Association, Funk brings a depth of knowledge about the world of motorsports and the people you find frequenting that world. 'A Nickel's Worth of Road Measles' is her debut work, one that touches upon the quirky characters found in garages and racetracks across the country. In this story, Funk weaves a love of reading engaging thrillers and mysteries with her experience in the automotive world. Funk holds degree in Creative Writing, and has many publishing credits in magazines and newspapers.

Read more at www.stephaniefunk.com.